Prais

THE SWISH

"A fashion-forward, creative story full of fun and friendship."
Lily, 13, Salisbury.

"Amazing. It shows so much about self-confidence
and to never give up."
Chloe Kearney, 15, Wiltshire.

"Laugh-out loud funny."
Sophia Lozano, 13, Maidstone.

"The Swish is amazing. From page one, I loved it."
Lola Compton, 12, Bideford.

"Funny and truthful. It shows what girls are made of.
It inspired me to pick up sewing again!"
Florence Richardson, 13, Chudleigh.

"Witty and fun."
Jessica Johnson, 13, Wilton.

"Truly inspiring. The illustrations are gorgeous!"
Megan Kelly, 15, Christchurch, New Zealand.

"Extremely exciting and funny.
Tash Bell is my new favourite author."
Asiya Ali, YouTube book reviewer.

"Showing girls it's OK to be yourself is so important. Kat's
strong and resilient... I absolutely loved this."
Ruby Hamilton, 15, Newcastle Upon Tyne.

The right of Tash Bell to be identified as the Author of the Work
has been asserted by her in accordance with the Copyright,
Designs and Patents Act 1988.

SECOND EDITION

© Tash Bell 2023
Illustrations © Poppy Freer 2023
Cover by Martin Baines 2023

Published by
Candy Jar Books, Mackintosh House
136 Newport Road, Cardiff, CF24 1DJ
www.candyjarbooks.co.uk

ISBN: 978-1-915439-40-6

Editor: Shaun Russell
Editorial: Keren Williams

Printed and bound in the UK by
Severn, Bristol Road, Gloucester, GL2 5EU
on responsibly sourced paper

THE SWiSH

TASH BELL

CANDY JAR BOOKS

For Rose

Do you have a way of escaping the bad stuff? A focus for your dreams when reality hits? We all get curveballs thrown at us – by life, by our parents (and don't get me started on school!). Some kids shout. Some kids run. Me? I rev my motor, put my foot down and... sew.

Vroom. I whizz round a buttonhole. Gran's old Singer sewing machine was built with the dinosaurs, so it can withstand even Mum going T-rex.

Almost.

'This debt!' Her shouts burst through my bedroom floor. 'It's become a monster. It's eating us alive!'

'So, stop feeding it,' Dad rumbles back.

'I'm feeding *us* is what I'm doing.' Mum clatters the cutlery drawer. 'I'm covering nursery costs so you can... do what exactly?'

'I'm working.'

'It's not work if no one pays you, Chris! It's you hiding behind your laptop. Eight hours I've been stood on that shop floor,' she yells, which sets the twins yelling too. 'I come home to find Daisy sucking on the remote control.

Lil's weed on the couch and— no, Lil, you do *not* win a sweet for it.'

Vroom. I race down my hem. The needle flies up and down, turning to a flicker of silver – like a fairy godmother's wand. No fairy godmother here, though, just me feeling angry my folks are so broke. Then guilty for making things worse. When Mum got in from work just now, I helped her unload the shopping. But I also tried to borrow a tenner.

'I've found this gorgeous Diesel jacket down the market.' I heaved her torn bag for life onto the kitchen counter. 'Proper vintage.'

'Second hand, you mean.'

'That's why it's ten quid! Distressed denim, but I can save it. Ewww…' I pulled out a cellophane bag full of squished, rank-looking leaves. 'What's *this*?'

'Half price, that's what.'

Mum tapped the yellow discount sticker. 'Salad,' she said with a frown. 'Though I admit it's starting to look more like soup. Soddit.'

She rummaged in the bag for a dented can of spaghetti hoops. 'Supper!'

She tugged at the ring pull – and snapped it clear off.

'*Mum.*' I yanked her back to my jacket. 'Remember those seed pearls Gran gave me? I could stitch them into the back – make myself a pair of wings!'

'Love,' said Mum, clawing back the sharp tin lid. 'Where am I going to find a tenner? Your dad's not earned in

2

months. Ow!' She cut her finger. Next thing she was leaning over the pile of dirty plates in the sink, trying to jam her bloody hand under the tap.

'Stop, Mum.' I rescued her sleeve. 'You're making it worse.'

'How could I make any of this worse?' She lurched round, flicking droplets of blood over the clutter on our kitchen table: the twins' spat-out dummies… their crusted breakfast bowls… the council tax bill she left for Dad to sort this morning.

'Come on, Mum. Things'll pick up.'

I swiftly slid the bill to the floor. 'It's nearly Christmas! Remember how we used to put up the tinsel – me, you and Dad – before *they* arrived.'

A thud sounded overhead. Then another, louder. And suddenly, it was snowing – in our kitchen! Soft white flakes appeared like magic, floating down onto my eyelashes, settling in Mum's frizzy hair. For a second, we looked like a family from the John Lewis ad – you know, all happy and loving, and about to buy a sofa. Then (*pfla pfla*) we were spitting out bits of ceiling plaster.

'The twins ARE JUMPING again!' Dad came storming down the stairs. 'I'm supposed to be writing up there.'

'*Supposed* to,' snorted Mum, 'you said it!'

Neither of them noticed me leaving. And now they're rowing so hard, not even my Singer can drown them out. So I try singing instead. 'La-la-laaaa!' OK, yelling. And I start on the pile of mending Mum's dumped on my bed. 'Deck the halls with boughs of—'

Grr, Lily's gone through the toes of her tights *again*. Ditto Daisy and her socks. I swear those two have got Hobbit feet. Darning done, I scoop up my sketchbook. The louder their shouts, the harder I scribble…

Stitch List

Upcycle my latest charity shop find: a sustainable style gem! No, the label's not STELLA MCCARTNEY. It's "£2 from SUE RYDER" (this tank top has seen action!), but hey, I've fixed worse. I'm thinking:

1. Shorten the straps.
2. Take in the side seams.
3. Stitch poppy motif across front of vest.

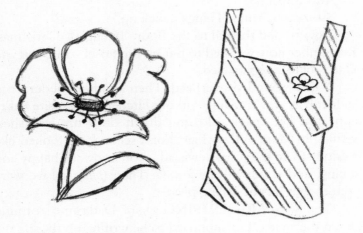

4. Find that length of frosted white lace Gran gave me...
   Snip out frosted flowers to make "snowflakes".
5. Scatter snowflakes over poppy, like it's hiding...
   waiting for the sun to come out.

I feed my top into the sewing machine, and put my foot down on the pedal. *Vroom* goes Kat Parker, chasing a dream down a seam.

Late for school, and it's the twins' fault again. They are ginger nut-jobs. People see their orange curls and freckly cheeks, and sigh, 'Ahh, aren't they like Orphan Annie from the musical?' Er, no actually, because:

a) There was only one of Annie, and
b) she didn't run round like a Teletubby who's drunk too many Fruit Shoots.

Also:

c) Annie mopped the floor occasionally. The twins just spill stuff on it.

Take this morning: *The second* Mum leaves for work, they pull their bowls of Coco Pops off the table. I go for the mop, while Daisy body-slides across the mess, crying, '*Wheeeeeee!*' Lil goes one better, and actually *does* a wee, all over the Coco Pops... and a bit of my foot. Agh, my sisters are not ready for potty-training! But we can't afford the nappies OR a kiddy-crunching cyborg to chase them to nursery (believe me, I've asked). So when I should be hogging the mirror, teasing my fringe and applying lip balm LIKE A NORMAL YEAR 10, I'm stuck poking two ginger furballs into a double buggy with the business end of my mop. It doesn't help that the seat straps are knackered; as soon as I get one twin in, her demented doppelganger slides out. It's like some crazy Japanese gameshow NO ONE CAN WIN.

Pushing them up the street, I wish Dad could take over. But we can only afford morning nursery sessions (says Mum) and my dad writes best first thing (says Dad), so it makes sense for:

a) Me to take the twins in, and
b) Dad *not* to tell Mum. She'll just worry (i.e. shout).

Handing the twins over to their nursery worker (is it me or has her hair turned white since they started here?) I give Daisy her special kiss, then duck away before Lil can wee on my shoes (SHE HAS GOT TO STOP). I'm bombing down Norbridge Hill to school when I feel the R3 loom up alongside like a pirate galleon rammed with Winsham Academy boys. On the top deck, Zack Melway rides up front with his guitar like some brooding hero! I blame those ridiculous razor-edge cheekbones of his. Chuck in a perpetually clenched jaw, and fierce green eyes fixed on a bleak horizon. Yep, Zack could pass for cool, if not for his mad mate veering alongside like a shipwreck about to happen.

'Kat?' he mouths through the glass. 'What are you *doing?*' Is it not obvious? Do I have to swing my arms and high-kick my legs in the international code for speed walk? I get a grin out of him at least. It disappears the second he checks his watch. 'Kat, you need to *run*.'

I run. But I don't factor in the wind blowing up my school kilt. As the bus pulls past, I hear whoops: Year 10 hockey boys Daniel Sanders and Liam Parkes are craning out the back, which means Jonah Kerridge must be up there too. Not yelling though.

Jonah's way too confident for that... and sensitive... and... *be still my heaving chest*, I really should go jogging more.

Wheezing towards the gates of St Edward's School for Girls, I realise registration is a lost hope. Staggering into the assembly hall, I *skiiiiiid*

down onto the end of the Year 10 row,

grin at my best mate Lisa, and

hoik my coat off quick

before the Tag-Hags catch the threads trailing from my sleeves. 'Ow,' mutters Lees, as I knock her, then, 'Give.' She sits on my coat, as our head teacher mounts the stage.

'Good morning, girls,' harrumphs Mrs Cribbs. "Camel" Cribbs, we call her. She's dead whiskery, and chews when she talks. She also has the permanent hump, so I'm not the only St Edward's student to double-take when she announces, 'I have GOOD news.'

'Hear that?' I nudge Lisa, who's back to scrolling down her phone for "Most Violent Hockey Goals". '*Good news*,' I whisper. 'Perhaps Cribbs is leaving?'

'Yeah right, for the Sahara,' mutters Lees. 'I pity those prickly pears.'

Cribbs starts chewing.

'Girls...' She peers into the gloom of the assembly hall. 'Many of you may be familiar with Darwin's Dental Health in Norbridge Mall.' Two hundred orthodontic braces glint back at her. 'Darwin kindly provided ALL the fizzy drinks and sweets for our Year 11 Summer Prom. Now they're offering to sponsor a Christmas party for our pre-GSCE cohort.'

'D'you hear that?' I clutch Lees.

'Yep. Nope.' Lees looks up from her phone. 'What's a cohort?'

'*Us*, you numpty! Shh.'

'The Winter Wonderland Ball will be open to girls in Years 9 and 10,' continues Cribbs, 'and will climax with an exciting and aspirational competition. Girls!' Our head raises her voice over the sound of three hundred girls whooping. 'You don't need me to remind you of our school motto.'

She does, it turns out. 'Strive for success!' she tells three hundred girls looking blank. 'I urge you to empower yourselves through competition, and enter our ball's fashion-forward finale: a catwalk contest for Most Dazzling Look, courtesy of Darwin's Dental Health. Prize is £500.'

'£500? Yessss!' A Mexican wave runs down our row. It breaks against the shiny blonde wall of Stella Harcourt. She's acting all "whatever", but you can tell she's excited because... yep, here comes the trademark hair-flick! Now the whole of her crew are flicking *their* hair too, even Keisha who's got braids. They're all giggling and saying, 'We're gonna rock this ball, girlfriend!' (Seriously, THEY TALK LIKE THIS! Like they're Hollywood Hills girls on a reality show, not a maths C-stream from Norbridge, Surrey.)

'As with our summer prom,' Cribbs continues, 'we'll hold the Winter Wonderland Ball here in our school gym, and open ticket sales to students at our twin school, Winsham Academy.' ('Yesss,' hiss the cool crew: THERE WILL BE BOYS.)

'We expect all of you students to socialise sensibly on the night,' Cribbs finishes up. 'Be creative with your gowns, but restrain your décolletage – and possibly...' She scans our row, stopping at Lees. '...brush your hair?'

Lees tosses her wild strawberry blonde curls and scowls. 'Our kind sponsor just wants pics of pretty girls with flouncy frocks and cute smiles,' she mutters. 'Darwin's Dental is going to get a lot of marketing material for their £500.'

It's only when we're filing out of assembly into double geography that girls get to worrying what a "décolletage" is. Stella Harcourt reckons it means something "down there", but then she thinks most things are either to do with "down there" or "up here" (i.e. boob-related). Mum says, 'That girl needs to spend more time studying maths, and less time taking selfies and picking on you.'

Well, Mum, that may be true, but the other girls follow Stella's every move. Me? Feels like I'm pursued by a bad smell most days. Yep, we live in different worlds, Stella and I. But maybe magic *can* happen. Play it right, and even a nobody like me can get into Winter Wonderland...

Can't I?

What we put on eBay today

1. Mum's laptop, *reserve price £50*.
2. Dad's bike, *reserve price £40*.
3. Mum's tailored coat.
   She used to wear it to Important
   executive meetings at her old job
   (her *cool* job). Gorgeous,
   isn't it? The colour of
   violets – and it's me
   who found it for her!

We'd go up to Covent Garden window-shopping (Mum for work, me because it was dress HEAVEN). And there it was – tucked away in the back of the Karen Millen store – the perfect coat for Mum's shape.

'I look ten years younger.' Mum span round in the changing room. '*And* it's given me back my waist! Now, can you find me a bijou blouse with a Peter

10

Pan collar that would appeal to a younger demographic?'

Yep, that's how she talked then. Mum had just grafted her way up to assistant buyer for an online clothes brand, and said she valued my input – on the fabrics, the cut… putting looks together. We were a team.

Then (*YAY, SURPRISE!*) the twins came along.

Mum was that shocked (and geriatric) she had to switch to flexitime. Only, it turned out her Important Executive Bosses weren't that flexible. Mum had to bail on her designer job, and go back to the shop floor.

Now she's a ladieswear assistant in Armitages, Norbridge's creaky old department store. It's got headless shop dummies in the window, and men's socks next to perfumes, and people only go in to use the key-cutters by the lift. But it pays better than H&M in the mall, and because no one else wants to work there, Mum can get double shifts. Which is like the opposite of flexitime, but she won't listen when I tell her to go knocking for her old job.

'Ach, someone younger, *cooler* than me will have it now. There's no going back, is there?' she says with a sigh. 'Not when you're wearing last year's coat and scuffed shoes.'

Seems you can't put those things on eBay either, so tonight it's her sharp suit (cut from the softest cashmere) has to go. The twins and I crowd into Mum and Dad's poky bedroom, as she slips the coat off the hanger. Spreading the arms out on the bed, she snaps away with her phone like we're on *Crime Scene Investigation*.

'Stop, Mum.' I panic. 'Won't you need this? Next time you want to dress up for somewhere nice.'

'*Nice?*' Mum grabs Daisy by the back of her nappy before she can bounce onto the bed. 'When am *I* going to go anywhere nice?'

'I dunno.' I haul Lil off the pillows. 'On a date with Dad?'

'You. Are. Kidding,' says Mum, like I'm stupid. Too young to understand, I just get to feel like *everyone else* is the star of their Instagram story, striking a pose in the Shop Window of Life. It's just my family stuck outside, noses pressed against the glass, crying, 'How did we get here?'

Because we *were* like everyone else, weren't we? Not flash, sure (Mum and I would try on every dress in Covent Garden, then come home with a belt). But we'd stop off at Starbucks by Norbridge station before catching our bus home, so Mum could grab a latte, plus a blueberry muffin for me.

Then it was just a muffin for me.

Next it was walking past Starbucks to save on the bus fare. Now we never hang out anywhere except the kitchen, and I'm told to double-dunk my teabag because, to quote Mum when she's moved on to the cider, 'We're not ruddy oligarchs.'

Stitch List
1. Take my beautiful rosebud blouse.
2. Remove Oxfam tag.
3. Steal kitchen scissors (resist urge to run with them).
4. Hack up leather jacket I found dumped by the Co-Op recycling bin.
5. Cut out leather letters (plus some big fat FULL STOPS).
6. Stitch hard words through my rosebuds:

YOU. ARE. KIDDING.

Tearing off my school shirt, I text Lisa.

Finished another make! Come round
with your phone. You know the drill!

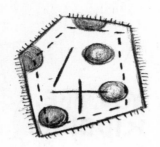

Go girl! Work that look,' cries the photographer. 'Let's see you *sashaaaay*.'

Summoning my inner supermodel, I strut down the fashion runway in:

- A scuffed pair of Doc Marten boots,
- A HOT pink punk kilt,
- Some recycled rosebuds, and
- A full-on pout.

'Er... what's with the mouth, Kat?' The photographer puts down her cameraphone. 'You look like a duck.'

Yep, that's how sustainable style rocks down the Katwalk. Of course, it isn't really a catwalk, just a smelly alley that runs down the side of our house.

'No place for kids,' Mum used to complain to the council. 'If they're not tripping over cracks in the tarmac, they're trying to dodge piles of dog crap AND ONLY MOSTLY MISSING.'

So today's shoot is not *haute couture*. The vibe is not achingly stylish, more "freezing cold Tuesday after school".

Plus, my photographer can't shoot AND walk backwards without tripping over her hockey stick. Downside to Lees coming straight from training – she dumps her kit *right* across the Katwalk. Upside? She's never once called it a dead end.

In fact, it's down to Lees we're working the Katwalk at all. The alley just used to be somewhere we hid when the twins started crying. Then, heading out one afternoon, Lisa grabbed a sweater I'd just finished reworking. An old navy crew neck of Zack's, it had gone through the wars, so I stitched gold braid around the collar and down the sleeves, military-style. The second Lisa yanked the sweater on, she snapped to "atten-SHUN!" Then she marched down the stairs, and paraded out onto the Katwalk. 'I call this a look, girl!' she saluted me.

Who cares if she was taking the mick? Why can't fashion be a laugh? For sure we both needed one.

And so Project Katwalk was launched. A year on, we've watched every episode of *RuPaul's Drag Race*. I've raided every charity shop in Norbridge, and sewn until my fingers bled (or Lisa's blown my ears off With 'BORED NOW!').

Then we pull on my makes, and get out there.

Well, down our tin-can alley at least. Lees and I have got good at skipping over the cracks.

As for filming on our phones? These pics we do *not* plan

to share. But I can't see what works until my clothes move. And Lisa can't double up laughing in the back of double maths if she's not scrolling through photos of a pink tartan mini skirt. 'You know that kilt is *majorly* tiny,' she now tells me.

'You said to go short!' I tug down my hem.

'When?'

'When we caught you Googling London Fashion Week.' I tighten my skirt buckles. 'You said you were doing research, remember?'

She looks at me blankly. 'Zack decided to wind you up,' I nudge her. 'Said you were gawping at hot models.'

'Ah!' A light comes on.

'Then you threw Wotsits at each other, while I finished my skirt.' I straighten the pleats – not real tartan, sadly (that'd be way out of my price range, plus I'm yet to find a Scottish Highland clan that produces kilts in hot pink #NOimagination #theirloss).

But hot pink it had to be! So I begged Zack's big brother Andy for one of the golf umbrellas that never sell off his stall: dead naff, bold pink check in flimsy polyester.

I ripped out the spokes, stitched in these pleats (plus two brassy buckles) and the rest is fashion history – well, it *would* be if we could record it.

Now Mum's traded in my smartphone for a Nokia brick,

Lisa gets to play photographer. (She's dropped her own phone that many times, only she can work the dents). Really it's Lees who should be modelling my clothes – she's got ATTITUDE covered. Whereas I'm like some sad Marvel character. You know, the Hopeless Case before she discovers she can fly? Only in my case (*thanks Mum*) no wings will be appearing any time soon.

Kerrang! The crash of a power chord, and Zack's head appears over the fence. The white collars of his shirt are rucked up under his black Winsham Academy blazer; his broad shoulders hunched over his guitar. Strumming furiously, he strolls towards us.

'Oi!' I bounce up and down in my Doc Martens. (OK, *Lisa's* Doc Martens – my footwear collection doesn't stretch past school shoes and an old verruca sock.) 'Keep the decibels down, can you?' I tell my guitar-wanging friend. Zack just wangs harder, thanks to a bright green electric cable that trails from his Fender back to his kitchen doorway like a lead he daren't slip.

Zack's my oldest mate. We've grown up together (though this past year, he's grown, like, a foot taller than me! I'm seeing A LOT more of the underside of his chin than I wish). The Melway brothers' house backs on to ours. Their garden holds the other side-gate onto the alley, so whenever Lees and I "work" the Katwalk, Zack considers it his job to:

a) Play LOUD rock.
b) Hang over the gate, and
c) wind us up.

'Woah, Kat, you've got legs! Who knew?' He grins at my kilt. 'You wearing that to the ball?'

'Hey.' Lees grabs her hockey stick and prods him with it. 'How do you know about Winter Wonderland?'

'We got the big announcement today,' he says as he dances away from her. 'Winsham Boys are expected to be *On Their Best Behaviour, and Socialise in A Mature Fashion.*' He grips his frets. 'So that'll be me playing guitar in my room.'

'No way.' I march up to his gate. 'You are NOT hiding from this one.'

'Who says I'm hiding?' He ducks behind the rose bush that rambles up the Melways' side of the fence. Their dad planted it years ago – for Zack's mum – and it grew into a crazy, gorgeous thing (like Zack's mum). Even now, in the dead of winter, one rose remains. White, soft as velvet, it brushes Zack's cheek as I pull him towards me.

'I get it, you guys have had it tough,' I say, 'but you can't lose yourself in your reverb forever.'

'Oh yeah?' He shies back, and sets off down his strings. 'Watch me try.'

'Fine. Lees and I will go without you! Soon as I talk Mum into buying me a dress.

'Ha!' Lisa snorts. 'And you diss *Zack* for ducking out?' Zack frowns at her. 'There's gonna be a catwalk contest,' she tells him. 'Most Dazzling Look. Winner gets £500.'

'Man.' Zack sends a power chord my way. 'What you could do with half a grand!'

'Er... BUY A BALL DRESS!' I kick a stone down the alley. 'No other way I'm going to win.'

'How can you say that?' Lees points her hockey stick at my kilt. 'Have you not just fashioned a skirt from an umbrella? Why *not* make a dress for the ball? You'd kill it!'

'I'd get slain, you mean. Tell her, Zack!'

'I'm with Lees,' he says with a grin. 'You could rock a bin bag, Kat.'

'*A bin-bag?*' I'm sticking Zack's head back into the rose bush when he's saved by his big brother.

'Curry's up!' Andy calls from their kitchen.

'Gotta go.' Raising his fretboard in farewell, Zack strolls towards the Melways' back door, cranking out the riff to "Foxy Lady" like he's Jimi Hendrix, but in a school shirt.

'He's right, you know,' says Lees. 'You're good at this stuff, Kat. Why hide in my phone?' She starts swiping through her photo gallery. 'Look at those jeans you embroidered! And that swish maxi-dress you made from your neighbour's old sari. And some weird halter-neck thingy…' She frowns. 'Okaaay, so not everything works.'

I try to snatch her phone. She holds it higher. 'You should be proud of your makes.'

'I am. It's just…'

'What?'

'Me,' I flush, 'wearing them – I can't pull it off.'

'But that's nuts.' She lowers her phone. 'You *made* them.'

'I *know*! I know how I feel when I'm sketching my designs, sewing them…'

'Go on.' She prods me. 'You feel…'

'Sure.' The word bursts from me. 'Like I've found one thing I *can* change. This…' I hug my arms around my wonky rosebud top. '…this is me. But when I think about going out in one of my makes, I just see Stella Harcourt and her crew of Tag-Hags sneering like I'm trash.'

'So? You put THE SWISH into trash, baby.' Tossing her curls, Lees strikes a pose. 'Forget the followers. Be your

19

own label.' She laughs – and her eyes shine bright enough for the both of us. For a second I can almost see it:

'Stop dreaming. Start walking.' Lisa turns her camera back on. 'Sashay *awaaaaay*!'

I shake back my hair, blink away the scrubby path, and set off down the Winter Wonderland catwalk in one of *my* creations! I am feisty, fearless and—

'CAT POO,' warns Lees.

I leap – and keep leaping. Hands on my hips, I start to kick up my legs in an Irish jig. As my mini-kilt starts flapping, my mate cracks up. She's got the maddest laugh, Lees, halfway between a baby's giggle and a smoker's cough. After the year she's had, I'll do anything to hear it. So I'm going for gold – whoops, here comes a star jump – when a front door slams in the street.

My front door.

I stop dancing. Lees puts away her phone. We look at each other through the gloom. Waiting. 'For Christ's sake, Kell!' it starts. 'Just leave it, can you?' Dad's voice carries from the kitchen. 'I *am* trying.'

'*Trying?* I get in from a ten-hour shift.'

Mum's reduced to a faint shriek. 'And you've not so much as loaded the dishwasher. There's baked beans *caked* to this pan. Chris?' A pause. The dull thud-thud-thud of someone heading upstairs. 'Don't walk away from me!'

I turn and trudge back down the alley for my coat. Scooping it off the fence, I look up at our attic window. Sure enough, the light comes on. A shadow moves across the glass. 'What are you doing in there?' Mum's fainter now; shut out. 'I've got Daisy hanging off one arm, a saucepan in the other...'

'Jeez,' says Lees. 'What is it with them? Your parents used to be so, you know...'

'Nice to each other?'

'Yeah! I mean, I get it – life's not exactly a picnic for people at the moment. Your dad could do with a break, but your mum—'

'She's never *not* working.'

'Exactly! So why so broke?'

'How would I know?' I yank on my coat. 'They don't talk to *me*, do they? I just catch scraps.' I thrust my arm through the frayed sleeve lining. My hand comes out snared in threads. 'Mum's always shrieking on about some monster debt they've got, like it's some evil pet they're hiding in the cupboard under the stairs. Dad says it's not *his* fault it's growing, eating us alive.'

'Jeez,' Lees says with a shiver, 'what the—'

'Twins, has to be.' I tug at my coat zip. 'Talk about evil pets! They trash everything, then eat what's left. *Nooo!* The zip chews into my top. 'You. Are. Kidding.' The harder I pull, the more rosebuds I ruin. When Lees tries to help, I elbow her away. 'I can *do* it.'

'Yeah, looks like.' Lisa peels off home, leaving me to fight it out – Kat versus zip.

Upstairs, my folks rage on.

From our kitchen, Lil starts bawling.

'S'OK Lil, *I'm coming.*' I'll have to cut my top free. So much for The Swish! 'Be Your Own Label?' I rattle open our gate. 'Just Wear It, more like.'

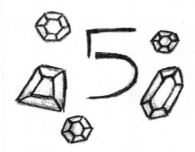

Funny, isn't it, how the 10W cool squad can only smell my "stinky" sandwiches when Lisa's off playing hockey?

Less funny when it's peeing it down. Fat raindrops plopping onto clingfilm, I unwrap today's lunch: yay, Marmite *again*. Who needs cheese strings or carrot batons? They are the playthings of the rich!

If I crane forward on my bench (best in the playground, natch) I can see into the brightly lit canteen. Watching the Tag-Hags gather round their usual table, I play my daily game of Lunch Break Lip Sync. First up, Carly – recoiling from something she's found in her baguette: 'Is that – *ew* – butter?' I mutter as her lips move. Next, I voice over Keisha, who is 'like, soooo dieting for the ball' in between slurps of banana Yazoo. I've got Jayden "crying off carbs" (and cracking into a giant bar of Dairy Milk) when all chat screeches to a halt. One by one, the girls bob up to greet the arrival of their Supreme Style Influencer aka...

Stella Harcourt aka...

10W's version of Beyoncé (only talentless and white).

Flicking her silky blonde hair, Stella waits for Keisha and Jayden to *shift*. Centre position vacated, she slides down onto the bench, pulls out her phone, and starts sharing. This time there's no need to lip sync, I can hear the squeals from here:

'Beautiful!'

'Stell, that dress would SO win for you!'

'Keep swiping!' As her thumbs glide over her phone, I can practically hear the silks rustling, the skirts swishing. We're all on the same countdown now, aren't we? Twelve days until Winter Wonderland. Twelve days to get our hands on a killer gown.

Lucky for me, today is the twenty-ninth of the month. That means payday at Armitages, which means my one chance to talk Mum into buying me a dress before another wage packet gets gobbled by *(cue horror music)* our MONSTER DEBT. Fortunately, I have a cunning, three-point plan for persuasion. I'm calling it *(swap horror music for drum roll)* my Cunning, Three-Point Plan for Persuasion...

1. Wait in kitchen for Mum to get home, then beg:
   'Just a cheap dress from New Look, Mum! Enough to transform me into a legit ball-goer *not* a sad meme @FashionFail #poorkid.'
2. Pause for Mum to put on kettle, and snort:

'So much for the next great generation of feminists! Aren't we over the whole Cinderella thing? And what's with the "hashtag poorkid"? You're a great kid! Bright, hardworking... anyone gives you a hard time, they're jealous.'

'Of *what* exactly?'

3. Launch into impassioned portrayal of St Edward's social pecking order – and how I'm at the bottom of it... getting *pecked.*

'I'm not sexy or sporty, Mum. I don't have a cool boyfriend or serious bling. I don't even have a "quirky" behavioural syndrome I can talk about at sleepovers. I just have smelly sandwiches and a coat that trails threads. So no, I'm not asking for a Cinderella dress. I don't *dare* stand out from the crowd. For one night only, I want to FIT IN.'

Heart-rending speech or what? How could any parent not instantly hand over £50 "for something sparkly"?

I WOULDN'T KNOW because when I *do* get home to argue the case for Looking Normal, I find Zack sat on our sofa, wearing a tea cosy on his head. He's playing his guitar (obvs), picking out the riff to 'Seven Nations Army', while my monster sisters jump up and down on the cushions in my old Disney Princess dresses.

I used to treasure every frill, now they're tattered and stained, their Velcro tabs stuck with ginger frizz. As the twins bounce, their bright pink and green skirts rise up like parachutes. 'Hey,' I catch Daisy before she lands on Zack's head. 'Who put *you* in charge of childcare again?'

''S no trouble.' He pushes back his tea cosy. 'Your dad had to go down the shop for candles.'

'Candles?' I grab Lil, who wriggles to get to Zack.

'Pwitty pwincess,' she clips a dangly pair of plastic earrings onto him. Daisy rams a broken tiara onto his head.

'PLAY GEEEEETAR!'

'Woah!' He scoops her up. 'Your mum's gone to grab a shower,' he tells me. 'Things got pretty messy when the twins joined in.'

Joined in with what? Looking closer, I see their sticky faces and arms are smeared with flour – and is that a melted chocolate button stuck to Lil's hair? I inhale the gooey, sweet smell of baking.

'Oh, Zack.' I sink down onto the sofa. 'How could I forget?' It's the 29th November. No wonder our house smells cosy for once.

Through the open door of our kitchen, I glimpse an explosion of mixing bowls and sugar-dusty sieves. In the centre sits a huge, wonky, Malteser-covered birthday cake – the same cake Mum makes *every* 29th November.

'I'm sorry, Zack,' I say.

''S all right.' He flattens his hands over his strings. 'No biggie.'

But it *is* a big deal, to all of us. 'I got so obsessed with this ball, I forgot.' I wipe a streak of white flour from his forehead. 'There's more important things than a stupid dress.'

'It's not stupid to you,' says Zack. 'Life goes on, yeah?'

Not always. Resting my head against his, I wonder if he can still see her in there? Can he smell the cocoa butter his mum used to rub into her skin; the spicy scents of cooking that would catch in her hair?

It's her laugh I remember best: Marie Melway and my mum would sit round the kitchen table, cackling away for hours, like life was an inside joke you couldn't get till you'd had kids and "kissed goodbye" to your pelvic floor. It was Mum who produced a birthday cake for Marie every year. And Mum who says, 'Now she's gone, all the more reason to celebrate she was here.'

For once, my parents agree. As Zack and I wait for Dad's key in the door, the twins tire. A mess of deflated skirts, they sink into my lap. Lil sucks her thumb, Daisy rests her head against Zack's shoulder. Gently, so as not to disturb her, he starts to pick out a tune on his guitar. The notes are slow, delicate… nothing I recognise. Until Lil starts humming. Then Daisy joins in, singing the words every child learns in their parents' lap: 'Happy birthday to you.'

It's dark by the time Zack's brother Andy gets in from the market. We light the candles and all cut the cake together in the Melways' kitchen. It's the usual scrum. My mum telling Dad he's holding the plate wrong and the twins 'blowing' out the candles (i.e. flobbing over Dad). But for once I don't want to strangle my family or moan about money. Watching the Melway brothers share out slices of burnt cake like they're the luckiest guys ever, I feel an ache in my chest.

How dare *I* ask for anything?

ew day, new me. Who needs to go to a stupid ball anyway? This girl's got better fish to fry! Or should that be flamingos? I found a flock of them in Franklins store. Not *actual* flamingos (Franklins sells fabrics, not feathers. Unless you count the kind you stick on a hat). But I swung by their shop after school, and found this beautiful remnant in the bargain bin: pink flamingos against a tropical sky. How could I *not* blow my last two quid on it?! Flying home, I fixed the twins' tea, then dug out a skirt I'd got aaaaages ago from the Cancer Research shop. It's denim (but not the cool kind. Forget Levi 501s, this is drab denim, denim that says, 'Sorry, can't talk fashion now, got to go sweep the prison yard'). I've cut and pinned my flamingo print into the central panel, and *pfla-pfla-pfla* (sound of wings flapping) it's virtually Versace!

Now to stitch down the edges on my Singer, and—

'Kat!' Dad sticks his head around my bedroom door.

'Am I glad to see you!'

'You are?' I take my foot off the pedal. 'Really?' I beam.

'For sure,' he beams back. 'You busy?'

'Just upcycling this skirt. See?' I flap my flamingos at him, and he ducks back behind the door. 'But it can wait!' I leap up after him, which is when I see he's holding Lil.

'Sorry.' He pulls a face. 'Her nappy's fit to burst – and it smells like a corker! Thanks, love.' Dad retreats to the attic, leaving *me* holding the baby. Except Lil's not a baby any more, is she? She's a toddler-sized BUTT-BOMB. Running to the bathroom (Daisy in tow) I whip off the one of the few nappies we have left, and *splat!* Lil explodes all over me.

Gah, gah. I'm gagging, but can't grumble – because Dad was racing back to his desk, wasn't he? I'm thinking –

1). A dad racing to get back to work is a dad who's got his mojo back. And,
2). Dads with mojos are statistically waaaaay more likely to buy their daughter a dress than dads who stare at the wall.

Yes, I know, I wasn't going to ask for anything! I was going to stay in my room upcycling rags FOR ALL ETERNITY. But as I change out of my crap-stained jeans into my worn-out leggings, I just want *for once* to have something new.

'Come on, you two.' I fasten Lil into a fresh nappy while Daisy tries to climb on my back. 'Time for *Dora the Explorer*.' Plonking the ginger chubsters down on the sofa with Nanny Netflix, I go back upstairs to Dad. Tickets for Winter Wonderland go on sale next week, and apart from Lisa (who says she won't attend any event that doesn't let her wear a tracksuit and/or gum guard) I am the only girl in 10W without a dress in her sights. Mum won't even commit to buying my ticket! To free up funds, I offered not to eat for, like, a *month*. 'Fine. You do that,' she said. 'I'll force baked beans up your nose WHEN YOU SLEEP.' (Not one of our best chats.)

An after-school job is out. I've tried, but the big stores aren't hiring. COVID killed off loads of the smaller ones, leaving just a few back-street shops. Before seeking solace in Fabricland today, I tried Patsy's Tea Parlour, Govinda's Crystals, Geoff's Pets... No one's hiring fourteen-year-olds. Why bother, when there's grown-ups like my mum ready to earn minimum wage? Meanwhile, I can't even get babysitting work because I'm stuck at home *doing it for free*.

Still, there's an upside to Mum working late at Armitages: it leaves Dad OPEN.

'Dad?' I knock on the attic door.

Nothing.

'Dad? You got a sec?'

Nudging open the door, I squeeze through the crack. Because you know those flash studio lofts you see on Pinterest, all skylights and steel beams? Well, *our* loft is basically a cupboard under the roof, with just enough space for one chair, one desk and my dad. He's sat hunched over his laptop, and only notices me when I whack him in the back trying to get in.

'Hey!' Dad pulls down his headphones. They're huge things – noise-cancelling ('family-cancelling,' says Mum.) As they come off, I catch his computer screen.

'Dad,' I frown at his Amazon book page. 'You've got to stop reading this stuff! You know what Mum says.'

'Yeah, well I'm not your mum, am I?' He scrolls down. 'I *care* what people think.' Which is the problem. Because you can't write books and not expect people to rate them. But scanning Dad's Amazon page, I see no rating has been posted for months. The last batch of reader reviews called his book "total dross"; "a huge disappointment". "It fails to match the magic of Chris Parker's first novel."

'You'll show 'em, Dad.' I rest my chin on his head. When did his hair get so thin? It smells musty. And sort of sad... like the armchair of a lonely person. A tinny noise comes up from him: 'Back in Black' by AC/DC – his favourite rock track. Dad used to blast it down the stairs; now it just leaks from his headphones. 'D'you remember how I used to crawl under your desk when I was little? You'd be writing away—'

'And you'd start sewing.' He nods knocking my chin. 'Your mum would bring home small fabric swatches from work and you'd turn them into dresses for your Barbie dolls. And that funny bag you stitched for me —'

'From purple felt,' I cringe. 'I made you put your pens in it!'

'Still do.' He points to a stack of discarded manuscript pages, crowned by a wonky pencil case. Seeing the dusty purple felt, and the babyish (egg yellow!) stitches, I want to cry suddenly. I remember how Dad would break off from writing to scoop me into his lap. I'd sew away while he spun out tales of his 'glory days' – how he snuck into a secret Blur gig; hitchhiked with his brothers to hear Oasis play at Knebworth; took Mum to her first (and only) 'Glasto'. 'World's maddest festival,' he shook his head, 'and your mum wore strappy heels and white capri pants. She spent three days stuck in the mud, screeching, "These are dry-clean only! And when are S Club 7 coming on?"'

He's good at telling stories, my dad. He used to write for the music press. When all the hip 'muso' newspapers

31

went under, he plucked up the courage to write a book. About an "imploding rock band", which sounded exciting. 'A bit *too* exciting,' Mum told me. 'Best read it when you're older.' (Apparently 'things happen' in a hot tub, and Mum's 'not sure the contraceptive message is sound'.) The critics loved it though. Mum stuck the press cuttings above Dad's desk. Their corners are curling and yellow now, but I can still see her pushing blobs of Blu-Tack onto the wall like she was pinning medals onto Dad's chest. 'Chris Parker has written a striking debut,' said the *Guardian* review. '*Bass Instincts* is a rattling great romp through the music industry,' said *The Times*. 'Work of genius,' beamed Mum, planting a smacker on Dad.

Who cares it didn't sell loads? It got Dad a book deal, meaning a publisher paid him for two more books *before he'd even written them.* How awesome is that?

Not so awesome, turns out.

The next thing Dad wrote was darker. Deeper, he says. Too deep, I'm thinking. Because no one liked it, and now all the money from his advance is gone and his publisher's not answering his calls. Dad hides up here, hugging his writer's block, while I'm left hanging off his shoulders like a poncho.

'What is it, Kat?' He shakes me off. 'Not this ball business? Your mum says you're after a dress.'

'Just a cheap one! Nothing fancy.'

'What's wrong with fancy?' Dad frowns.

'Really?' I feel hope catch in my ribs. 'You mean it?'

'Of course.' He peers at his screen. 'You're getting pretty good on that old sewing machine of your gran's.' He clicks off his Amazon page and on to a Word doc. 'I'm sure you can knock out something amazing.'

'*Knock out* a ball dress?' What *is* it with these people? 'Yes,

I can sew a skirt – or rework a top—'

'Great. So stitch the skirt to the top and bingo – you've got a dress!'

'It doesn't *work* like that, Dad! You can't patch together a ballgown, you need to find the right fabric, follow a design.'

'So open your sketchbook.' He starts tapping at his laptop. 'You've drawn a thousand swirling skirts.'

'When did *you* last see my designs?' I thump his chair. 'These days you only come into my room to dump the twins on me!'

'Christ, Kat.' He spins round. 'Can you stop blaming the twins?'

I stumble back. 'W-what?'

'You're always complaining about them! It's not your sisters' fault, this fix we're in. Now let me get on.' He swings back to his screen. 'Can't you see I'm writing?'

He's *writing*? I hold my breath, so as not to break the spell. Tentatively Dad runs his fingers over the keyboard, like it's a piano he's remembering how to play.

Forget my stupid dress. Dad's writing again? For one ragged heartbeat, I dare to dream. Then I bend to kiss the top of his head, and see he's just hitting backspace.

'**O**pen up!' Furious banging sounds on the front door. 'Now!'

I drop the pan I'm scrubbing into the sink. It all goes quiet for a second. Then the letterbox clatters. 'Can you hear me? Or do I—' *(BOOF)* 'Have to—' *(BOOF)*

'Wait!' I dry my hands on my school kilt.

'*BATTER YOUR DOOR DOWN!*'

'Isss Leeeesa!' The twins bounce in their high chairs. 'She BATTERIN'!'

'Coming!' I shout.

'We TUMMIN' TOO.' Chubby legs kicking, the twins slide out of their high chairs. Together we hit the hall, stumbling over parcels piled up for posting: Mum's violet coat, sold to the highest bidder; ditto her laptop, plus any clothes the twins have outgrown and *not* set fire to. Gah, I give them a kick (clothes, not twins, though it's close) and yank open the door. Lisa is crouched at letterbox height, shouting, 'You guys REALLY need to fix your doorbell! Oh, you're in.' She jerks upright, nearly taking my eye out with her hockey stick. She's got her skort rucked up and her crazy curls scraped into a sweaty top-knot. As she comes inside, I note several mud splatters and a nifty chin bruise.

'Good game, was it?' I ask, swiftly confiscating her stick. (Lisa tends to swing it about a bit. Recently bewailing the 'criminal overpricing of gumshields', she put such a dent in my wall we had to stick a big poster of Chris Hemsworth over it. And a small Tom Holland.)

'S not Lisa's fault, this new hockey obsession. She just needed a break from her mum, who's "clinically depressed" according to her GP, and "cries when making our tea", according to Lees ('I wouldn't mind, but it makes the sausages dead salty.')

So I suggested she check out some after-school clubs. By the time Lees got round to applying, though, the only places left were in Hockey and Christian Union. Clearly Christian Union was out ('How can *I* believe in eternal love,' said Lisa, 'when Dad left me and Mum for Sheila, the satsuma-coloured SEX BAG?')

But hockey? How was *that* going to work? Lees had spent months playing the divorce card to get out of PE. ('Sorry, miss, I can't run round the track due to emotional weakness in my legs'; 'Sorry, miss, I've lost my football boots somewhere in my BROKEN HOME.')

Sure enough, three weeks into hockey training, Lisa was mostly using her stick as a support aid. So the coach told her: 'Perform in today's match, or you're out.' What happened next is the stuff of St Edward's legend.

Two minutes from final whistle, we're 0-0 with Southbridge Academy (infamous shin-whackers). Lisa hasn't got near the ball, but *has* caught three Fruit Pastilles in her mouth, thanks to the sharp aim of her two cheerleaders. Energy snacks hurled, Zack and I are huddling together against the wind. (Why *is* that, by the way? Calm skies overhead, but walk out onto a hockey pitch, and whoops, your hair's blown off.) Then Zack spots a bald bloke trotting from the car park with a video camera. 'That's not...?'

'Lisa's dad! *Lees,*' I wave at her. 'Your dad's here!'

'And he's not on his own,' notes Zack.

Teetering after him in leopard-skin leggings and orange high heels is Sheila, aka the satsuma-coloured sex bag. Fake tan glowing, she plonks herself RIGHT behind the opposing team's goal. Lisa can't miss her.

Uh-oh, I gulp, *please miss her*. Because Lisa has scooped the ball off a passing defender, and is now charging full pelt towards Sheila. Raising her stick, Lisa WHACKS the ball straight into goal.

St Edward's fans storm the pitch! Zack and I jump on Lees (partly to 'hold her down,' mutters Zack, 'and get that stick off her'). While Sheila's led away by St John's Ambulance, Lisa leaves the pitch a hero and, more importantly, gets bumped up into the U15 Mixed Hockey Squad: welcome to *Popularity Big Time!* Picture St Edward's coolest girls teamed with Winsham Academy's fittest boys. Chuck in a shed-load of hormones and a few cans of body spray, and you've got *Love Island* with gumshields. Not that Lisa wanted to bump gumshields with anyone, not till recently, that is.

'Hey, dudes.' She scoops up the twins. 'You missed an EPIC showdown against Drydale College.' Daisy and Lil roar with delight as she swings them round our tiny hall. 'Guess who scored her fourth hat-trick of the season?'

'Awesome!' I catch Lil before she torpedoes into the coat pegs. 'You won, then?'

'We should've,' she snorts. 'Except your precious Jonah put himself up to take the crucial, last-minute penalty.'

'Jonah?' I feel my cheeks flush. 'He's not *my*—'

'I swear he can't see through that fluffy blond fringe of

his. His shot went about ten metres wide! We lost the game in overtime. Means there's no time for me to go home and change.' Flinging Daisy over her shoulder, she starts up the stairs. 'And I NEED to change!'

'Why?' I follow with Lil. 'If anyone can rock a trackie, it's you.' No lie, Lisa's got limbs of steels from all this sport. Plus, her cheeks are perma-rosy. Chuck in big blue eyes and that mass of strawberry-blonde curls? Her label is "Angel in Nike"!

Lisa can't see it, though. In training sessions, she doesn't note how every Winsham boy wants her on his team (or rushes to tackle her if she's not). Her sights are on—

'Gina,' says Lisa. 'You need to help me, Kat, she's going to be there!'

'Where?' I follow her into my room.

'Pizza Express.' She checks her phone. 'In half an hour! Team meal, and I need to look HOT.' Dumping Daisy onto the bed, Lees hops across my floor, dodging sequinned scraps. 'See you're at work!'

'Was, till I had to get the twins' tea.' Planting Lil with Daisy, I tidy away the scarlet scarf I'd started cutting up for a skirt (snipping off the "50p" tag as I went!). '*Careful,*' I cry as Lisa starts to rifle through my clothes rail – it's already teetering under the weight of my makes: floaty frocks I've sewn from old duvet covers, preppy kilts cut down from charity shop skirts, a glittery halter-neck I upcycled from an old "disco" top of Mum's – hardly "high fashion" (I cut out the shoulders, and laced up the back!) But still, *my* makes. My super sustainable Katwalk collection. 'What look are you going for?' I ask Lisa.

'FULL impact. Your yellow shirt maybe, or this vest with the beading?' She swishes my hangers. 'Your slogan tees are cool'. She pulls out a t-shirt I upcycled for last year's

Pride: tie-dyed it rainbow colours, then stitched gold satin letters across the front:

'That'll show Gina,' I say with a grin.

'Er, maybe not.' Lees shoves it back. 'We're going for pizza, not a parade. Oooh...' She pulls out an old favourite. 'I *love* this velvet bodice! Or will I get cheese on it?'

'Cheese away! The velvet's faux, but...' I hold it up against her. 'The bodice is so you. Just watch out for—'

'Pins, I know!' She pulls off her hockey shirt and hoiks on my bodice like the trusty in-house model she is. *Hours* she's spent stood in her underwear while I drape stuff over her, and jab her with pins. Lisa doesn't care. Give her a bag of Hula Hoops, and she'll munter on about hockey or Gina (or Hula Hoops) while I snip and pin a pillowcase into a mini skirt, or dismember a jacket I bought for £1 at a car-boot sale. (Arms? *Chop*. Neck? *Slice*. Result? Bodice!).

'Hang on,' I say. 'It needs to come in a bit.' Threading a needle from my sewing box, I pinch an inch of velvet round the back, and stitch in a couple of quick tucks. 'Perfect!' I spin her round to the mirror.

'You sure? Not too much?' She frowns. 'Should we run it past your—'

'Nope, she's out.' I give a brisk tug (yeah, like that'll bring her back!). Mum used to sit in the kitchen, a ginger frizzball clamped to each breast, as Lisa and I strutted out to the Katwalk. She'd give us a weary thumbs-up, then later I'd find a fiver stuck to my pillow with a Post-it note: *pin money!*

That's what bought the faux-velvet jacket. Vintage (OK, second-hand) but deep purple like royalty would wear. Maybe that's what gave me the idea of a princess bodice?

'Wow...' Lisa runs her hands down her slinky new shape.

'D'you

'Er, *yeah*. Unless she's nuts.'

'She's not nuts!'

'Just saying.' I raise my hand. 'She does wear a nose-ring.'

'That's not *nuts*.'

'It is if you spend your life playing hockey.' Gina Baxter only started at St Edward's last term. Apparently "something bad went down" at her previous school. Forced to wear a fabric plaster over her right nostril during play, Gina can't run onto the pitch without spectators debating:

a) Has she had an accident sniffing glue?

b) Gone overkill on the spot-squeezing, or

c) Been attacked by a fruit bat? (Can you tell Zack and I get bored when we've worked through the Fruit Pastilles?)

Pair her bandaged nose with a ruthless tackling streak, and Gina is NOT to be messed with. Plus, she wears her hair in a wedge-cut, and draws her eyeliner on super-fierce. Result? Of course Lisa fancies her! Now we just need *Gina* to figure it out. 'If you like her, let her know,' I tell Lisa for like the billionth time.

'But how?' says Lisa (also hitting the billion mark). 'I can't just bring it up when we're at the lockers.'

'Why not?' I straighten her top. 'Next time Coach gets you all into a hockey huddle, you volunteer to try a couple of new positions: Wing Attack, maybe – and oh yeah, being a lesbian?'

Lisa snorts – but she's listening. 'Go on.'

'So…' I pull the tatty rubber band from her hair. 'Coach sprints off to consult her Rule Book on Sexual Non-Discrimination in an AstroTurf Setting, and *you* clock Gina.' I scrunch her curls. 'Is she a) reeling in horror OR b) humming Katy Perry? If she's applying cherry chapstick, you're in!'

'I wish. Gina's not the problem, though, is she?' She tugs her head away. 'Stella Harcourt is.' She's not wrong. Stella RULES Year 10 like some crazy military leader, marshalling her Tag-Hag army to perform random acts of verbal cruelty, revenge-snogging and backstabbing. Stalking social media in her Nasty Gal boots and Stüssy jeans, Stella is our Dictator of Cool (and mercy is *not* her bag). If Lees comes out, sure Stella *might* decree her 'cool gay' like Cara Delevingne. But judging from the black looks she shoots Lees whenever she scores, she's more likely to kick up a stink in the girls' showers, then shriek, 'She was checking my pubes!' through the evil echo chambers of Snapchat.

'How does she get away with it?' Lisa yanks on my one pair of good jeans. 'It's like she marched into school one day and seized power.'

'Correction,' I say. 'Her daddy bought it for her. Stella wasn't always cool, remember?' I dart into my parents' room. 'BACK IN YEAR 7, SHE WAS PART OF THAT GIGGLY GANG,' I shout from their wardrobe, 'WHO FOLLOWED ZAYN MALIK… AND PLAYED NETBALL…' I swish through Mum's hangers for a cool scarf or belt, 'AND OBSESSED ABOUT LUSH BATH-BOMBS DURING DOUBLE MATHS.'

Nothing. (I swear Mum used to have more clothes than this. What else is downstairs in those eBay parcels?) Turning to my parents' bed, I see Dad's pillows have not migrated any nearer to Mum's since I last checked. But at least her stack of shoeboxes hasn't gone down. I bet Stella sleeps surrounded by TOWERS of them. When her folks split, she got *two* allowances – and started Year 8 flashing new blonde highlights and a Tommy Hilfiger jacket. Dropping netball for mixed hockey with Winsham Academy, she started wearing super-short skorts (like she wanted ALL the boys to notice her) plus full make-up (like she didn't want them looking too close). Now Stella's our official style queen, she punishes any girl who can't trail a label. She's got the Tag-Hags calling me "trashy" or "skank". Also "Alley Kat", which is ironic, because Stella does NOT know about me working the Katwalk.

'No way,' says Lisa when I return clutching a pair of black boots from Hobbs. 'I can't wear these out. Your mum loves them!'

'She loves you more. Besides…' I buff the boot leather with my sleeve. '…she's not worn them in ages. Says she can't get them on over her bunions.'

'Bunions?'

'Like onions…' I grin. '…but they grow on your feet. You get them from standing up in a shop all day, serving people like Stella. *She* sees you're wearing label heels?' I thrust the boots at her. 'She won't question the bodice.'

Lisa forces her feet into the shoes. What other option has she got? Don't get me wrong, Lisa's not scared of Stella (Lisa's pretty much the only girl in our class who isn't). But she doesn't want the whole school knowing her business before she's figured it out for herself.

I'm not like Lisa. I *am* scared. Not of what I can do with a needle. I know I can create kick-ass clothes. I just daren't wear them out… not after last time. The flashbacks still burn me, make my stomach turn inside out, make me want to rip up everything I've made, and never sew again.

Yep, there's a reason my designs don't make it off the Katwalk.

Halfway through Year 9 was when it happened. I remember it like it was yesterday. John Kerridge and his Winsham squad had fixed to hook up with Stella and the Tag-Hags at Norbridge Bowls. Only, this time, Lisa got asked along too. New star of U15 Mixed Hockey, she'd been blessed by the hand of inter-school cool (not that Lisa would notice a hand of anything unless it was passing her crisps).

Unfortunately, Lees doesn't *get* bowling. 'It's just a load of cannonballs. Without the fun of a cannon.' But I forced her to go and (crucially) take me, so I could hang with Jonah Kerridge. OK, sit close to him. OK, not *that* close to him. But in the same general area, looking casual (having spent all of Saturday finalising my look).

Nothing casual about the Tag-Hags though. While Lisa paid for us to get in, then proceeded to buy EVERYTHING on the hot dog counter, I felt the back of my neck burn. Heard the crackle of chat. Sure, Stella's squad had seen me round town enough weekends. They'd be striding into Urban Outfitters as I emerged from Fabricland in my patched dungarees (Sniggers Would Be heard). But this was

my first time "coming out"… in clothes I'd made myself.
Looking "Swish". As Lees led us to Stella's table, I shook
off my coat (and kept shaking!) Ate my hot dog, and hung
with the popular crowd. Can't hide in the crowd forever
though, can you?

'Hey, Alley Kat,' said Stella. 'Your turn to bowl.'

'Oi,' reared Lees. 'Don't you call her—'

"S fine.' I moved towards the ball rack, passing the
Winsham boys' bench. Gross Daniel and potty-mouth Paul
started whooping like they'd never seen a girl before. Not
Jonah, though… Sorry, Lees, but it seems to me Jonah sees
a lot through that dreamy blond fringe
of his. While Stella is all lip gloss
And "Look at me!" Jonah Kerridge
quietly looks *at you*. His eyes are so
soft – and sky-blue – you can just
tell he's sensitive. But strong,
too, I reckon. So that night at
Norbridge Bowls, I
finally did it. I dared
to look up…

And he was smiling.

At me?

AT ME!

I checked Stella. She'd seen it too.
Tossing her hair, she gave me The
Flick. But for once it didn't sting. Suddenly I felt as cool as
her. Cool as my cute, floral skater skirt! Not that I'd skated
in it (unless skidding down the stairs counts?) But I'd
chopped it down from a "mumsie" second-hand skirt, and
run a clashing pink strip around the hem to give it an edge.
So I was feeling sharp as I took up the bowling ball. Blowing
a wisp of hair from my eyes, I bent to take my shot.

'*You. Are. Kidding.*' Stella swooped down on me. 'Check the label, girls!' She clawed at the tab sticking up from my waistband. 'BhS. *British Home Stores?*' crowed Stella. 'That saddo shop shut down years ago!'

The Tag-Hags screeched round me. '*Sooo* charity shop—'

'So lame—'

'The shame!'

'Get *off*.' I twisted.

'Why?' Stella's nails scraped my skin. 'Scared we'll get a whiff of your skirt? Bet it reeks of old lady wee. Look, boys, the freak's *freaking out!*'

The Winsham crew were on us. Next thing I knew Stella had let go suddenly. Twirling round, I knew who I'd see—

'Lees?!' My mate had gone full Thor: one arm gripping Stella, the other raised to catch a flying hammer (slash hockey stick).

'You pair of freaks.' Stella twisted free. 'I'm outta here! Before I *catch* something. That skirt is skanksville.' She led her crew up the stairs, sniggering. 'Someone pass me the hand sanitiser!'

By the time I'd straightened my skirt, they'd all split. Tag-Hags and Winsham boys, they followed Stella to a bowling lane far, far away... on the other side of the social galaxy. When Jonah looked back, I tried to smile, but my face wouldn't work. I could only watch as he disappeared behind his fringe.

'Come on, this rack is paid for,' said Lisa. 'Cannonbaaaall!' she set off down the run. Scoring a strike, she turned and punched the air. 'Can't let the other side think you're beat.'

'Yeah, true.' I took the next ball. 'And *I* can't turn down free stuff.'

ut where do flashbacks get you? This isn't the movies. It's Norbridge, a week away from Winter Wonderland, and I'm dress-less...

Hopeless...

Down *with no gown.*

Still, it's Friday night, and I'm off to meet my hot date! Shame she's seventy-four and can't get out of her chair. 'All right, Gran?' I breeze into her room at Acorns Residential Home. 'Ready to go large?'

Gran nods, but she's always nodding now. It's her Parkinson's Disease; the doctors say the connections between her brain and body are starting to go a bit haywire, and they'll keep getting worse until—

LA, LA, LA, DON'T WANT TO THINK ABOUT IT.

She's been put on drugs that help but "can cause inhibition loss". Conversation-wise, it means Gran has no filter. Like now. 'Ooh, you've got such *strong* arms,' she tells the carer who's plumping her cushions. 'And a *very* macho moustache.'

'Hiya, Carlotta,' I greet the nice Spanish lady who looks after her. Luckily Carlotta loves Gran (and does have a fair bit of face fur, so perhaps appreciates the check-in?) 'Who's the old bird been winding up this week?'

'Only the council inspector,' Carlotta bustles out. 'She came round to do her tour, and your gran kept congratulating her on the size of her bottom.'

'It was gigantic! The size of, you know,' Gran waves a crabbed hand, 'those things you get in swimming pools.'

'An inflatable?' I swipe a biscuit off her plate.

'A whale.'

I cough up crumbs. 'That's some swimming pool, Gran.'

'It was some bottom.' She chuckles, nudging the plate towards me.

I like visiting Gran because every visit is exactly the same. Her room always smells of lavender and custard creams (and let's be honest, a fair whack of Febreze). Gran always sits by her bed waiting for me and, best of all, the twins aren't allowed. Acorns banned them after Daisy knocked over a glass of water holding old Mr Martin's dentures. While Mum mopped Mr Martin's crotch WHICH WAS BAD ENOUGH, Lil toddled off to post his teeth down the loo.

Besides, Gran doesn't "do" babies any more. ('Not now I can't pick them up, the wee dotes,' she says with a sigh. 'I'd rather chat to you.') She beams as I bounce onto her bed. 'No Zack today?' she asks.

'Next week.' I munch a second custard cream from the plate. 'He's helping Andy shift gear from the market tonight. He says to nick a biscuit for him.' I pocket custard cream number three. 'And to give you this.' I plant a kiss on her paper-soft cheek, and feel her skin crinkle up into a smile.

'Oh,' I remember, 'Mum's washed your blouses. Here.' I pop down the bag containing her carefully-folded fresh shirts. The laundry at Acorns always sends Gran's blouses back a bit crumpled and grey ('which makes *her* feel crumpled and grey,' says Mum, smoothing them out under her iron). Appearances are important to Gran. She's always got a twinkle in her eye, and asks Carlotta to do her 'lipstick and powder' every morning. Suddenly (weirdly) it strikes me that Stella would approve.

'Ach, what's with the frown?' says Gran. 'That wee madam at school causing trouble again?' I shrug. 'Well, you know what I say.' She pats my hand. 'Keep your friends close, but your enemies closer". Let's get out the googly wotsit!'

That's "iPad" to you and me. Acorns have got one for "communal use". It's in hot demand with the old folk, who use it mostly as a tea tray. Since Mum returned my smartphone to the store, Carlotta tries to smuggle the tablet to Gran when I come visit. Wiping the mug-rings off the screen, I now prop it on Gran's lap, and enter the Stella Harcourt Gallery of Gorgeousness where hair is always shiny, smiles are always "shared", and popular girls reign. With every swipe, I feel myself shrinking: a sad Alice who doesn't belong in their Wonderland.

'Ach, you're mad as a hatter to worry about this lot!' says Gran. 'Look at that pinched face.' She jabs a knobbly finger at Stella. 'Yes, she's got big hair, but her lips are thin. No wonder she's slavering them in that shiny muck. And what's with *this* poor creature?'

It's Carly, pulling a trout pout.

'She looks like someone slammed a door in her face,' huffs Gran. 'Her mum should rub some Savlon on her.'

Bless my gran and her "uninhibited responses". She's the Stormzy of Acorns, speaking her lyrical truth. So what'll she make of "Hockey Allstars @ Pizza Express"? I swipe to the pics posted from Lisa's team dinner: Stella flanked by Winsham boys; Natalie giving her dough balls to Jonah. I tap the familiar, floppy fringe. *'That's* the one I like.'

'Och, what a honey-pot! And such dreamy blue eyes,' clucks Gran. '*What* did you say her name was?'

Aargh! Luckily Carlotta comes back in with Gran's tea. Left alone to roam through the harsh and unforgiving landscape of social media, I meet girl after girl trying on gowns @WinterWonderland #killingit. 'Why the sad face?' Gran peers over her cup of tea at me. 'Thought you liked looking at clothes?'

'I do. I *did*. I just—'

'Spit it out, dear! I could be dead any second. Worse...' Her cup wobbles. '...I might phone your mother.'

'No!' I don't want her worrying Mum, or whomever else she gets through to. (Gran's dialling hand is that shaky, she's now best friends with "The Golden Lotus" takeaway in Aberdeen. And a strange man called Pat.) So I put away the iPad, and spill – about the ball, and the catwalk contest – and how everyone's got a shot but me. 'Which I'm *fine* with' (Gran's cup has started to rattle in its saucer) 'I'd be mad to think—'

'Ach, whoever got anywhere by thinking? It's *dreams* that transport you.' She waves her hand. 'Dreams that transform!'

But she's forgotten she's holding her tea, hasn't she? By the time I've tidied her up, there's no getting back to Winter Wonderland. Which is OK by me. We've got better places to go! 'Ready, dear?' says Gran.

It's *my* turn to nod. 'That's my girl.' Rattling open a door in her bedside table, she presses a tiny brass key into my palm.

Crossing the little room, I reach her huge wardrobe. The only *proper* thing Gran got to keep after selling her flat, it's massive and made of mahogany like a dark, fairy-tale vault.

But if you know the secret – and look hard enough – there's a tiny brass lock set into the door.

Carefully, very carefully, I insert the key.

Big news. BALL news. When Camel Cribbs makes the shock announcement in assembly, Zack's the first person I call (this news is too big for a text!) He doesn't pick up, of course (too busy playing guitar riffs in his head to hear his phone). So I have to hold it in all day, fearing I MIGHT BURST. Hopefully over one of the Tag-Hags. It's got so you can't walk down a corridor without crashing into one of them hunched over her phone, stabbing 'BUY! BUY!' Talk about *un*sustainable fashion – every Mumbai sweatshop is now shipping a strapless dress to the Norbridge area.

Yep, Stella's called it: her look for the ball will be "hot, but not try-hard". Keywords are "shimmer", "streamline" and "mermaid". Now everyone's trawling the net for frocks with a fishtail.

Not every catch lands. It seems Carly's gown flopped out of its packaging yesterday looking *very* different to what the photo promised. According to Lees (who fills me in on the goss as we stream out of school), Carly tried it on and panicked. Worse, she sent a selfie to Stella. Now the only pics getting shared around the hockey locker room are

#frockhorror and #human jellyfish.

'Ouch,' I say. 'That must sting.'

'For Carly,' says Lisa. 'But for you, it means one less rival on the catwalk!'

''S that easy, is it?'

'Well, obviously you've got to sit down at your sewing machine and do some...' She waves her hockey stick. '...you know—'

'Sewing?'

'Yes!'

'Wow, thanks for the tip.' I laugh. 'You'd never know your head was full of sprinkles.'

'What can I say?' She grins. ''S not every day Gina asks me to split a toffee banoffee with her. And it's all down to you! NO IDEA she had me down as a Tag-Hag 'cause of these.' She shakes her strawberry-blonde curls. ''S only when I tipped up to Pizza Express in your "bomb bodice" – Gina's words – that she saw I was *not* some sad Stella clone.'

'Suffering Sappho!' I cross my wrists like Wonder Woman. 'Unleash the BODICE POWER.'

She shoves me, giggling. 'It's *you* who's got bodice power, Kat. Those Tag-Hags can stuff their online shopping baskets. They'll still look like cheap Stella Harcourt knock-offs. You're the only one who can design something that's, you know...'

'What?'

'*You.*'

'Right,' I puff. 'A saddo with a needle! I can't afford so much as a new bit of trimming.'

'Jeez, enough with the tragedy.' Lees raises her stick and starts to draw it like a bow across an imaginary violin. I swing my bag at her. Repeatedly.

'Oi, watch the face!' She batters me off. 'Sprinkles is

calling.' As she peels off down the high street to find Gina, I imagine what it'd be like to have Jonah waiting for me, his face lighting up as I dazzle the room.

I veer off without thinking. Normally my walk home takes in the charity shops on Eddison Road: the British Heart Foundation, the Trussell Trust, Barnardos. (If the clothes don't speak to me, the cosy shop staff do!). Tonight, though, I'm not feeling the thrift. All those glittery gowns the other girls are swiping? They've got to me. So I divert down Charlton Mews, a cobbled street lined with swanky boutiques. The windows are plush – classy mannequins draped in backless gowns and silky, floor-length shifts. Pressing my face against the glass of a gorgeous gown shop, I play my new favourite game: 'I Wish'. *Swish,* a dress appears, like I conjured it up: a golden mermaid gown with a glittering fishtail. There's just one catch:

It contains Stella.

Striking a pose outside the changing room, she struts across the shopfloor. Keisha and Jayden are *literally* applauding, while an assistant tucks a luxi price tag into the dress, then bobs away like She's Not Worthy.

Now *that's* "bodice power".

I turn away before they can see me. As I trudge back to the high street, the drizzle hardens to rain, turning the bright lights blurry. How can *I* dream of storming the school catwalk? It's the Bank of Mum or Dad that buys "Most Dazzling Look".

Crossing the road, my shoes start to leak. Sinking into a puddle outside Poundland, my socks turn to soup. As I splosh past shops filled with phoney snowmen and fake-fur coats, it hits me. Hits me *like a speeding reindeer in the face*: Santa sucks.

Forget Christmas being a festive free-for-all. It's a

ticketed event, at the coolest club in town. Inside, music's pumping, everyone's laughing and dancing and snogging under the mistletoe. Everyone except me. I stop to take in the chaos. 'Sorry, love, you're not coming in.' Santa blocks the door like a bouncer in a super-lame suit. 'Your name's not on the list.'

Scrap being naughty or nice. No one cares. Like a rubbish RuPaul, I sashay *awaaaaay* from the Christmas sparkle. My path is down the back streets, past the dodgy chicken shops... the boarded-up barber's... the children's hospice shop... the job centre... and the church. Shivering outside St Thomas's, a vicar-type bloke hands out mince pies. 'Christ is coming!' he shouts. So I eat mine quick before Baby Jesus can grab it. Sorry, but I am *over* "miracle births".

'Hallelujah!' everyone said when the twins came along. 'Answers to a prayer!' Yet when Mum and Dad remember getting pregnant with *me*? Whole other story: 'All those terrible years of trying,' Dad groans. 'Heartbreak after heartbreak,' recalls Mum, 'I swear that's when your dad started losing his hair.' Then they look at each other and shudder just like they did that time our toilet got blocked, and the man from Drain Wizard had to come and pump "years of blocked waste" from the pipes. Ironic, as that's pretty much what the doctors did, with Mum, I mean. Poked about with her pipes for years, before she finally got me through IVF. On, like, the seventh go. "Bless the NHS", and all that. You'd think I was the miracle! But no, ten years later, out pop the twins. 'God's plan,' said the midwife, but I've always pictured it more like that stomach-busting scene from *Alien*.

Twice.

Getting home, I find my sisters strapped into their high chairs, screaming so hard their faces are purple. Their orange curls are sticky with sweat.

'Ssh, ssh,' I try to soothe them. But Lil's back is arched that rigid, I can't get her out. Now I'm panicking too. 'Muuu-um? Daaa-ad?'

'I swear, Chris...' Mum's screams come down the stairs. '...say that ONE MORE TIME, and I will—'

'What? Shout at me?' His voice is muffled by the attic door. 'Change the record, Kell.'

'RECORD?!' Mum spirals. 'Who listens to *records* anymore?'

'Ssh, I'll be back,' I tell the twins. Running upstairs, I find Mum resting her head against Dad's door. 'The world's changed, Chris. Everything's broken. *We're* broken.'

I turn back down to the kitchen. I manage to unstrap Lil, who clings to me, throttling me with her hot arms as I fight to free Daisy. Now they're both bouncing in my arms, like this is fun! Can't they see I'm RIGID WITH RESENTMENT as I lower them carefully to the floor? Can't they feel me EMANATE HOSTILITY as I tuck them into their red duffle coats, and FURIOUSLY tug down the sleeves so their little fingers don't freeze?

'*ZackandAndys, ZackandAndys!*' they shout with joy as I pull on their little yellow wellies. I herd them towards the back door, but (*ugh*) it's stuck again. (Dad blames the damp. Mum blames Dad. Meanwhile, there's mushrooms growing out of the woodwork; sadly *not* the kind we can fry up for our tea.) Gritting my teeth, I yank hard. Twins at my heels, I leap the back step and run to my safe place.

Zack.

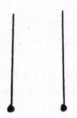

Feels like forever I've been climbing over the back fence to the Melways. Then two years ago Dad tore through it, mad as the winter wind that had been banging at our windows all day. He'd just got back from the hospital: Marie Melway had asked him to be there when the consultant brought her test results. Hours Mum and I had been waiting for him to get back. But he strode past us, out into our tiny patch of garden, his face grey and hard like the sky. Tearing off his coat, then his shirt, he wrenched at our back fence like the Hulk, which is *so* not Dad! You could see *actual muscles* bulging in his back as he yanked at the wood, and then CRACK.

Everything splintered.

Mum saved things (she still could then). 'Chris, you're so stong!' She'd pretended to swoon. Catching her, Dad had laughed, then practically collapsed through the gap in the fence. He didn't drop her, though.

Looking back, that was the last time things felt normal.

Except they weren't, were they? Normal, I mean. The twins were due any day, so Mum's stomach was out to HERE, and Marie Melway's tumour was growing. Now the doctors could see dark spots on her lungs, Everything they'd thrown at it – the chemo that hurt her skin; the special tea Andy made her drink; the oranges Zack blew his pocket money on? The cancer just laughed.

That's why Dad attacked the fence. Zack and I had been climbing over it since his sixth birthday. He'd BEGGED his parents for a slide. Propped it against their side of the fence, and dropped the ladder down ours. Worked a treat for years! But when Marie got proper sick and Mum started to worry Zack would do himself an injury – all six foot of him trying to climb over in the dark. Andy was nineteen then.

On her bad nights, the nurses would let him stay over at the hospital, and Zack would appear at our back door. Mum would put a big dinner down in front of him (she had time to cook back then: huge, squidgy lasagnes, crispy roast chicken). Zack would wolf the lot while Dad went upstairs to blow up the air mattress. That's when our spare room was just for junk. Boxes of expensive baby kit were piling up, but Zack made a nest for himself among Dad's old gear: "Teach Yourself" books (*How to Play the Beatles*; *Easy Oasis*) and the guitar he'd never learned to play. My folks put off turning the room into a nursery until Mum came back from the hospital.

And Zack's mum didn't.

The day after Marie's funeral, Dad gave his guitar to Zack. Said he'd heard him learning to play it quietly at night.

He's still quiet, Zack. Until he picks up his guitar. Then he thrashes the strings like it's way more than a riff he's ripping up – he could tear the whole damn world apart. When Andy's not disconnecting his amp. ('You and that guitar?' he says. 'You're gonna do all kinds of damage! But at least this way I can hear the footy.')

'*ZackandAndys, ZackandAndys!*' I help the twins through the gap in the fence, then they're off, waddling in their wellies like ducks up the Melways path.

By the time I catch up, they've shot through the kitchen into the boys' front room. The footy's on the TV. Andy's afro is sticking up from the back of the sofa, next to a ruffled blonde head... a *lady* head! The girls love him. Lees reckons it's down to Andy being so cool. I think it's 'cause he's kind. Mum says, 'They want him because they can't have him'. Lily's clearly not got the message. Climbing over the sofa, she whacks Ruffled Blonde in the face with her yellow wellies. 'Aargh!' cries the girl, then, 'ahh,' as Daisy follows over. 'Identical twins?' she coos. 'They're so sweet!'

'They're savages,' says Andy, catching Daisy before she can nose-dive onto the rug. Without taking his eyes off the footy, he raises his arm and grips my hand in the famous Andy-Melway-Bone-Crush. 'Got your wings yet, girl?'

'Almost,' I fudge. It's Andy who found the old Diesel jacket for me. He used to be a serious style player himself. Now he scouts cool thrift for me down the market.

'Neat idea to stitch in your gran's seed pearls,' he says. 'Your mum go for it?'

'Er, yeah. Soon as her next pay cheque comes in, she says.'

'Sure?'

'Sure.' I squeeze his hand. No way am I letting Andy lend me cash. He's already working all hours on the stall to keep his little brother in guitar strings.

'Nooo!' The wrong side scores. Andy lets go, leaving me to head upstairs... towards the elastic-band sound of an electric guitar being played without its amp.

Pushing open Zack's door, I throw myself down on his bed. The boy barely looks up, intent on picking his way through the opening lick of AC/DC's 'Thunderstruck.' Forget *Easy Oasis*, he's onto the hard stuff. Mm, is that why

58

he's starting to *look* hard too? His jaw flexes above his white school collar. His arms work against the thin polyester of his shirt. Rummaging through the homework Zack's dumped onto his duvet (*yesss,* Fruit Pastilles) I furrow my brow at the former playfellow of my youth.

'What?' says Zack.

'You.' I chuck him a Fruit Pastille.

'*Man,* you know I hate the red ones.' He chews through a power chord.

'Look at you,' I laugh. 'Acting cool like you do not care.'

'I don't.'

'But still, you're getting all, you know.' I stick out my jaw.

'Dislocated?'

'*Chiselled.*'

'Jeez, Kat.' Blushing, he ducks his head back over his strings. That's when I see it, what's changed.

'Andy's had the clippers out!' Zack's new crop is sharp ... and so are his cheekbones. Zack gets them from his dad. Plus, his dad was white, so Zack's skin's a bit lighter than Andy's ('diluuuuuted,' Andy teases him) and his eyes are this mad emerald colour. When they catch the light, or lock on to you – like now...

'*Zing!*' my mum used to say to Marie. 'Your boy's going to be a heartbreaker.' Of course the only thing *I've* seen Zack breaking is guitar strings. *Ping!* He snaps one now.

He swears, then checks his mum hasn't heard. He does this without realising, glances at her picture by his bed when he's stewing over homework or trying to master a lick.

She was ace, Marie. Always smiling like in this photo: a dimple in each cheek and lights dancing in her eyes. She had a strict side, though, too. Bringing up two boys on her own, she was forever shouting, 'Think before you jump, child!' or 'Watch how you go.' Round her neck she wore a small, silver St Christopher medal. 'To protect us on our journey,' she told me. 'Every day is an adventure.'

Now Andy wears her chain. But he's given up his adventures to wave Zack off on his. 'Watch how you go, bro,' he rubs the medal with his thumb. 'Don't look back.'

'According to Camel Cribbs,' I tell Zack, 'not a single Winsham boy is trying for Most Dazzling Look. Can you believe it?'

'Er, yeah,' says Zack with a laugh and fishing out a new guitar string. 'This is Norbridge we're talking about. You'll be lucky to get the lads into a tux.'

'Whatever. Boys are useless. But now school's decided to chuck in a talent contest,' I bounce on the bed. 'Winter Wonderland committee are holding auditions next Monday. Any student from St Edward's or Winsham Academy can enter, individually or in a group. Winner gets to perform at the ball in front of two hundred kids. Not bad for your first gig!'

'My *what*?' He looks up from threading his string.

'You heard me. What else have you been practising for?

Here's your chance to get up on stage and finally *play* that thing!'

'It's called a guitar.'

'Correction, it's a rock guitar. And *you*, my green-eyed

goon, need to start looking the part.' Jumping off the bed, I fly out the door. '*ANDY!*' I shout down the stairs.

'*What?*' he shouts up.

'You know that biker jacket you got ages ago – scuffed suede, classic zip?'

'Yeah.'

'Can Zack have it?'

'No.'

Hmm. Time to ramp up my feminine powers of persuasion. 'Oh, Andy...' I lean over the banisters. '*Go onnnn!*'

Silence.

Then an explosion of sound from the front room. I can't tell who's going crazier – 90,000 fans in Wembley Stadium, or Andy and the twins.

'GOAL!' yells Lil.

'*Yessss!*' cries Andy.

'Thank you,' I mouth back. Then I make like a stealth panther and creep past the top of the stairs to Andy's room. It's smaller than Zack's. Andy insisted they swap last year to allow for his little brother's growing collection of amps. Now you can't get past Andy's clothes rail without ramming your shins on his bed (a double with one flattened pillow. Andy never asks girls to stay over. If I come round for breakfast, it's just the Melway boys chucking cornflakes at each other).

Along the wall, Andy's categorised his beloved collection of trainers (scruffy for work / muddy from footy / GLOWING WHITE for the ladies). On top of the bed, he's tossed his pair of pinstriped trousers. Despite their classy tailoring, Andy wears them like jeans (scruffy for work / hoovering round Zack's homework / loving the ladies). No wonder the hems are fraying. Poor pinstripes.

Smoothing out each leg, I pinch the central crease back into line and realise that these weren't designed to flop over a pair of Reeboks. No wonder they look forlorn, they're *suit* trousers, missing their other half! Where…? I rifle through Andy's clothes rail. There! A super-sharp, pinstriped jacket.

As I shake it, a memory flies out: Andy buying the suit to celebrate getting his internship at the architect's firm. 'No more uni student.' He snapped on the jacket for his mum. 'I'm off to build castles!'

Before the year was out, he was wearing the suit to her funeral. Then he hung up his jacket and went to work for Fat Bloke. Not his real name (at least I hope not) but he's the size of a sumo wrestler, and he runs a massive patch in

Market Square on Tuesdays and Saturdays – plus some stalls down by the railway arches – flogging plastic mops, cheap tea towels and knock-off bottles of Toilet Duck. Andy's his best worker. Never misses a shift and takes time with the old ladies. If little Moggy's wee'd on your best rug, then Andy's your man! Just not the man he planned to be.

Returning the suit hanger to the rail, I grab what I came for: Andy's biker jacket. He found it in Camden Market, so it's proper vintage – with a twist: instead of black leather, it's made from the softest brown suede. A slim brass zip runs up the front, forcing the collars up into a hard flick. I show it to Zack. 'Rock star or what?'

He recoils. 'I can't take Andy's jacket. I wanna pay him back,' he says, 'not nick his stuff.'

'Relax. I've heard you shred enough chords.' I buff up the suede. 'I know the plan.' Zack's gonna make music, then make it big! Big enough to save *both* Melway brothers. 'But if you want to get your brother off the market stall, and back to building castles, you've got to stop practising and start playing. Get out there.'

'Be judged, you mean?'

'Earn your dues.' I chuck the biker jacket at him. He lets it slide to the floor.

So I sink back down on the bed. He picks out a tune. I dole out more Fruit Pastilles. I'm kicking my legs when he puts down his guitar.

Shrugs on the jacket.

It looks good on him. Rolling his shoulders, Zack gets a feel for it, and it's like I can feel it too – how the soft suede strains across his back, how the sleeves ride up his wrists when he goes for his guitar. Slicing through the opening riff of 'Thunderstruck', Zack looks up at me and smiles.

Game on.

Zack's only gone and put a band together! He comes through the Melways' back door FULL OF IT. 'But...' I clear space for him to prop his guitar against the kitchen table. '...I only gave you the jacket yesterday!'

'Well, it worked.' He flicks up his collar. 'I'm a rock star!'

'Hey.' I stop him sitting on my homework. 'Watch where you put your rock star butt.'

'Sorry!' He leaps up, and helps me collect my sketches, scattered over the table and chairs. 'Latest textiles project?' he asks. I nod.

'Miss Bloxam wants to see our ethical fashion designs, but I can't work at home. The twins have decided they're flesh-eating cannibals, and kept trying to take a bite out of my leg.'

As Zack laughs, I flip my pencil case so he can't see the "Skank" that someone's scrawled on it. 'Cool colours,' he studies my drawings. 'Detail's amazing.'

'You think?' I blush.

'Those are swallowtails, yeah? And that's a Red Admiral. Dad knew them all,' he explains. 'He used to walk me down the canal when Andy was at footy practice. Showed me how to spot a dragonfly from a damsel.' He wiggles his eyebrows at me.

'This band of yours.' I laugh. 'Who's in it?'

'A couple of Year 12s,' he turns serious. 'I knew they played, so I suggested we get together after school; kill it for the next three days...' He shakes off his biker jacket. '...and give this audition a shot.'

'Great.'

'Yeah.' He rolls up his shirt sleeves. 'S'just—'

'What?'

'One of the guys.' He runs his hand over his crop. 'Turns out you know his sister.' Before I can ask more, the Melways' back door crashes open.

'It's OVER.' Lisa slams into the kitchen clutching her school bag, sports kit, hockey stick, Domino's pizza box and a giant bottle of Fanta Orange. 'I have NOTHING!'

Exploding her stuff all over the kitchen, Lisa proceeds to chug down two litres of fizzy orange in an effort to "re-stabilise", while Zack and I fall on the family-size Meat Feast. (Caring for Lisa requires carbs: *we* know it, she knows it.)

'So,' I say as I chomp down my cheese, 'What's up?'

'Gina,' she gasps between glugs. '*Gina's* what's up. I'm walking back from hockey practice, *gutted* because Gina hasn't shown, when I go past Sprinkles – and there's Gina hogging a booth WITH A BOY.'

'But...' I beat Zack off my olives. '...you told me that you and Gina hung out round the mall, all weekend. She held your hand.'

'She *did*, I thought, but was it me holding *hers*?'

'Oh, Lees.' As my mate lets out a "Burp of Ultimate Sadness", I rub her on the back, like I did with the twins when they were babies. 'Isn't it time you took the plunge?'

Lees has known she likes girls since she first saw Miley Cyrus on that wrecking ball. To check she didn't like boys too, she waited for Nina Bixby's fourteenth birthday party at Norbridge Rink, then went on a snogging rampage. Pretty brave for someone who is a) Emotionally Cautious, and b) wearing ice skates.

By the time she was escorted off the ice by management, Lees had:

(i)   Fallen over fourteen times.
(ii) Got BADLY wedged behind an inflatable penguin, and
(iii) Snogged three different boys (but one of them was Scott 'the grot' Dilbert, so hardly a litmus test).

Lisa went home encased in Tubigrips and swore she'd never kiss a boy again. Problem is, the *only* girl she wants to kiss is Gina. 'Just ask her to the ball,' I tell her.

'Kat's right.' Zack tears into his thick-crust. 'So what if Gina has a Sprinkles habit? Doesn't mean she's got a boyfriend.'

'Doesn't mean she wants a *girlfriend* though, does it?' puffs Lees. 'I mean, look at Kat.'

'Me?' I choke on my cheese.

'*You've* not kissed a boy yet. Granted, it's probably because you're always hiding in that smelly alley outside your house—'

'Standing in cat poo,' nods Zack.

'So how do you know you're not gay? And no...' Lees pulls a face. '...your sad hots for Jonah do NOT count.'

'Jonah?' Zack looks up at me. 'You fancy *Jonah Kerridge*? He's a total—'

'Tool? Airhead?' helps Lees. 'Fringe muppet?'

'Great,' I glower at Lees. '*Now* you're good with

words?' Zack however is struggling.

'Jonah… but… he hangs out with *Stella*. He's like the fool to her hot blonde princess.'

I feel myself burn up. 'You think STELLA'S HOT?'

'We're not talking about Stella! Jeez, Kat.' He shakes his head. 'Why didn't you say?'

'Say *what*? We don't have to tell each other everything, do we?'

'No.' He eyeballs me. 'Seems we don't.'

He flips shut the pizza lid. Conversation closed, which is Fine. By. Me.

Just not with Lees. 'My poor deluded chicken.' Draining the dregs of her Fanta, she upends the bottle and starts bonking me over the head with it. 'Must I… knock… the sense… into… you? Clearly, you've been BRAINWASHED (*double bonk*) by sexual stereotyping!'

'Ow.' I yank the bottle off her while I set about "presenting the evidence":

> When younger, I had not *just* a Barbie doll (bad enough) but a Ken.
> I fancied Ken.
> When Mum was mega-pregnant with the twins, she made me watch *The Princess Bride* with her, like, a thousand times (it's her favourite film, plus she couldn't get off the sofa).

And the damage was done. Now, to Lisa, I can ONLY fancy skinny white boys with floppy blond hair (hopefully not called Westley. No girl wants that coming up on her phone). Thanks two litres of "Carbonated Truth Juice"!

At this point Zack picks up his guitar, leaving Lees and I to gauge our gayometers in proper scientific fashion: by listing Hot Celebs We Fancy.

I write down:

1. Harry Styles. Because no boy *styles* it like Harry. *(Geddit?)* Seriously, did you see that dress he wore on the cover of *Vogue?* Cool doesn't *cover* it. *(Again, geddit?)*
2. A dancer from *Strictly* whose name I don't know but he's fit, and
3. Marcus Rashford. He scores goals, feeds schoolkids *and* looks hot. *(Phewee, he needs to rest up! While I embroider his sweatpants.)*

By contrast, Lisa's hotlist compiles:
1. Rihanna.
2. The England ladies' football captain.
3. Rihanna again.
4. Orlando Bloom *and*
5. Katy Perry.

'There you go. Conclusive proof…' Zack strikes a power chord. '…you're both nuts, and shouldn't be allowed to snog anyone EVER.' But it's me he's looking at when the reverb hits.

'So,' I ask him, 'who's on *your* list?'

His green eyes flash. 'Who says I need a list?'

Stitch List
1. Rummage under bed. Nope, no dress has been left overnight by the fashion fairies, so
2. Pull out my rag bag. (MUST think of better name for it: Ethical Textiles Container? Sustainable Swag Sack?)

It *was* an XL t-shirt, until I snipped off the sleeves, and cut a fringe along the bottom. Knotted the tassels together to make a bag, which is now RAMMED with...

3. Scraps; need sorting. Currently a mad tangle of:
    discount-shop remnants.
    cut-up charity clothes.
    twins' outgrown dungarees (yellow gingham).
    Lisa's old hoodie (tomato red).
    Dad's worn-out PJ bottoms
    (jazzy green stripe).
    Rags to everyone
    else, but to me?
    Riches!

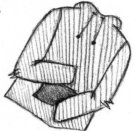

4. Find a length of stretchy fabric... Black, I'm feeling.
5. Cut fabric in half. Loop each piece and put in a seam. Hellooo, "twin" tube-tops!
6. Back to my rag bag: Tear, twist and turn bright strips of cloth into a rainbow.
7. Stitch rainbow across front of first tube-top – for Lees when she's ready. When she can wear it with Pride.
8. Smooth out second tube-top – this one's for me. How far can I stretch it? What's *MY* two-finger salute to the world? Grab my jar of silver sequins, and let rip!

ulp, it's happening. Posters appear around school this morning. Watching a big Darwin's banner go up in the gym, Lees and I agree on two things:

    1. This contest is *ON*, and

    2. the winner will be collecting £500 from beneath a giant set of gums.

'Come on, tickets go on sale today.' Lisa marches me to the school office as the lunch bell sounds. 'Never mind that Gina's crapped on *my* dreams, let's get you yours.'

'But I can't afford the ticket – and I still don't have a dress!'

'So make one.' She pulls a crumpled £20 note from her bag. 'I'll cover the rest.'

'But, that's the last of your allowance till Christmas.' I pull at her sleeve. 'You can't—'

'Can. Two tickets please!' She leans over the unattended reception counter. 'OR DO I START HEADBUTTING THIS DESK?'

'Two tickets?' I say, as Miss Bottle our receptionist scuttles out.. 'Lees, you're coming too?!'

'Well, *someone's* got to get you over yourself. And past

YEARS 9 AND 10 ARE INVITED TO ATTEND

The St Edward's and Winsham Academy

Winter Wonderland Ball

Friday 18th December, 7-9pm

£500 prize for MOST DAZZLING LOOK

Sponsored by DARWIN'S DENTAL HEALTH for all your orthodontic needs. Online discount for fixed braces, use code 'GUM'

that lot.' She nods over my shoulder. Turning, I choke on an incoming cloud of hairspray. It's Stella Harcourt leading the Tag-Hags on a ticket charge. She practically catches fire when she sees we've got here first. As Miss Bottle our receptionist scuttles out with her ticket strips, Lisa slaps down £20.

'Ta, miss.' She tears the first two tickets off Miss Bottle's strip off the first two tickets. Handing me #001, Lees grins and marches us me past the line of scowling Tag-Hags. 'Strut, girl.' She grins. 'How does it feel to come first?'

Er, scary. Especially when Lisa bolts for lunchtime hockey, leaving me to hide out alone in the locker room. The Hag-Tags smell blood (or maybe it's my Marmite sandwiches?). 'You've got some cheek.' Olivia leads the swarm. 'Holding up the queue while you sponge a ticket.'

'You gonna *beg* a gown from somewhere too?' jabs Jayden. 'Or try Oxfam: buy a dress someone's died in.'

I stick my head in my locker until they buzz off. Forcing down my sandwiches, I feel my guts churn. Fear? Maybe. Period on its way? Please no.

Stuffing my sandwiches back into my bag, I do the maths. Three weeks and counting... it can't be?

Could be.

Checking the corridor's clear, I walk quickly to Pastoral. I don't *want* to stage another smash 'n' grab on free sanitary supplies, but the Tampax ran out at home weeks ago. No surprise! Mum only has a period once in a blue moon. Meanwhile, she's trying to feed a family of five from the Co-op yellow-sticker trolley? I can't ask her to blow two quid on a packet of tampons – two quid for what exactly? Cardboard tubes stuffed with cotton wool mice.

'Mousey!' squealed Daisy, pulling my last one from the box by its tail. 'Go splash!' She dunked it in her bath by the tail.

'Aw.' Nat and Keisha round the corner. 'You off to Pastoral?' says Nat.

'What's the problem this time?' Keisha fakes concern. 'Need a tissue? Or bus fare home?'

'Funny.' I back away – too fast. Tripping over my feet, I shed a shoe. Quick as a flash, Natalie's on it.

'Gross!' She hooks a nail into my heel, holding it away from her like she might catch something. 'These stink! Talk about tramp shoes, *aargh!*' She flings my shoe at Keisha. 'There's something inside!'

'*Ew!*' Keisha bats it up into the air. When a rat *doesn't* fall out, she catches it. Inserts a long, lacquered nail into the toe, and extracts a damp, stinking ball of—

'Sellotape, that's all.' I snatch. She whips back her hand.

'Stuffed into your shoe because...?'

'None of your business. Give—'

'It's a patch-up job!' crows Keisha, waving my shoe at Nat. The sole starts to flap. 'Ha! Even her shoes are laughing at her. See this, Stell!'

I skid around to find Stella. Skidding around, I find Stella shooting me daggers. 'I can't *believe* they sold you a ticket,' she says.

'Catch!' Keisha hurls my shoe down at me. As I drop for it, she slaps the Sellotape ball to the side of my head.

'Classy,' says Stella, as I stand up and pull the tape from my hair. 'You gonna stick yourself together for the ball too?' Pushing past, she takes off down the school hall, *her* runway.

As I bend down to put on my shoe, Nat and Keisha batter past me with their bags, dropping word-bombs down the back of my neck...

I burn the whole way home.

Running upstairs, I pull off my school shirt like it's on fire. Instead I pull on my cool, black tube-top. I finished the sequins last night; the slogan pretty much stitched itself! Tiny pieces of silver scattered across the dark, they spell...

'*That's* the message you want to put out?' says Mum. Stood in my bedroom doorway, she screws up her eyes, like the sequins are pricking her.

"S just a top,' I say, feeling bad suddenly. Like I've hurt

her when it's *me* that's hurt. *Me* that's getting kicked down all the time.

Me that feels broke.

'Oh, Kat.' She rubs her face, scrapes back her wiry scrub of hair. 'Come on.' She turns and plods down the stairs, heavy like the world's poured concrete into her. 'Let's have a cuppa. And a talk.'

'Yay, *finally*!' I run after her. 'Because this dress situation is getting desperate. I need you, Mum.'

'Well, here I am.' She clips into the kitchen and flicks on the kettle. Which is when I realise she's wearing her Armitages uniform.

'Aren't you supposed to be on a late-night shift?'

'Yeah, well...' She scoops last night's potato peelings out of the sink. 'Ladieswear was empty, cruisewear was *dead*...' She pedals open the bin. '...and ladies' shoes were hardly dancing off the shelves.' She dumps the scrapings. 'So I told my manager I had a migraine, and here I am. Totally available.' She sticks her head in a cupboard. Re-emerges clutching three mugs. 'Ready to talk ball.'

'Really?'

'Really! Pass us the teabags, can you?' She lines up the mugs. 'Armitages Christmas bash is in a couple of weeks, and boy, do I need a party!' Skimping on the milk, Mum slops in the steaming water. 'All these double shifts I've been pulling.' She rips open the crumpled packet. 'I reckon we can afford to let out our breath. *Pah.*' She sighs at the last teabag.

'Yay,' I fish it out. 'We godda teabag!'

She laughs, swills the teabag in the first mug, squishes into the second, then *grinds* it into the third. 'The pre-Christmas sales have started. What do you say we get down to New Look?' She does a little shimmy. 'Find us *both* a dress!'

'Hey.' Dad comes in from the front room. 'Thanks, love.' He cradles the mug Mum passes him. 'What are we celebrating?'

'Nothing, it's just something to say I love you.'

'Er... Really?'

They exchange a look.

'Crikey, Kat,' says Mum with a laugh. 'We're not *that* bad.'

'No.' I hug them both. 'You're brilliant.'

'*Waah!*' A crash comes from the front room. We freeze, then we break apart as two the toddlers start wailing. 'I *told* them not to climb on the telly.' Dad turns back to the front room to go to them, shoving his mug at Mum.

'Hey!' she cries, as tea goes everywhere.

'I'm sorry!'

'How does *that* help?' Mum frantically wipes scalding liquid from her chest. 'This is my last good shirt. I'll have to soak it in the bath.'

She stomps upstairs. As I go to the twins (and Dad picks up the telly) I hear her running the taps. She keeps running. 'What are you doing up there, Kell?' Dad shouts up the stairs. 'It sounds like Niagara Falls!'

'Oh Chris, the water...' Mum sounds far away, like she's drowning. 'It won't run hot.'

Please like and share – the Christmas Party look has landed! See supermodel Yvonne rock the house in the Parker kitchen in:

Oily dungarees,

A hip-hugging tool-belt, and
(watch out Gigi Hadid),

A spanner.

Yvonne – "Von" to her mates – works with Mum at Armitages, but is training part-time to be a plumber. (She's "yet to get her head round a toilet plunger". She says she'll do "anything to escape another winter in Men's Pants.) Mum called Von around as soon we realised the heating was down. But since tipping up, so far she's not done much more than hoik her tool-belt and demolish our ginger nuts. *Correction*, she's also banged our boiler with her spanner and shaken her head a lot (she's going to be an excellent plumber).

'Sorry, Kell,' she says finally. 'The masterboard has gone.'

Mum frowns. 'Meaning?'

'You freeze to death. Or you get a new boiler.'

Mum goes pale. 'How much will that set us back?'

'State of your pipework?' Von sucks her teeth. 'Could be looking at a grand.'

'A *thousand pounds*? How do we find that?' says Mum. 'We're already struggling to give the kids Christmas.' Her frown goes wobbly, like she's about to cry.

Mum never cries.

'*Do something*,' I say to Von.

'Er...' Von scratches her head with the spanner. 'You say it's your husband got the boiler installed? Perhaps he did the smart thing, and paid for an extended warranty.'

He didn't, turns out.

'Sorry, Kell love.' Dad returns from B&Q, dragging a huge cardboard box. 'Thought you'd want me to save the money. Look!' He pulls a grubby fan heater from the box. 'They sold me a showroom model – half price.' He beams proudly at Mum. 'What are you thinking?'

'I'm thinking...' Mum says slowly. 'HOW IS THIS GOING TO HEAT A *HOUSE*?'

As the shouting starts, Von makes a run for it. Time to split. Fleeing to Gran's, I leave Dad tugging at the heater cord. Stabbing the plug into a wall socket he mutters, 'Electrocute me *now*.'

'So that's blown it.' I crash into Gran's room at Acorns. 'My one chance.'

'To do what, dear?'

'Escape! To Winter Wonderland.' I throw off my coat. 'For *one night*, I'd get to forget all their NOISE.' I'm vibrating with it, shaking as my ears are still ringing. My hands trembling as they tug up my tube-top. 'No way I can beg Mum and Dad for a ball dress now.'

'Quite right,' says Gran with a nod. 'You've not come

from a long line of working women to start sponging now.'

'Hey,' I protest. 'I'm still a kid!'

'So?' She sniffs. 'Mozart composed his first sonata when he was nine. Twiggy was spotted when she was sixteen.'

'Twiggy?' I dump myself on the bed. 'Who's Twiggy?'

'Only the world's first supermodel!' Gran harrumphs. 'One day just a skinny north London girl like me, then *whoosh!* She turned into the face of the swinging sixties. Big baby-blue eyes, she had, with lovely, long lashes. They'd have *fluttered* at the chance to wear a sparkly number like this!' Gran bumps a shaky fist at my sequin top. 'Broke?' she ponders. 'Maybe it's *you* who need the magic, dear.'

Eyes twinkling, she opens her gnarled hand to reveal the tiny brass key.

I go to unlock the mahogany wardrobe. This time, I pull out two heavy, leather-bound volumes. Just holding them calms me, like things *can* have weight. Sliding them gently on to Gran's bird-like lap, I perch on her armchair to open the first book: my parents' wedding album.

'Dad looks so dashing.' I turn the pages for her like I have a hundred times. 'He could be a film star.'

'Too nervous for a film star that,' says Gran with a chuckle. 'He's holding your mum's hand like she might fly away.'

'That's because you made her dress so light! All that white lace...' I run my hand over the laughing girl on the page. 'She's floating like she's in a dream.' Then I recall how I left my folks fighting over the fan heater, and slam their story shut.

Instead, I pull open the second album: 'MY GIRLS' Gran's written smartly across the front. More wedding photos, but a different bride and groom each time. The pics start out black and white (men in stiff suits; women in veils) but soon turn to colour. One happy couple is running into the sea, the next jumping from a helicopter, but every bride wears a dress made by Gran. 'I can't believe you had your shop for forty years!'

'But time flies,' she says with a nod. 'I'd make a wedding dress for some wee girl. Turn round and there she was again, asking me to make over the dress for her daughter! What I loved best, though, was seeing one of my gowns passed down from mother to daughter, to grand-daughter! A good garment is made, like love—'

'To last,' I finish the lesson. Gran started to teach me when my "chubby fingers first closed round a pin. Years we sewed together. Then the Parkinson's set in. Suddenly I was picking up *all* her pins. Gran had to pack up the shop, then her little flat above it.

Moving to Acorns, she gave me her precious Singer sewing machine and her dressmaker's shears; her tins of silver needles and rainbow spools of thread. But the secrets of her sparkle...?

I return to the wardrobe and pull open the doors: it's an Aladdin's cave of treasures. Glass tubs filled with a thousand bright beads, gleaming gems and seed pearls line the shelves like candy jars in an old-fashioned sweet shop. Gran dispenses me a liberal handful every birthday and Christmas. But on nights like these? Opening a jar of gold sequins, I rest it carefully on Gran's lap, then guide her trembling hand inside. Her knobbly fingers come out covered in glitter. She touches my face, sprinkling me in magic! Laughing, I go back for more. Whirling out of the wardrobe, I send satin ribbons spilling over her shoulders and trail lace trimmings across her lap. 'Oh yes,' she strokes the tiny, frosted flowers. 'This was Lucy. And these pointy stars...' Her fingers read the tiny bumps like braille. '...that's Jessica.' This is how she knows her dresses – by the girls they transformed. 'Because no matter how old the bride, dear, she's always a girl on her wedding day.'

She's starting to forget things, Gran. What she had for tea yesterday. Where she put her bag. The point of the Kardashians ('and how do we make them stop?') But the feel of fabric can focus her. Touching the tools of her trade, she starts to piece herself back together. Which is why I save the best for last.

A roll of cloth is propped behind the wardrobe door, like a sentry standing guard over Gran's fading past. Heaving it out, I pull on the roll and release shimmering waves of Indian silk. 'Such a beautiful blue,' murmurs Gran, as a sea of shining aquamarine spills over her dry hands.

She bought the silk years ago, to make up a set of bridesmaid's dresses. When the bride called off the wedding ('A good thing too. , apparently. The groom was a *rat*.') Gran couldn't bear to sell it. Now her hands start to tremble at its touch.

'Can you feel the magic rippling through it, dear? Waiting for someone to make it...

'Gran... you OK?' She's proper shaking now, jerking

the roll back at me.

'Take it,' she says. 'Do as I taught you. *Make* your gown.'

'But, our lessons stopped, remember?' I nudge her gently. 'You never showed me how to put in a zip!' But Gran's done with Memory Lane.

'Take off, dear. Transform yourself.' She pushes the silk at me. 'Go!'

'All right, all right.' I back off as Carlotta bustles back in. 'I'm going!'

Hoisting the roll over my shoulder, I head for home. All I need now is for Jonah Kerrigan to see me trudging through town like Burglar Bill. I *pray* Jonah Kerrigan does not see me channeling Burglar Bill. But as bundle the bolt of silk through our front door, I feel like Gran's planted something in me. Not magic exactly, but a tiny hope.

Could I stitch my way into Winter Wonderland?

'You ARE KIDDING!' Mum's voice comes from our kitchen.

'Calm down, Kell!' shouts Dad. 'I've not done anything yet.'

'That I *can* believe!'

'Lots of people take out payday loans—'

'Because *they get paydays.*'

'I'd not go crazy,' pleads Dad. 'Just borrow enough for the boiler, and to buy the kids a few presents. Come on, Kel, love.' I hear chair legs scrape across the kitchen floor. 'We could do with a good Christmas, couldn't we? A bit of joy to tide us over—'

'Sink us, you mean. The interest that lot charge. We're drowning in debt as it is.'

'And whose fault is that?' Dad mutters.

'Don't pull that one on me,' says Mum. 'You've not earned in months.'

'I'm trying.'

'Well, you're failing. Failing to write a book that no one, *no one even wants.*' The chair legs scrape back. 'We can't afford dreams any more, Chris,' says Mum. 'You need to get a job – any job. Cleaning toilets, sweeping streets—'

'On a basic wage?' Dad gives a hollow laugh. 'How will *that* make a dent on the debts you've racked up.'

'Don't put this on me! She's *our* daughter.'

'But it's *you* who went overboard! Throwing cash at fertility workshops.' I freeze. I can barely hear him over the pounding in my ears. 'Yoga retreats, acupuncture treatments sessions. All that before we paid for the IVF clinic!'

Paid for IVF? But I was their miracle NHS baby, Mum said.

'Cycle after cycle of treatment,' groans Dad. 'Each one hurting more than the one before, costing more. Then, when we did get her, you had to have the best crib, the best pram—'

'She was our miracle!'

'She was seven years of trying, and a £50,000 bill.'

Gran's silk slips through my fingers. 'Keep your voice down,' hisses Mum. 'How can you *say* that?'

'Because it's true! Christ, Kell, I'd pay that ten times over to have our Kat, you know I would. But once she was born, it was time for us to get real – tighten our belts and start paying back what we'd borrowed. But no, *you* had to have it all – the family holidays, the family car, this house…'

'So?' Mum's voice catches. 'We've been happy here, haven't we?'

'And now we're paying the price.'

The pounding wins. The roll of silk starts to dance in my arms – I'm shaking, I realise. 'Kat? My Kat?' Daisy cries from the front room. 'We cold!'

'Froat hurty,' croaks Lil. 'Need juice.'

Still hugging the stupid silk, I bolt from the house. The wails of the twins pursue me, but it's not their fault, is it? None of this is their fault.

It's mine.

15

Crashing through the Melways' back door, I'm enveloped by warmth.

'Yo, Needle Girl. You hungry?' Andy turns from a pan he's got sizzling on the cooker. 'I'm doing Mum's famous jerk chicken.'

'Hey.' Zack strolls in from the hall. 'You OK?' He disappears in a burning haze of spots. 'Kat!'

Everything goes blurry. I'm spinning out of control until his arms lock round me, and I feel safe. For like a nano-second, then I skid on some jerk sauce, and bring us both down.

'Is she all right?' I hear him saying.

'Easy, girl.' Andy's getting me up onto a chair. 'You're white as a ghost. When did you last eat?'

'Er...' I blink and see more spots – huge, they are. And... *gold?* 'Baubles!' I sit up. Then I feel woozy again, and Andy tells me not to try ANYTHING until I've finished a plate of his jerk chicken. I munch through it, admiring the decorations on the Christmas tree the boys have set up. It stands proud in Marie's corner: between the fridge and the blocked-up fireplace, it's where she stuck up her best pics of her "best boys".

'*Man*…' Zack props Gran's roll by the tree. '…this weighs a ton.'

'That's 'cause it's quality,' says Andy. '*Not* made for dragging down alley ways.'

He waves a damp cloth at me, then bends down to dab grubby marks from the silk. 'Gently, yeah?' He shows Zack, then rises up to let him work, knocking a picture frame as he goes. Together, the brothers right it: a photo of Marie Melway with her two bouncing babies (well, *Zack's* a baby. Andy's bouncing a ball off his head).

Beneath this pic (now draped in silver tinsel!) hangs Andy's graduation portrait. He's dressed up like some Mediaeval dude in a fur-collared robe, looking dead earnest and clutching a scroll tied with purple ribbon. Next to him is a small pic of Mike Melway. Actually Mike was massive – tall as a tree (well, seemed like it to me). He gave Zack his broad shoulders, and his big, easy grin. But he gave Andy the camera. Mike was the one who spotted his gangly stepson's knack "for how things look". I was there when Andy, proud as punch, took the photo of his stepdad: Mike's stood outside Southbridge fire station in full uniform, yellow helmet tucked under his arm. 'My man…' Marie would say, 'is a *good* man. He'd give you the shirt off his back.'

Except firefighters have to give more than their shirts, don't they? A couple of years after Andy took that pic, there was a fire across town that seemed to swallow the sky. Trying to save one more kid, Mike Melway went back into the burning tower block that killed him. Now his boys are stuck salvaging *me*? 'I am evil!' I hiccup, bringing up a dollop of jerk chicken onto my top. How I've ruined Mum and Dad's life, screwed the twins' future, and broken the boiler "*just by being borrrrn!*"

Somehow Andy gets my jumper off me — and into the washing machine — leaving Zack to steer me upstairs. 'Kat...' He plonks me down on his bed. '...you need to change.'

'I *know*,' I bawl. 'I am eeev—'

'Your shirt,' he says. 'There's puke on it. I'll be back in a sec.'

As he nips back downstairs, I peel off my vomity top. Fishing through the pile of clothes by Zack's bed, I find his Jimi Hendrix t-shirt. A long-ago gift from my dad, the colours are faded, the cotton softened by use. Kicking off my shoes, I snuggle into it. 'Looks good,' says Zack with a grin, returning with a cup of tea. 'Camomile. It's calming, apparently.'

'Great.' I take the mug of hot, yellow water. 'I'm suffering post-traumatic shock, and you forget the milk?'

He rolls his eyes. Then rolls up his shirt sleeves and waits for me to take a sip.

'Oh, Zack.' I slurp. 'You should've heard them. Dad was so angry! This mess I've got them into. All the time blaming the twins, torturing my parents to buy me some *sick gown*, when they've blown everything on buying *me*.'

'They got you from IVF, Kat, not TK Maxx.'

'Yeah, and what did they get for their fifty grand?'

'Er...' He cocks an eyebrow. 'A beautiful and talented Child of Sunshine?'

I put down my tea, and prod him with my foot. He grabs it. 'Kat.' He pulls my leg. 'It's not a one-way deal with your folks. You do their laundry, mend their clothes…' He pulls harder. '…watch the twins—'

'Stop it!' He slides me off the bed.

'AND you've taken a billion mugs of coffee to your dad.'

'Rubbish.' He bumps me down on to the floor.

'*Not* rubbish, though you could work on your coffee.' He bumps down on the floor beside me. 'It tastes like soup.'

I shove him with my shoulder. He shoves me back. I nudge him. He returns it. I stop fighting, and rest my head against his. We stay there for what feels like forever. Then, slowly, his face turns towards mine—

'Still a school night, Kat.' Andy sticks his head round the door. 'Home!'

Heading downstairs, we conduct negotiations. Andy wants to tell my folks that I know about the IVF.

I don't.

Andy insists.

I REFUSE. Then break down and blub like a blubber whale from Blubsville.

Andy re-thinks. He will not tell my folks so long as I promise *not* to turn into a Troubled Teenage Glue-Sniffer.

'O-kay,' I say with a sniff. SNIFF, GEDDIT?!

He steers me out the back door.

'Hey,' Zack grabs my bolt of silk, 'you forgetting something?'

'Yeah, sorry.' I blush, taking it from him. 'Gran's got this mad idea I can make my own ball gown.'

'What's mad about that?'

'Er, look at me,' I struggle with the roll. 'I'm ruining it already!'

'We'll take care of the silk.' Andy lifts it from me. 'You start on your design.'

'But—'

88

'You do *have* paper in your house?' he says.

'Rude letters from the bank, mostly.'

'Perfect,' chips in Zack. 'The Beatles wrote their best songs on the back of an envelope. Get sketching, Needle Girl.' He topples me off their back step.

'Hey!' The Melway boys, they don't give up, do they? On life. On me...

As I head down their path, clouds shoot past the moon. The side-gate rattles, then swings open like it's been waiting for me. The alley, it's turned into a shining, silver runway! Laughing, I take off down the Katwalk. Golden leaves billowing around me, I shout into the wind, 'I'm Needle Girl!'

I fling out my arms and spin, becoming a swish of shimmering skirts. My veins tingle, like electricity is surging through me, like I could dazzle Winter Wonderland just *by being me.*

Too soon, I reach the runway's end. As I turn onto our dark street, it's like a light goes out. Who cares? Moon shining at my back, I break into a run. Screw waiting for life to hand me the fairy tale.

I'm gonna earn it.

'Yay!' Lees jumps up and down when I tell her. 'You're gonna *wreck* this catwalk contest.'

'If it doesn't wreck *me*.' I steer her towards our lockers. 'I've got less than a week till the ball. Six days to create a kick-ass gown.'

'Sheesh.' Reality hits her. 'You can't upcycle your mum's jeans for this one, can you? You're gonna need, you know…' Lisa rubs her fingers together. '…swishy stuff.'

'Fabric?'

'That's the job.'

'I'm on it.' Thanks to the Melway boys. Zack dropped Gran's freshly spruced silk round this morning.

Andy says, 'Look after it this time.' Zack pulls his best stern face. 'Plus I'm to check your desk for glue. A-ha!' He picks up an ancient Pritt stick. Pockets it like Evidence, article 1, then grins and chucks me my coat. 'I'm to walk you to school, so you don't throw yourself under a bus.'

I took a snip of Gran's silk before we left. Now I pull it from my coat pocket to show Lees.

'Wow, that *is* SWISH,' she says, then bites her lip and frowns. 'But, Kat…'

'Yes?'

'You'll need more than this.'

'You reckon?' I say with a laugh. But yeah, I'm planning to go in *fierce* at the waist, then flare out into a mad swoosh of skirts.'

'With your dark hair and pale skin?' Lees nods. 'You'll look gorgeous! Soon as you've sorted out the pink eye.'

'Wha——?' I put my hand to my face.

'Your eyes are red from crying — and your eyebags are *well* baggy. Clear signs of a midnight meltdown. I've been there, remember? Well, now I'm here for *you*.' Lisa squeezes my hand. 'For the next thirty seconds, then I'm off down the hockey pitch.'

Lees turns to her locker, giving me space to spill (while *she* pulls out 50,000 dirty socks in search of her sports vest).

'OK,' I admit, 'there has been *some* nose-blowing at my end.' And not much sleep. Last night saw me riding a rollercoaster. One minute I was winning Winter Wonderland, the next I was listening to my parents argue about me having ruined their lives. So I tell her what I overheard; my parents rowing about the IVF, and how much it cost them. 'All this time they've been fighting about their MONSTER DEBT.' I gulp. 'And the monster turns out to be me! I've ruined their life.'

'Seems they're doing that nicely themselves.' Lisa pulls out a vest and sniffs it. Recoils, recovers and starts tugging it on.

'I've been Googling.' I chuck her skort at her. 'Guess THE number one reason for divorce in the UK today.'

'Er… sex? No, don't tell me.' She yanks on her skort. 'Hobbies!'

'*Hobbies?*'

'When Dad left Mum – *oof*.' She tugs on a sock. 'He said

they had nothing in common. Mum was always working down her allotment – *oof…*' Second sock. '…while Dad just wanted to, you know—'

'Make sweet love to Sheila?'

'See? SEX!' She jumps up. 'My first answer was correct. Please give me double points and a commemorative fountain pen.'

'Cash,' I say instead. 'That's what kills love – *not* having it, I mean. Things are bad out there, Lees. It's not just *us* getting rained on. Guess how many pay cheques the average person is away from being homeless?' Lisa opens her mouth. 'Three!' I shut it for her. '*Three* months without a job, and anyone could be out on the street.'

'Or getting their wife to work all hours at Armitages. *You've* not screwed your folks, Kat.' She pulls on her boots. 'They've shafted *you*.'

'But—'

'But nothing! They *knew* they'd got into debt having you, so why was your mum out buying Bugaboo prams and hand-carved rattles? Why did your dad pack in his job to write?'

'It was his dream—'

'Now what about yours?' she asks. 'So, yeah, it's not Nobel-Prize-winning stuff. You want to wear a hot frock to a dodgy ball. In the hope some super dodgy boy finally sees you.'

'Jonah's not super—'

'Too right. He's not *super* anything,' she says with a snort, 'but how could you know when you've barely spoken to him? Seriously, you need to forget Jonah.' She grabs her hockey stick. 'Forget your parents. Do this for yourself and, Kat Parker…' She waves her stick at me like a giant wand. 'You *shall* go to the ball!' Then she ruins it by whacking me round the head. 'Try not to look like a pumpkin.'

'*Ha,* who's a pumpkin?' Stella swishes into the locker room. When we don't answer ('Me, me! I'm a pumpkin!') she shrugs and gets out her phone. As the Tag-Hags cluster round, Stella starts scrolling through prom dresses.

'Hey.' Keisha shoves me away. 'What *you* looking at, loser?'

'*Oi,* less of the loser,' says Lisa. 'Just you watch.'

'Watch what?' Stella looks up.

'Winter Wonderland,' says Lees. 'It is ON. Kat's going to win that £500.'

'Oh, yeah?' says Stella.

'In a gown she's made herself.'

'Nooo!' The Tag-Hags erupt. 'Freaky frock time,' cries Nat.

'You do *know* it's a ball?' Keisha asks me, 'not a sack race?'

Stella laughs, but her eyes go to the scrap in my hand – and I see something glitter in them. Not full-on fear (*as if*)...

... But a flicker.

Stitch List

1. Dump my sketch book (I ran out of pages at 4.00am this morning). Draw final design on back of angry letter from the bank. (Genius idea, Andy! I rifled through Mum's pile of mail, and found the angrier the bank gets, the thicker their paper. Ditto mortgage people, council tax people and the Gas Man. Sketch-wise, I am LAUGHING.)

2. Sharpen pencils, they're down to *stumps*.

3. Splash my genius brow with cold water. (Hot is still OFF. Von promised to source us a super cheap boiler: "Just you wait!"

   Still waiting. Also shivering + wearing bobble hats to bed.)

4. Apply killer tweaks to design: tighter fit to waist, fuller flare to skirts. *Bejazzle* bodice with beads? Nah, too much.

5. Swipe Dad's fountain pen to ink in my lines. How are they looking? Super sharp?

Nailed it.

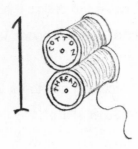

’m rushing! Just five days to turn my paper dream into catwalk reality. Sketching is the easy part. It takes engineering to convert liquid silk into solid style. How to get my skirts to swish up, for starters. And no, Lees, I cannot "eat baked beans until the ball".

I spend most of PSHE drafting ideas (*go mad with layering? Helter-skelter frills?*). Means I'm playing catch-up when Miss Lipscombe starts to recruit girls for the ball committee – duties to include making TOILET signs, and manning the snack tables.

'So only losers without a date need apply,' says Stella from the back row. Sniggers roll down the class, washing *right* over Bossy Harriet as she sticks up her hand.

'That's the spirit!' beams Miss Lipscombe. 'Who wants to buddy up with Harriet here?' A few eager girls are itching to, I can tell. They dart looks at Stella who dead-eyes them back.

No one volunteers.

'No one? Really? Poor Harriet!' Miss Lipscombe tries to make a joke of it, but Miss Lipscombe can't see Harriet's gone rigid: Stella's frozen the class.

Then a hand goes up. Zara Khan in the second row.

She's my partner in textiles class – wouldn't normally say "boo" to a goose. Now she's taking on the Tag-Hags?

'Saddo alert,' cackles Stella. 'Those two sneak into my Story on ball night, there will be No Filter Strong Enough.'

'She is *definitely* hiding something under there,' Olivia nods at Zara's headscarf.

'Greasy hair,' reckons Jayden.

'Nits,' squeals Keisha.

'*Eugh!*' the bitch chorus goes up. 'Gross.'

How can Miss Lipscombe not hear? Zara has, for sure. She pulls down her arm, then pats the forehead of her hijab, like she's returning the pressure of a comforting hand. 'Miss Lipscombe,' she murmurs.

'Yes?'

'Put me down for toilet signs AND snacks.' Louder now. 'My mum makes a mean samosa.'

Squawks from the back. I turn round to see Natalie wrapping her school sweater around her head. 'Girls...' She strikes a pose. '...you like my hijab?'

'Love it,' crows Carly, rushing to do the same. 'Check my turban, Stella!'

Stella's eyes narrow and she grins widely. She shoots a glance at Zara, who's hunched over Miss Lipscombe's sign-up form but bound to look round *any second*.

'I'll help!' Leaping up, I body-block the back row. 'Let's hear it for toilet signs! All the single LADIES, all the—'

'Lower your arms, Kat!' yells Miss Lipscombe, as Carly and Nat whip off their headgear. 'You're volunteering for the ball committee, not trying to take off.'

She then traps us all in one of her interminable Powerpoint presentations. "Say no to bullying," Miss Lipscombe tells us, while the Tag-Hags shoot me death stares, and I pray for the next period to start: Double

Textiles, it's the only class worth taking. Today, we file into Tech Room 1, and find it filled with a hundred technicoloured wings.

'Wow…' Zara goes ahead of me. '…it's a butterfly garden!'

'It's *metamorphosis*, thad's whad,' drawls our textiles teacher, emerging from the stock cupboard rattling a plastic tub. Miss Bloxam is an OBA (Officially Brilliant Australian). This means she has a tattoo of a koala across her shoulder, and is rude to our faces (rather than over the top of our heads like most grown-ups). 'Time to focus yer whacked TikTok brains on our sustainable fashion project. Yer unfinished designs got me so mad,' she scowls at Nat and Keisha, 'I threw myself into the recycling bin.' She whips the lid off her tub. 'See what I found!'

A heap of plastic bottles and tin cans. At least that's how they must've *started* life. Miss Bloxam has curled back the bouncy plastic and soft aluminium to create crazy wings. Red Coca-Cola butterflies tumble round the tub, sisters to the sparkling Sprite moths that decorate the studio walls. Going to our desks, I feel happiness bubble up inside me. Zack would love this! A Lilt dragonfly hovers above the whiteboard, its tin wings sprayed a thousand shimmering greens. Evian bluebottles buzz over a pile of textbooks. Zara strokes a golden "Caffeine-Free" Coke butterfly that's settled on our sewing machine. Meanwhile, Miss Bloxam darts round clipping wings onto the backs of everyone's chairs... bags... sleeves.

'Ugh,' says Keisha.

'Strewth!' Miss Bloxam slaps a fat, furry moth on her. '*Smile*, can yer? I've seen a bigger crack on a wallaby's bottom.'

I love Miss Bloxam. Why she chose to leave sunny Oz to teach in a crap school in Nowheresville Norbridge is a mystery. (Perhaps she's on the run? She certainly seems to have a casual attitude to school property. I can't remember a lesson when Miss Bloxam *hasn't* snuck a bit of trimming into my bag. 'Relax, gal, it's the Outback way,' she winks. 'Now you look over there while I slide in these pinking shears and, ooh, three metres of reinforced stretch.')

When she's not nicking stuff, she's sharing her ninja sewing skills. It's Miss Bloxam who showed me how to put darts into a top; how to cinch a waist, and almost (*almost*) how to handle a zip. Best of all, she didn't laugh when Lees swung by to show Miss Bloxam our Katwalk pics. Before I could wrestle the phone back, Miss Bloxam was fully scrolling. 'Kat, your gear is BONZA.'

Bonza means "good", right?

Ow! A bulldog clip hits me on the back of my head. Turning, I find Keisha, arm raised. 'Here.' She hurls another at Zara. 'Fashion freebie!'

Deftly Zara catches it. 'Netball.' She smiles shyly at me. 'Goal defence.' Straightening the butterfly's wings, she perches it on my shoulder.

'SO sad.' Natalie snaps the moment on her phone. We turn our backs on her, but can't ignore the sound of acrylic nails click-clacking away. 'Ha!' She gets a text back. Stella says, *'Laughing face, crying face. Kat scrounging bulldog clips to hold her ballgown together?'* Nat and Keisha crack up.

'Ignore them,' says Zara. 'They want a rise out of you.'

'They've got one.' I fly up like Miss Bloxam's butterflies. Bad enough the Tag-Hags poison every other lesson, they're NOT ruining textiles. 'Screw being a target.' I shoot towards the fabric shelf. 'I want to win.' I release a bolt of muslin from the bottom of the heap. Thin, white cotton, it's the "poor girl" of the fabric community. 'Yet it props up the finest fashion houses,' says Miss Bloxam. Before rocking up here, she used to be a seamstress in *"haute couture"* ateliers (that's workshops to you and me) in Milan and Paris. 'A designer gown doesn't appear by magic,' she told me and Zara, 'it starts as a muslin mock-up.' We looked blank. 'Pieced together in cotton.'

'Ah.' I got it. 'Like a shadow dress?' She nodded.

'Last chance for designers to perfect the cut before they *rip* into the fancy fabric and shower down the Swarovski crystals.'

Well, crystals I don't have. But I know all about working in the shadows! Rolling the white cotton out onto my desk, I refer back to the draft I sketched in PSHE. Measuring by eye, I chalk the outline for each segment — three pieces for the bodice, triple that for the skirts. Zara hands me the scissors. I pause. She nudges my elbow and I'm off!

'So yer going for it?' Miss Bloxam appears as I finish pinning my cut-outs together. 'This catwalk contest?'

'Er... yeah.' I feel myself go red. 'D'you think I'm mad?'

'Never medda a designer who wasn't.' She grins. 'Wanna hand?'

'Please.'

'Right, let's swap out these pins.' She bends over the muslin, all business suddenly. 'Want your shadow dress to move? Yer tack it together, with big, easy stitches.' She threads a needle. Zara takes it.

'Committee girls stick together.' Zara tells me, and just like that we've got ourselves a sewing bee. Chat hums as we tack down seams together. Popping out pins, Zara and I pluck up the courage to ask Miss Bloxam about her koala tattoo.

'Jeez, thad's nothing,' she says, pulling down her jeans to show a crazy big scar. 'Where a koala bit my butt.'

Now Zara's sharing too – pics of her little nephews chomping down on her mum's homemade samosas. Which gets *me* describing Daisy and Lil, and their latest developmental milestone (synchronised headbutting).

'Ta-da!' cries Miss Bloxam. 'We have a dress.'

'A *shadow* dress.' I shake out the white cotton skirts.

'Five minutes till the bell goes.' Miss Bloxam checks the clock. 'Enough time to try it on.'

'Here? No way!'

'Go on,' Zara checks over her shoulder. 'No one's looking at you.'

'Duh. No one does,' I say, 'unless it's to laugh.'

'So...' says Miss Bloxam. 'Waddya gonna do about it?'

I glance back. The other girls are bent over their work;

Nat and Keisha are giggling over their phones. 'Change,' I say. 'Fast'.

Zara and Miss Bloxam screen me. I strip down to my bra and school tights, and shake the muslin mock-up over my head. As I disappear into a cloud of white cotton, Zara fans out the floor-length skirts.

'Wow,' I say with a giggle. 'The look is definitely "bed sheet.'

'But the cut is dead on.' Miss Bloxam pins a quick tuck in the bodice. 'You've really brought out your shape.'

'Get me, taking shape!' Twirling round in my holey tights and cotton skirts, I picture myself rocking the ball.

When I open my eyes, it's to see Natalie and Keisha turning their phones on me.

By lunchtime I'm *the* Instagram story.

Cinderella rocks an old sheet

Lisa shows me the worst on her phone. The pics hurt, but the comments kill.

Count the holes in her tights!
Has she rolled round in toilet paper?
Those bra straps are *grey*.

Laughing face after laughing face. Everyone from St Ed's to Winsham Academy is hating on me, feels like, but I'm hooked, scrolling for more.

Watch out, catwalk. Here she comes!

A new story flashes up. I'm a faceless blur of "toilet paper".

Stella hearts it.

I turn away before I see Jonah's heart too.

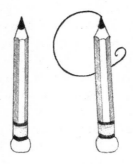

When the final bell goes, I race home like I could outrun the photos.

Who am I kidding?

The R3 bus whistles past, and all I see is Winsham boys working their phones, checking me out in my grey bra and bed sheet. I shiver, and tug my coat tight. When a gust of wind billows open my bag, my mock-up gown tries to escape. I let myself into our house, and find it colder than the street outside.

The twins are huddled together on the sofa, watching Christmas ads on the TV. Lily licks snot bubbles off her top lip. Daisy coughs quietly so as not to compete with a £49.99 singing robot bear.

Tucking a blanket over them, I wipe the worst of the green muck off Lily's face, and go to the kitchen. Dad's rummaging in the cupboard where we keep the thermometer and the plasters. His jumper's got a hole in the elbow. The bald patch on the top of his head has grown, I notice, but Mum's only got eyes for the bills.

'Great.' She tears through post at the table. 'Another letter from the tax officer. "Dear Mrs Parker,"' she reads out word for word, '"having reviewed your case, I cannot increase your levels of Universal Credit. But I *can* keep your Child Benefit laughably low, what with being THE CHRISTMAS GRINCH."'

OK, so not *exactly* word for word.

'Oh, Chris. It's hopeless.' Mum chucks the letter down. 'We'll never get the cash together for this new boiler.' She chews her lip. 'There might be something floggable in my stack of shoeboxes. Plus, there's your bike – that's still on eBay, right?'

'Right.' From out of the cupboard, Dad pulls a sticky-looking bottle of pink Calpol. Keeping his back to Mum, he gives the contents a furious shake. When he squeezes past me to the front room, I see there's barely a spoonful of pink left. 'Who's looking worst?' he mouths at me.

'Lil,' I mouth back.

I go to Mum, who's started shuffling coins and crumpled £5 notes between brown envelopes marked 'Food', 'Kids', ~~'Clothes'~~ 'Medicine'. I realise it's the first time we've been together since the other night.

The night I learned how much I cost her.

'What is it, Kat?' She snaps an elastic band round an envelope.

'Nothing, I—'

'What?'

'Dad, have you seen,' I bluster, 'he's losing his hair?'

'Let's hope he's selling it.' She folds up a fiver. 'Tonight's Lidl night, and we've less for our weekly shop than most families would spend on a takeaway. Now scoot,' I'm leaning on her pile of bills. 'Before you send everything crashing!'

I go to my room. Ignore Gran's roll of silk, and don't
    look at my sewing machine. What's the point? Just
dumping my bag on the bed, I feel my hands turn to ice.
        Wind rattles my window. I lean my forehead
            against the freezing glass. No moonlight
        shines down the Katwalk tonight. But through
            the darkness, a light shines in Zack's room.
            I can see his shoulders braced over his
            Fender guitar; can practically feel the
            tension in his arms. He's working it,
            isn't he? This audition, it could be the
            start of something. If Zack can just
        produce the talent – screw that, the drive.
    Talent's the easy part. I turn back to my ice-box room.
I can't *afford* to feel sorry for myself. And you know what?
That's OK. Let the Tag-Hags play with their phones, this
girl's got work to do. *Ker-rang,* 'Thunderstruck' is playing in
my head now! Possibly a sign of hypothermia, so I fish my
bobble hat out from under my pillow, and ram it on. Then
I yank my rag bag from under my bed. Extracting a jumper
I outgrew last year, I cut off the sleeve ends. Then I snip a
hole in each cuff, so I can poke my thumb through as I pull
them on: fingerless gloves! I grab Gran's silk roll, and…

Whoosh, I let fly a bolt of shimmering blue.

Whip, it catches on the draught.

Flop, it hits the floor.

Fine. "Flop" I can work with.
("Flop" is what I know!) Smoothing
Gran's silk out on the floor, I take
my crumpled mock-up dress,
and snip out the tacking stitches.
Time to re-assemble: One by one, I
pin each muslin segment into the silk

105

– like jigsaw pieces for a puzzle only I can put together. Goodbye shadow dress, let's get real!

The world fades around me: I hear Dad creaking up to the attic, Mum shouting that she's off to the Co-op for more Calpol. It takes a furious (familiar) banging to bring me out of myself. And down the stairs to our front door. Peering through the letterbox, and get a hockey stick between the eyeballs. 'Still no doorbell?' growls Lees.

'Hey,' I open up. 'What are you doing here?' She's not come alone, turns out. On the step beside Lisa is a bulging bin bag and an (even more) bulging Auntie Sheila. Lisa's stepmum-in-waiting is caked in bright orange foundation and (forget it's mid-December) is dressed for a beach party. We're talking...

1) High-heeled, canary yellow sandals.
2) Tight apricot leggings, and
3) a tangerine boob tube (only the tube is NO match for the boobs).

'Sorry,' says Lees. 'I couldn't stop them.'

I assume she's talking about Sheila's titanic tangerines until she adds, 'Dad's just parking up.'

'*Here?* Why?'

'Because,' Sheila shoulders in, 'I've got a nephew goes to Winsham. You, madam, are getting shared. Parading around Snapchat in nothing but your skimpies!'

'Her *skimpies?*' Lisa rolls her eyes. But Sheila's too busy staring at me, like she's looking for something. And worried what she might find.

I stare back, can't help it. Sheila normally keeps out of the way when we're round at Lisa's dad's. She's just a voice Lisa shouts at; a large dent left in the sofa, a make-up bag spilling into the bath. This is the first time I've seen beneath the foundation. Her skin, it's cracked with eczema. Painful-looking patches she's tried to hide. All that make-up must make it worse, though? And her eyes don't "go" with the rest of her. They're soft, almost grey. 'You OK, love?' she asks.

'COME ON, WOMAN!' A car door slams. 'The lads are expecting us at the club.'

Lisa's dad walks around his gleaming Ford Mondeo. Tucking his shiny shirt into his shiny trousers, he pulls another bin bag out of the boot, twin to the one Sheila now holds up to me. I watch in horror as the contents spill out. 'What the—?'

'Emptied my closets, didn't I?' Sheila stuffs down a tangle of neon-coloured viscose. 'Put together some *proper* party gear for you.'

'I'm sorry, Kat.' Lisa groans. 'I tried. I *told* her—'

'*Half the street* heard what you told me,' says Sheila, her face flaming bright orange. 'But I came here for Kat.' She grips my hand. 'I *get* you want to design your own ball dress, love, but wanting don't work. Believe me.' I feel her brassy rings cut into her flesh. 'You go for the fairy tale; you get chased by trolls. *They* knock you down,' she lets go, 'you don't ever get up.'

'Evening, ladies!' Terry Mathews puffs up the path. Dropping his bin-bag on the step, he sidles in between Sheila and Lees. 'Ready for a date with your old man?'

Lees looks shocked, then delighted, then realises he means Sheila. *She's* turned back into a sex-bag, all bouncing boobs and teetering heels. 'Less of the "old", Terry!' She giggles. Together they head back to the car, Terry striding manfully, Sheila hanging onto his arm.

Lees and I stand shell-shocked, the doorstep between

us. 'Wanna play fright night with the twins?' I shake my bin bag at her.

'Can't, sorry.' Lisa backs down the path, raising her hockey stick. 'Coach has called a practice.'

'Not another one?'

'Snow's on its way – they've had to move regionals up to Friday.'

'*This* Friday?'

'I *know! We*'re not ready.' She whacks her stick into our hedge. 'Me and Gina are the only ones training our butts off.'

'But Friday's Winter Wonderland.' My mate disappears in a shower of yellow leaves. 'You'd better make it back in time! I can't do this on my own,' my stomach cramps with panic. 'If you dump me just so you can —'

'What? Muck about with a puck? Dribble down a pitch? Jeez, Kat…' She turns off down our street. '…you're not the only one busting a gut round here.'

'Lees.' I run after her. 'I'm sorry. It's these pics – they've got me spinning out.'

'So stop.'

'Stop?'

'This business with the ballgown.' She stops. Swings round. 'Bin it.'

'But—' I can't believe this. 'You're the one who told me to go for it!'

'I know, *I know*. Your designs always look cool to me, but those pics.' She whacks her stick into a fresh bit of hedge. 'You can't wear that thing to the ball, Kat. It's—'

'A WORK IN PROGRESS.' I explode. 'Or did you expect me to *magic* a dress out of thin air? I'm trying here, Lees, but it's hard. *So hard*. Which you'd know if you… if you…'

'What?' She pokes at our branches. I hear something snap.

'We don't go down the Katwalk anymore. Lees, you don't answer my texts—'

'I'm training,' she says.

'You never want to hang out.'

'There's no time!'

'You find time for Gina... as if she cared.'

'Meaning?'

'Lees, you don't even know she *likes* you.'

'She likes me.'

'You hope. So you're dumping me—'

'Don't.' Lisa swings her stick. '*Don't* guilt-trip me, when we both know you'd chuck everything if Fantasy Fringe Boy so much as looked at you. In fact, he's probably looking at you right now. They all are.' She fires a parting shot. 'Don't trash Sheila's stuff. Those pics were bad.'

Agh! I rage back to our house, grabbing both bin bags. Up in my room, I let rip. Shred the black plastic, and release a storm of laddered tights and trashy slit-skirts. Dropping to my knees, I swirl my hands through Sheila's super-cheap, super-bright threads...

...and feel the rage fizzle out of me. 'You poor things.' I stroke the tortured tops and baggy bottoms. Every garment has lost its "give". Every seam shows the strain, except for one: a brand new mini-dress, it still bears its Primark shop tag. 'Size 10, SUMMER SALE'. Summer madness, more like. How could Auntie Sheila think she'd fit into *this*?

Shaking out the skimpy black slip, I picture all the blonde, skinny girls who sashay through summer while Sheila sweats to keep up. Dazzled by the lights of her favourite store, she's sucked in by a little black dress, and thinks, 'That's *me*.'

Flashing her payment card, Sheila races home with the piece that'll transform her. Wrestling it on, she turns to her mirror, and sees the truth — the truth that confronts every one of us too fat, too plain or too poor to buy into the dream: 'That'll *never* be me.'

'*I GIVE UP*.' Mum slams back into the house. 'Sodding Co-op's out of Calpol.' The twins start coughing again; my cue to get down there. I'm shovelling Sheila's cast-offs into a bag for the charity shop when I feel a crackle of static. Between me and the black dress, something sparks.

Quickly, I shed my school uniform, and pull it on. I yank down the tight skirt, and *ba-doing*, it rides right up again.

'Kat,' Mum yells up the stairs. 'Help me get the twins in the car! If I've got to drive to the pharmacy, might as well get them looked at.' My sisters start to wail as the telly goes off. 'Snot should NOT be this colour.'

'Coming.' I check myself in the mirror. The cut is so bad, the dress manages to be both tight *and* saggy at the same time. 'It needs to come in *here*,' I gather the excess fabric into a knot at the back. I'm fastening it with my hairband when Mum shouts from halfway up the stairs.

'Kat, do I need to drag you out?'

'*No*.' I rifle round for my jeans, but it's clothes carnage up here. I have to settle for chucking on my coat. *Just* about holding it together (zip's still bust) I run downstairs to find the front door gaping. I slam it shut behind me, and head out to the car. My sisters are strapped into the back, sneezing into their little red duffle coats. As I get into the front, Mum gives a grim nod.

'Time to assume the Parker Prayer Position.' Sticking her key into the ignition, she lowers her head onto the steering wheel: 'Please, car, *please* have enough petrol to get us to Sainsbury's Savacentre.'

She turns the key.

Nothing.

She bangs her head against the wheel. Dandruff shudders down onto her shoulders. She tries again, both of us praying this time. The car gurgles into gear, and Mum and I grin at each other, like we DID that? 'Road trip!' I cry.

'Destination twenty-four-hour pharmacy.' She hits the gas. 'I can't stand another night of those two coughing.' She frowns into her rear-view mirror. 'Poor mites.'

'Watch it!' I yelp as she nearly clips a bus. Now Mum's swearing; the twins are roaring. 'Toons,' I cry, 'we need TOONS!' Fiddling with the car stereo, I get a burst of white noise, then Mariah Carey warbling that all she wants for Christmas is "yooooooou".

'*I don't need to haaaaang my stocking,*' I sing along, '*there upon the fireplace...*' Leaning into the back, I grab Lily's sticky paws and start patting them together in time to Mariah.

'Look, Mummy,' squeals Lil, 'we CAPPING!' Daisy starts clapping too (well, slapping herself in the face, but it's rhythmic). They're both giggling and kicking their little red shoes as I slide back into my seat.

'Thanks, love,' says Mum. 'Good to have *one* other adult around.' She gives me a glance, so tired... so sore. So I smile for us both as she steers our little car round the giant Savacentre ring road. I smile till it aches, and when I can't take the ache any more, I sing. '*Make my wish come trooooooo...*' As we turn into the car park, the twins are starting up: '*All I womp for Kwissmuss is oooooooo!*'

Even Mum joins in.

We head into the store, swinging Lil and Daisy between us. '*We don't need no Christmas pre-sents,*' sings Mum, flipping a bird at the toy displays.

'Mum!' I fold her finger down, which makes her laugh. Even a mile-long queue for the pharmacy counter can't knock her mood. 'Good to know we're not the only ones suffering.' She diverts us down the food aisles, lifting the twins into our trolley ('taxi service,' she tickles them, 'for snot-bags'). When Lil tugs a family bag of Wotsits off the shelf, Mum doesn't hurl it back. And when her phone starts to ring, she does a little jig. 'Von! You found us a boiler?'

A beat.

'But Von,' she sags like a sail in a storm, 'you swore—'

What? What did Von swear? I crane in to catch snatches:

'Rookie error, Kell, I could kick myself...'

'The price I quoted for your boiler? Turns out it's a trade discount.'

'I can... my Plumbfix card, but the discount... it expires in five days.'

'No,' gasps Mum. 'We'll never get the cash in time. How much will the price go up?'

I don't hear Von's answer, just Mum's cry as she takes off. Phone clamped under her chin, she grips the bar of the trolley, white-knuckles like she's riding a roller coaster. Careering towards the "discounted items" shelf, she yanks the Wotsits bag off Lil and chucks it at the stacks of expired food.

'Gimme!' yells Lil.

'Hurty,' yelps Daisy as Mum starts hurling dented cans of discount beans into the trolley. Quickly I scoop her out of harm's way.

'Down you go.' I set her on the floor. 'Let Mummy do her shopping.' But when I try to pull out Lil, she starts kicking. 'Me womp WOTSITS.'

'Come on, Lil.' She kicks harder. I feel her little legs scrape against the trolley wires as I pull. I want to cry too.

Instead I drop her roughly down beside Lil, and strain back to hear Von.

'Cost breakdowns...' The tinny voice of doom comes from Mum's phone. *'Hidden extras... PANIC STATIONS.'*

'Go!' Mum shoos me away to tend to the twins, who've *obviously* run off. Muttering mutinously, I trudge back to the Wotsits shelf. No twins. I trail down the snacks aisle. Shuffle past cereals, then confectionery...

    ... rice and pasta *(I pick up speed)*...
   tinned foods...
     teas & coffee *(I'm running now)*...
       'Daisy? Lil? WHERE ARE YOU?'

They've vanished.

ricochet off other shoppers. Startled mums grab at their kids, old ladies clutch at their bags. 'Have you seen two girls? Tiny,' I cry. 'Holding hands.' I skid to a halt at the store entrance. Automatic doors open to reveal a world of darkness, spitting with rain, roaring with traffic...

The road! It'll kill them. I set off at a sprint, crashing into a woman entering with a trolley. She recoils as I start to twist and writhe like someone possessed. 'Get away,' she shrieks. 'Let go!'

'I can't. My coat, it's caught in your trolley!' I'm trapped by the threads of my tatty coat lining. The harder I try to get free, the tighter I'm snared.

Agh, I slip out of my coat.

'Hey.' The woman shouts after me. 'You can't just *leave* it—'

'*Girls!*' I hit the exit ramp. '*WHERE ARE YOU?*' The ring road roars back at me, swirling angry torrents of traffic. Sheeting rain distorts the oncoming headlights. 'Please,' I beg shadow-faced strangers. 'Have you seen my sisters?'

'HERE!'

I spin round.

'BY THE LIGHTS!' I squint through the rain. Across the road, there's a gang of schoolboys huddled in a bus shelter. Their leader's waving at me. Through lightning-fast breaks in the thundering traffic, I catch a sweep of blond... the upturned collars of a Burberry coat. *Jonah?*

'These two yours?' he shouts. The twins toddle out from behind him, their red hoods pelted by rain.

'DAISY!' I yell. 'LIL!'

'Kat, our Kat!' They jump for joy. In a massive puddle. Whisking back his coat, Jonah shakes his head like "this is NOT happening!"

A sudden lull in traffic, and I realise he's laughing, gesturing at the lights. 'They turned green for them. Got a clear run as far as the bus shelter, then started kicking the crap out of Daniel.'

'STAY THERE, GIRLS!' I tell them. 'Don't run to me!'

They always run to me.

'Please,' I cry to Jonah. 'Hold their hands.' But he's playing to his crew, ragging Daniel.

'Look, Kat!' Lil toddles towards the road. 'I WUNNING.' Ginger curls bobbing, she hurls herself at four lanes of angry traffic.

'NO!' I shriek as cars swerve. Brakes scream. A juggernaut thunders between us.

'*Lil!*'

The world turns to slow-mo. I plough forward, powerless to stop the crushing progress of the tanker. With a bone-breaking judder, the huge wheels roll past me to reveal ...

Jonah poised on the kerb, holding my little sister up like a trophy. His squad are whooping and Lil's *loving* it. Daisy's kicking him in the shins, and my heart wants to burst.

True, this *may* be from sprinting across four lanes of traffic. Blasted by car horns, I throw myself at my sisters. Crushing their little bodies into mine, I can't bear to set them down. When they do wriggle free, I rise up to thank Jonah, and see Daniel nudge him. Liam whistles. As another car hoots, a cold trickle runs down my back ...

I'm not wearing my coat, am I?

I'm soaked through, bare-legged and wearing Sheila's dress. It sticks to me like a skanky second skin. When I yank the skirt back down, Jonah's crew rustle in their hoods like I'm putting on a show for them.

'Yay!' cries Daisy. 'Pitty dwess.'

'Pretty,' says Jonah with a smile, 'doesn't cover it.'

'Guess that was the plan.' Stella Harcourt swings out from behind the bus shelter. Keisha and Nat follow, looking cold and wet. Unlike Stella, who's swathed in black faux fur like a cat that got the cream.

Now here I am curdling it. 'You get around, don't you?' She curls her lip at me. 'First you're all over Insta. Now you're streaking through the Savacentre.'

'Desperate or what?' Keisha sneers.

'She's got some cheek for a freak.' Nat turns to Stella, pleased with herself. But Stella's found two new friends.

'Poor things. Feel their little hands!' She bends over the twins, all fake concern. 'They're frozen. Why aren't they home – or, I dunno, strapped *into* something?' She appeals to Jonah. 'You've seen that crappy buggy she's always pushing round town.'

Jonah shrugs. His fringe falls down over his eyes, and I'm on my own again — no, strike that, I'm surrounded. Then Jonah raises his hand. Slowly, he brushes back his hair, so no one can miss the look he gives me:

Approval.

I shiver. He laughs. 'Here...' He shakes off his Burberry coat. '...take this'. He steps closer, draping it over my shoulders. I hear raindrops popping off the expensive fabric. Feel the weight of the coat bear down on me, then the soft fall of Jonah's fringe on my cheek.

'*KAT! You are heading for SO MUCH TROUBLE.*'

Mum. I spin round to see her slaloming down the ramp from the Savacentre. She looks like a crazy woman, nothing in her trolley but a couple of tins and my tattered coat. As Nat and Keisha start to snigger, I want to make myself *invisible*...

For none of that to be mine.

But first, I want to keep Mum AWAY FROM JONAH. Grabbing the twins, I'm marching us back to the crossing when a gust of wind hits. It practically rips Jonah's coat off me! But I've got my sisters' soft, squishy hands in mine. The Winsham boys can whistle; I'm not letting go.

'Laters, Kat,' Jonah shouts over the catcalls.

'Yeah, sure!' I twist round, and my skirt rides up again. *Gah,* this dress is NOT my friend.

But it's got Jonah treating me like one.

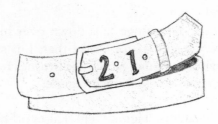

I wake up next day feeling different. Happy and... what's the other word? Oh yeah, warm! I nestle deeper into Jonah's flash coat. So it's not designed to be a sleeping bag, but then my room's not *supposed* to be an icebox.

Plus, (I discovered last night) the coat's got a quilted liner buttoned in. Clearly Jonah's trying to

    a) chunk up like The Rock (*ha*, as if Jonah worries how he looks!) Or he

    b) feels the cold, which is *another* thing we've got in common! Other things being (fangirl alert now: I *am* sniffing his coat) a lover of salt and vinegar crisps... and, ooh, is that a cheeky undertone of Twix?

'Kat!' yells Mum from the kitchen. 'You up?'

'Yep!' I roll out of bed. Kicking Sheila's bin bags outta my way, I strut to the bathroom mirror to check my new look. Mmm, maybe lose the bobble hat? Also the rest of my nightwear. Hanging Jonah's coat on a towel peg, I shed

    1) Thick sweater.

    2) Thin sweater.

    3) Thermal vest.

    4) Dad's old football socks.

5) Mum's old PJ bottoms, and

6) Knickers (MY OWN! Hand-me-downs have their limits).

Leaping *gazelle-like* into the shower, I fall out again FAST 'cause it's freezing. School uniform on, I snuggle back into Jonah's coat. The fabric feels class; the tailoring's totally sharp. Buckling the belt, I strike a pose. The way Jonah looked at me last night—

He saw something, didn't he?

Er, he saw *a lot*. I pull the belt tighter – and find the belt loop's torn. (Have St Edward's girls been *literally* mobbing him?) Thrusting my hands into the pockets, I pull out fistfuls of boy rubbish: old Refresher wrappers... shredded homework assignments... a crumpled page from *Men's Fitness* magazine. Opening it up, I find two sachets of "Power Protein". And Lees says he *doesn't* take his hockey training seriously! Well, if Jonah can mean business, so can I.

First I bag up every sorry scrap of Sheila's. Then I focus on Gran's silk. Cutting out my "jigsaw puzzle" shapes, I prop the shimmering pattern pieces against my sewing machine – one killer gown ready to be activated.

'Stick a rocket up it, Kat.' Mum yells from downstairs.

'Just watch me!' Silk stacked, I smooth back the checked lapels of my Burberry, and strut down the stairs like I'm at the Met Gala. A breakout designer with a dreamy boyf—

'Hold up.' Mum stops me in the hall. 'What are you still doing in that coat?'

'Nothing! Just...' I slide past her '...returning it.'

'Not so fast.' She grabs my collar.

'Oi!'

'I want a feel.' She strokes the soft gabardine lapel. 'You know it takes the best part of a month to produce a Burberry coat?'

'A *month*?'

'Minimum. One mill up north makes them — has done for over a hundred years. *Supposedly*...' She can tell I'm hooked. '...Thomas Burberry invented waterproof gabardine for *one particular* type of customer. Any guesses?'

'Er.' I go back a century. 'Rich gents going hunting? Posh ladies off to the races?'

'Nope. Soldiers,' she straightens my shoulders, 'off to the First World War.'

The penny drops. '*That's* why it's called a trench coat?'

'Burberry wanted to protect doomed, young heroes.' Her face hardens. 'Not floppy-haired rich boys who ponce round the Savacentre eyeing up girls who should know better.'

'Meaning?'

'The rain wasn't coming down *that* strong, love! I could see—'

'What? It was just a dress.'

'Dress?' snorts Mum. 'I've worn bigger socks.'

'THOCKS.' The twins toddle out from the kitchen. 'FOR FEEEEEET.'

'The talent you've got, Kat,' says Mum, 'yet *that's* what you trade on?'

'No!' I blush. 'It's not like that. Jonah's different.'

'I bet.' She scoops up the twins. 'Well, this Jonah Whatshisname... Porridge?'

'Kerridge.'

'Let *him* swan round like Norbridge's answer to Romeo Beckham. *We* can't afford to pay for dry-cleaning. Give the boy back his coat,' she dumps the twins on me, 'before this pair poo in the pocket.' Then she goes to work, leaving me to get the twins off to nursery IN MY BURBERRY (*IN*

YOUR FACE, MUM!).

I only take it off when I reach Norbridge Hill. The R3 bus could bomb past, and I do *not* want to be spotted in Jonah's coat by the cool squad – worse, by Jonah. *What would he think?* Short answer: no idea. But I know we just need a chance to chat. When my phone rings, my fingers fumble for it. *Has Jonah magically got my number?*

'Zack,' I try not to sound disappointed. 'Y'all right?'

'Yeah. You?'

''course. Why shouldn't I be?'

''S just . . .' Zack sucks in his breath. 'Lees told me about the Instagram thing. How you—'

'What?'

'Had a re-think about this "Dazzling Look" contest. Screw wearing a dress to the ball,' he deadpans, 'you're going full toga.'

I snort despite myself. 'I've just been "outed" in a bedsheet, Zack. Shouldn't you be worrying about my mental state?'

'Nah, way too late for that.' I can hear him grinning down the phone. 'Just wanna check you're still working on this gown of yours. The real one.'

I flashback to last night – how Sheila's rank dress stuck to my thighs and the look Jonah gave me. 'Yeah, I'm still working on it. I've gotta go, Zack.'

'But—'

'Heading into school, sorry!' I hang up. Zack doesn't want to hear about me and Jonah. He's made that much clear. As for my butt-skimming, black dress? I don't need Zack to tell me: it's a red flag to the Tag-Hags.

Sure enough, I walk into a cloakroom full of hot sniggers, plus a cold shoulder from Lees. 'Sorry.' I say, as she rams her key into her locker. 'For yesterday. *Of course* hockey regionals matter more than my stupid dress—'

'They don't matter *more*.' She swings around. 'They just—'

'Matter. I get it, sorry.' I pull a face. Keep pulling it.

'You can drop the constipated frog face.' She shoves me. 'I'll be your friend again. But only because you *clearly* need one.' She eyes the huddle of haters at my back. 'What you done now, stolen someone's boyfriend?'

'No!' I clutch my bag to my chest. Jonah's coat sleeve flops out.

'Proof!' Lisa falls on it. 'You've kidnapped a Winsham boy for your pervy pleasures. You do *know* those lads are not worth the trouble? And that's not me talking as a...' Eyebrows wiggling, she mouths the word, 'Lesbian.'

Giggling, I tell her how I got stuck outside the Savacentre in a skimpy sock-frock, aka:

The Heroic Chronicle of How Jonah Saved My Sister *AND LENT ME HIS COAT*!

'Yeah right,' says Lees, 'after he clocked you in the sock-frock.'

'Don't be stupid. He was just being nice.'

'What's stupid? You've got a great bod. Again, that's *NOT* me talking as a—'

'What? Tell us!' Stella struts over, making Lees flush up into her strawberry-gold curls. Which Stella *loves*. 'Don't be shy, Lisa! You're saying you're a—?'

'Mate.' I step in front of Lees. 'She was saying *she's my mate*.'

'Ah, sweet.' Stella pouts at me. 'Just don't go thinking anyone else likes you — or your gutter girl style.' She spots

Jonah's sleeve dangling from my bag. 'You do know this is, like, Burberry? Or do you have to trash *everything* you touch?' She takes out her phone.

'What are you doing?' I ask.

'What d'you think? Telling Jonah you've mashed his coat, but I'll return it after school.' Texting, she wafts off to registration. 'You can carry it around till then.'

I turn back to find Lisa headbutting her locker. '*Aargh!*' she roars. 'How do we let her *do* that?'

'We don't.' I stuff Jonah's coat sleeve back into my bag. 'We're playing the long game.' The length (to be precise) of double English, double maths, double science and final period PSHE. By the time the end-of-school bell rings, we have formulated our plan.

'Coat,' demands Nat, as we walk out past the toilets.

'Give.' Keisha holds out her hand. Lees whacks her hockey stick into it. 'Ow!' squeals Keisha. 'What are you doing?'

'Testing your reflexes,' says Lees. 'Now if you came to hockey practise more—'

'Just give us Jonah's coat,' demands Nat, shooting nervous looks over her shoulder: Stella's about to strut from the toilet, make-up done, and wanting results.

'Sorry,' I say, 'but *I'm* giving Jonah his coat back.'

'Ha!' Keisha looks rattled. 'Knows that, does he? You made a date?'

'No need.' Lisa swings her stick. Keisha ducks behind Nat. 'The boy practically lives in McDonald's. If I didn't chase him around a pitch occasionally, he'd look like a pufferfish. See?' Lees blows out her cheeks and *puff*, scatters them both with saliva.

'Did you have to do that?' I march her off.

'What? We had a plan—'

123

'To call Jonah a pufferfish?'

'Just saying,' she says with a shrug. 'He's not got killer cheekbones like Zack.'

'*Zack?*' I stop. 'We're talking about Jonah.'

'*You* are. I'd rather talk about your massive levels of NUTS-ness.'

'My what?'

'Nuts-ness. It's a thing.' She walks off. 'Trust me.'

'And I've got it?' I run after her.

'Jeez, yeah. What else explains your *wicked* sense of style versus your *weirdo* taste in boys?'

'My...? Wait! Where you going?'

'McDonald's, remember?' She swings out of school. 'You gotta a hot date.'

Every prince needs a realm, doesn't he? Prince Wills has Buckingham Palace; Thor swings his hammer round Ragnarok. Well, Jonah Kerridge rules Norbridge McDonald's. Every day after school, he settles into his "throne zone" by the stairs. Shooting paper straws across the tables, his squad suck their teeth at the plain girls, and show off for the pretty ones. If I am to enter their realm, verily, I must flick back my hair and roll up my kilt.

'How do I look?' I ask Lees.

'Like you've got your skirt snagged up your bum.' She tugs it down. 'Now go...' She pushes me into the restaurant. '...find Golden Boy.'

'Shhh, he'll hear you.' Jonah's stood by the stairs in a new coat. A dark navy duffle, it sets off his blond hair. 'D'you think he's seen us?'

'Through *that* fringe? Fat chance,' snorts Lisa. I elbow her. Too hard...

Her stick jerks up, clipping the tray of some passing kid. As his cheeseburger goes flying, the boy sets up a wail. Jonah looks over.

'Crap.' I back into Lees, who's caught the cheeseburger

mid-flight ('Saaaave!') and is now trying to perform a victory fist-bump on a terrified eight-year-old.

'Stop,' I hiss. 'You're making me look bad. *What do I say to him?*'

'Mmm…' Lisa chews on a bit of gherkin. 'How about, "*Wow, fab fringe! Can I lend you a hair slide?*"' Her phone beeps with a message. 'It's Gina.' Lisa's face lights up with her screen. 'She wants to meet me at—'

'Sprinkles?' I guess.

Already she's texting. 'C U in 5.'

'Noooo.' I grab her sleeve as she goes. 'You can't leave me.' Lisa gives me a funny look. 'Thought I was making you look bad.'

'I didn't mean—'

'I *know* what you meant.' She unhooks my hand. 'Just be yourself, yeah? Before you forget what that looks like.'

The door swings closed behind her. 'Kat,' Jonah calls, 'you coming over?'

Legs shaking, I move through the crowd surrounding him. Mouth dry, I croak out a 'hiya'. He gives me that smile of his: half-cocky, half-shy, but *fully* on me. And, I can't lie, my knees go. Seriously, I'd keel over if the seats weren't already taken by his squad. Daniel, Liam and the usual suspects are perched on the seat-backs, looking like bargain basement versions of Jonah – all greasy fringes and skewed school ties – apart from two guys who've actually sat down at the table to play cards. 'Hey,' I greet them. 'Big Mike, Little Mickey.'

'Kat? Sweet!' Little Mickey leaps up, scattering cards. We used to hang together when Zack played on the school soccer team.

'You good?' Big Mike enfolds me in a massive goalkeeper's hug. 'And Zack – still playing?' We both know he doesn't mean football. Zack packed all that in when Marie died. But Marie used to go to the same church as Big Mike's mum, so Mike knows the score. 'Still swinging that electric axe of his?' I nod.

'Like he could take out the world.'

'Hey.' Jonah moves in. 'You guys know Kat?'

'Know her?' says Big Mike. 'We *owe* her.'

'She sewed our team strip,' says Little Mickey with a grin. 'Took our old shirts, and did some needle ju-jitsu on them.' He feigns a karate chop. 'Now we're playing with pimped-up cuffs and a gold flash on our backs.'

'Still can't score a goal, though,' chuckles Big Mike. 'Kat, you need to talk our star striker Zack back into—'

A squeal cuts him off. The Tag-Hags enter the restaurant, creating maximum noise for maximum impact. Stella's the only one playing it cool. Dispatching Jayden and Natalie to the food counter, she glides our way.

'Jonah,' I say quickly. 'Thanks for... you know.' I whip out his coat... now a crumpled rag.

'*Man!*' Daniel cracks up. Jonah looks horrified.

'What've you *done* to it?'

'Nothing. See?' I shake out the folds of gabardine, sending plastic cup lids skidding across the table. Burger wrappers whirl into the air.

'Nice moves,' sniggers Daniel, 'but we preferred your action last night, Kit.'

'Kat,' I flush. 'My name's *Kat.*'

'Here, Kitty, Kitty.' Leaning down from his seat-back, Liam flicks my kilt with his straw. 'Show us your legs.'

'Hey!' Big Mike rises up, but Little Mickey's quicker. A quick elbow, and Liam's toppled off his perch. While his mates whoop over him, Jonah looks at me.

'Sorry,' I hold out his coat. 'If you hang it up—'

'S fine; it was getting tired anyway.' Jonah chucks it down on the seats. Then he shakes back his fringe like, "change of subject". 'Winter Wonderland,' he says. 'You going?'

'Yeah. No. What?' His beautiful Burberry is sliding off the seat towards a sticky puddle of Coke.

'This ball, it's lame, yeah?'

'Lame? Yeah,' I snatch up his coat.

'Still, could be a laugh,' he's saying. 'The whole crew's going – wanna come?'

'Er, sure.'

'Cool.' He shakes back his fringe. 'And Kat...'

'Yeah?'

'Wear that dress. From last night.' His fringe falls into his eyes. 'You looked hot.'

Hot? My face burns. My palms sweat. It's almost a relief when Stella breezes over. 'Kat! *Finally*...' She wafts scent at me like we're "Best Friends Forevvs". '...you've come to hang with us.'

She's kidding, right? I look round for an ambush, but Jayden and Natalie are up at the counter. Stella flicks her hair, and it's like a whip crack to the Winsham boys. Daniel and Paul sit their butts down at the table; even Liam springs up off the floor. When Jayden and Nat arrive with their trays, Stella is all, like, 'Make room for Kat!' Then she makes sure I'm stuck down the opposite end to Jonah. 'Not eating, Kat?' she cackles down the table.

'No. I— '

'Can't afford it?' She throws me a pity pout. 'To put on weight, I mean! Not if you wanna wear that tight black number to the ball. *We're* all eating, though.' She extracts a skinny fry from Daniel's packet. And points it at me. 'Don't make us look bad.'

'As if,' mutters Jayden. Nat giggles.

'Kat,' Big Mike gets up. 'I'm shouting Little Mickey a meal deal. You want his fries?'

'I'm fine.'

'He always leaves them—

'*No!*' It comes out louder than I meant. 'Sorry, Mike, I—'

But he's lumbering off already, Little Mickey in his wake, looking hurt for the both of them. Tag-Hags swoop into their place. Carly leans into Liam; Keisha flicks her braids into Daniel's Filet-O-Fish. All fix their eyes on me.

'Mmm...' Jayden bites into her burger. 'So good.'

Natalie takes a loooong, rattly slurp on her milkshake. The boys laugh. Not Jonah – he's busy playing with his phone, leaving Stella free to strike. 'OMG, Kat,' she flicks her nails at me, 'you are so—'

She stops, stares right past me, across the restaurant. So does Nat, then Keisha. Everyone's gawping at the entrance. Like something's blown in from the cold.

I turn around and see Zack. Guitar slung over one shoulder, he's wearing Andy's biker jacket in place of a blazer. Making his way over to our table, his green eyes blaze. His cheekbones look sharp enough to do damage. The Winsham squad slide down in their seats, but the Tag-Hags sit up in theirs. Jayden touches her hair; Natalie sneaks a look at Stella, who's suddenly toying with her  Pandora pendant like it's THE most important thing in the world. Until it's not; beneath their glossy black lashes, her eyes find Zack's.

I see a muscle flex in his jaw. 'Needle Girl,' he says. 'You done here?'

'Erm…' I look up the table, but Jonah's now ninety-nine per cent fringe. And I sense Stella won't be sharing her lip balm with me soon. 'Yep, I'm coming.'

I grab my bag. We don't speak again until we're out on the high street. 'You're shivering,' says Zack. 'What happened to your coat?'

'Don't ask.'

'Here.' He swings down his guitar. 'Take my jacket.'

'No way. You'll freeze.'

'I'm cool.' He tugs his sleeves. 'I'm a rock star, remember?'

We both start giggling as Zack tries (fails) to get my arms into his coat.

'OK, I'll do it!' I zip myself in.

'Suits you,' he grins. Then he slings his arm round my shoulder ('I need your warmth') and we swagger through the Christmas crowds like we rule the world. All these jostling grown-ups? They're just fools who don't know it yet.

The long walk home takes us back to ourselves. No ball, no Jonah, just me and Zack shooting the breeze and splitting his Fruit Pastilles. It's only when we reach our block, and the dusk is taking off our edges, that I ask, 'How come you were in McDonald's? Thought you'd stopped hanging out with that crew.'

'Lisa texted,' he shrugs. 'Said you might need back-up.' Something in his voice makes me look up. A cloud moves across the moon, turning him into a stranger: the broad shoulders, the sudden height of him – it's like I don't know my mate anymore. Don't know how to *feel* about him. I panic, pulling him towards me.

'Woah.' He vibrates. Then pulls out his phone. 'Godda

go – band practice.'

'Wait.' I tug off Zack's biker jacket. 'You'll be wanting this. Audition's tomorrow, yeah?'

'4.00pm, St Edwards gym.' He hands me his guitar to hold. 'I'm bricking it.'

'Rubbish, you've just got butterflies.' Watching him shrug on his jacket, I can feel them myself! 'It's a sign the magic's about to happen.'

'You reckon?'

'Of course! 'S not like we don't want it enough.'

'But that's just it. ' He shakes his head. 'What *do* you want, Kat? You sew away, making these incredible clothes, then fall over yourself to get in with a bunch of losers.' He zips his collar up against the wind. 'Stella Harcourt, Jonah Kerridge. The whole "popular" crew. What d'you *see* in them?'

I shrug.

He waits.

'I dunno! They just seem... sorted. Like they have all the answers. They've got this swagger.'

'I hear you,' he nods. 'Chucking fries, blowing straws? Those guys *own* McDonald's.'

I give him a shove.

'All right, I'm gone!' He swings his guitar over his shoulder. 'But you're Needle Girl, remember?' His eyes lock on to mine. 'Screw swagger. You've got the swish.'

I race home. *Zack thinks I've got the swish. Whatever THAT means.* Did Lees tell him about my label?

Tearing into my room, I run my hands over my crazy upcycles; the skirt I made from a flowery pillowcase; the jeans I chopped down into Daisy Duke shorts; the skimpy sweater I reworked into a halter neck top. So maybe I *won't* save the planet, but can't I start? Here. Now.

With me.

Flicking the light on my sewing machine, I feel my face glow. *Jonah thinks I'm hot. Whatever THAT means...*

I do NOT glance at the corner of my room where I threw Sheila's damp dress last night. I do NOT need to remember how it slithered up my legs. Ball's calling; clock's ticking. Time to show Jonah what good looks like!

Stitch List

1. Assemble back panels of my gown. Try to work in a zip. It can't be THAT hard!
2. OK, it's quite hard. Zip's super long for starters. I unpicked it from an old dress of Gran's, but the

colour's wrong. Means I can't just fix it in, I have to hide it.

3. Hatch plan to create a cunning, zip-concealing flap!
4. Aargh, needle runs away from me. Now silk's snagged, back of gown is RUCKED.
5. Unpick zip while wailing, 'CAN NO ONE HELP ME?!'
6. Shout at twins for coming in to help me. Put them to bed.
7. Return to sewing machine. Hear crash from twins' cot.
8. Shout at twins for coming to help me AGAIN.
9. Return to sewing machine. Hear crash from cot. Shout at twins for coming in to—
10. Give up. Let twins go to sleep in my bed. (I won't be using it tonight, will I?)
11. Decide to FORGET ZIP for now, and focus on skirts (after all, there's enough of them!)
12. Check time: 2.00am. Check progress:

Hmm...

My bodice seams sit snug. I've sewn the skirts panels together, and fixed them to waistband. Shaking out the shimmering blue silk, I can start to believe it's a dress (just as long as I don't look round the back!) But step into its folds, and there's a piece of magic missing:

The swish.

When I dance round the room, my skirts don't dance with me. I froth them up with my hands, but let go and...

Flop.

Seems I can't work with it after all. Shattered, I step out of my non-gown. Draping it over my Singer, I go face the corner. Shivering, punishing myself, I peel on Sheila's cold black dress.

'So, now you're in our crew for the ball.' Stella stops me at the end of school. 'Begged Jonah to let you tag along?'

'Er, no.' I try to get past. Jayden blocks me.

'So you're *not* coming then?'

'I'm not begging.'

'That'll make a first.' Jayden and Olivia snigger. Then Stella gets up in my grill, like I'm an insect stuck to her lip gloss. She sneers and—

Wow, *Stella's* got spots? Little clusters of acne around her nostrils. Close-up I can see her cover-up's cracking.

'Excuse *me*,' I push back. 'I'm needed in the gym. Talent auditions.' My Nokia brick buzzes in my bag. Harriet getting antsy, I bet. 'Ball committee are judging.'

'Ha, as if you could be the judge of *anyone*,' says Olivia. Jayden smirks as their leader steps back to deliver the killer blow.

'Since when do *you* know Zack Melway?' says Stella.

That I am NOT expecting.

'He should come down McDonald's more often.' Olivia giggles to Jayden. 'When did Zack Melway get so fit?'

'I know!' Jayden sighs. 'Didn't his mum die or something?'

'Sad times,' pouts Olivia. 'But now he plays guitar. In a band!'

'With my brother,' says Stella. 'Oh, did Zack not tell you?' She widens her doll-blue eyes at me. '*Branded*, they're called – they've been practising round at ours all week. Except, times I'm there, Zack seems to be on a permanent Diet Coke break!' She laughs, as if there's some private joke they share. 'He never mentioned *you*.'

'What's to say? We're mates, that's all.' I barge through the lot of them. *Zack's hanging out with Stella? What else has he not told me?*

'Watch out!' Lisa yells, as I crash into her outside the gym.

'Sorry! I... what are *you* doing here?' I say. 'And what's that on your jumper?'

'My new label.' She pats a white sticker on her chest: BALL COMMITTEE. 'Bossy Harriet slapped it on. Quite hard actually.' She frowns. 'My right boob might *never* boing back.'

'Yay! You've signed up,' I cry. 'For me? Oh, Lees.' I hug her.

'*Boob!*' She shoves me back. 'But, yeah. These talent auditions could be a laugh. Plus I felt bad for bailing on you at McDonald's yesterday – not that I didn't send in reinforcements. Zack handled Stella all right?'

'About that...' I follow her into the gym, then stop short. 'Hang on, where *is* everyone?'

So much for a heaving mass of talent. The hall is empty apart from the judges' table. Which is empty apart from Zara Khan (who looks *a bit* like she wants to cry) plus a stack of clipboards that screams 'Harriet'.

'Where is she?' I ask. 'Our esteemed chairman, I mean.'

'Shouting at the talent. Harriet herded all the acts in there.' Lisa nods towards the changing rooms. 'To be fair, the warm-up *was* carnage. Think *High School Musical* meets *The Rocky Horror Picture Show*. Then chuck in the Winsham gym team.' She does a star-jump by way of explanation. 'Six big boys stretching out in their leotards.'

'*Leotards?*'

'Shorty shorts, whatever.' She drops into a lunge. 'Harriet could *just* about cope with them doing the splits. But when the boys started on their burpees, she turned purple, and marched ALL the auditionees off for a lecture on health and safety.'

A low-level ranting noise comes from the changing room.

'Zack's in there?' I ask.

'Trailing his guitar lead. But forget Zack.' She tugs me back. 'How did it go with Jonah yesterday? I've messaged you like a gazillion times! You gone off-grid?'

'Sort of. I—' I feel my palms go sweaty. 'I wanted to tell you myself, 's all. Then I got into school and remembered you were off on your—'

'Geography field trip.' She shudders. '*Why?* Why must we count pedestrians in Norbridge town centre? Leave the poor people be, or at least help them round Poundland—.' I cut her off with a MEANINGFUL LOOK.

'So… Jonah,' she says. 'What happened?'

'Nothing. 'S just,' I blush. 'He asked me to the ball.'

'But this is big,' Lisa staggers. 'BEYOND big. Of course, he *remains* in my eyes a pufferfish, but—'

'He wants me to wear that dress.'

'What dress?'

'You know, from the other night at the Savacentre.'

She stops. 'Not Auntie Sheila's Skimpy Sock-Frock?'

'Well, he didn't *call* it that…'

'Who *cares* what he called it? Boys are DUMB.' She crosses her arms. 'But you're dumber.'

'Me? What've *I* done?'

'Well, you've not punched him for starters. Why does Jonah get off telling you what to wear? What century are we in, woman?! Or were you *planning* to come in a farthingale hoop?'

'Ha, I could *do* things with a hoop.' I snap. 'All night I was up sewing my gown, but I've totally botched the back — and the skirts won't swish.'

'But your design—'

'Looks good on paper, sure. But fashion is 3D, Lees. I need to engineer the fit and flare, or my gown will flop. I'll lose the contest *and* Jonah.'

'But…'

'But nothing.' I wrap my arms around myself. 'Wear that little black dress, and at least I'll get Jonah.'

'And then what?' Lisa snorts. 'You gonna live all your days in a lycra mini-skirt? You'll *so* get thrush.'

'Ew!'

'Just saying.' A slam echoes around the gym. We jump round to see Bossy Harriet marching towards us. Red-faced ('An improvement on purple,' murmurs Lees), she bats us to the judging table. Zara looks relieved when we sit down with her.

'I'm more nervous than the acts,' she says. 'I hate judging people.'

137

'Really? I love it!' Harriet consults her clipboard. 'We've got seven acts lined up. Just one no-show.'

'Make that two.' I nod at an empty chair beside Lees. 'Are we missing a judge?'

On cue, the gym doors swing open. In stomps Gina, nose-ring glinting; eyeliner hard. 'Ah, perfect timing!' croaks Harriet. 'Mrs Cribbs warned me, I mean, told me you'd be joining us.' She rattles on nervously, as Gina takes the last seat. 'You're our "alternative" vote.'

'Great. See these?' Gina pulls out two sharp-looking pencils. 'When I stick them both in my eyeballs, it's a "no" from me.' Then Gina slumps down in her chair, making it clear she's *not* here for the love of youth talent and variety acts, but has racked up three detentions and WILL be dropped from the hockey team unless she does community service on the committee.

Ramming in her earbuds, Gina misses a big, goofy look from Lees.

I don't. '*This* is why you signed up to the ball committee?' I hiss at my mate. 'Nothing to do with me!'

'*Shh.* I need visual confirmation.' Lisa checks Gina's lost to Spotify. '*Does* she rate boys?'

'What about hockey practice?' I glower at Gina, scrolling through her playlist of Hard Jungle Beatz. 'It is a *mixed* team you two play on.'

'That's different,' says Lisa. 'Those boys are our team-mates – loud, spotty shapes we pass a ball to. This lot...' She nods at the changing room. '...they're talent. In skinny jeans.'

'Or shorty shorts?' I say drily.

'Exactly. If Gina swoons at the first boy to crack into the splits—

'Or break into song—'

138

'Then she's not the girl for me,' sighs Lees. 'Obviously Zack is a triple threat. He rocks up, slinging his guitar and—'

'Zack?' Harriet pricks up her ears. 'Zack Melway? He's just pulled out.'

'What?' Lees and I swivel in unison.

'*Branded*, that's his band?' Harriet puts a scratch through her list. 'They cleared off before I could finish the fire drill.'

I turn to Lees in panic. 'Go,' she says. 'Find the moody-eyed muppet. I'll stall Harriet.'

Heart racing, I bomb towards the changing room. Pausing at the door, I see Lisa doubling up: 'Cramp,' she moans. 'I've got a cramp!'

'Where?' demands Harriet. 'Stomach?'

'Legs!' Lisa sticks both out in front of her, and starts scissoring. 'I'm in SPASM.' As Harriet tries to catch at her shins, Gina pulls out her earbuds.

'If you'd kicked off like this in yesterday's match, Lees,' she says, 'we might've got that extra goal.'

I push open the changing-room door, and get hit with a fug of BO, hairspray and Haribos. The auditionees are practising in nervous huddles. When a juggling ball flies over my head, I grab the small Winsham boy who threw it.

'Hey,' I say. 'D'you know Zack Melway? Year 10. Electric guitar, green eyes?'

'Suede jacket? Yeah.' He nods at the door to the fire exit. 'They went that way.'

Rattling open the door, I take the fire-stairs three at a time, and erupt into the yard LIKE AN ACTION HERO. '*Oof.*' I trip over a guitar amp. 'What the—?'

I follow the lead to a stack of band kit by the bike sheds. Two Year 11 Winsham lads are huddled over it. One's vaping, the other's chewing on a Mars bar. A third boy sits slouched on an amp.

'*Zack.*' I go to him. 'What are you doing down here?'

'Relax,' says his vaping friend. 'No one can see us.'

'*I* can see you.' Through the smoke, he's all smirk and dirty blond hair. 'I will have Camel Cribbs on you in a NANO-SECOND if you don't haul your sad cookies back upstairs.'

His mate, a chubby Asian guy, chokes on his chocolate. 'Who the f— is Camel Cribbs?'

'A strict disciplinarian! In camel form,' I say. 'You do not want to give her the hump.'

'Hey.' Dirty Blond flares his nostrils, shooting fumes at me. "'S not me or Sam who called this.'

The smoke clears. 'You're Nick Harcourt,' I say. 'Stella's brother?'

'For my sins.' He sucks on his vape, then offers it to Zack, who shakes his head. Not looking at me, Zack stands and swings up his guitar.

'Come on,' he grabs his amp. 'Let's split.'

'No!' I run ahead of him, blocking his way. 'Zack, what happened?'

'I lost it! OK?' He halts in my arms. 'I *lost it*. Mum's chain – her St Christopher medal.'

'Oh, Zack…'

'She wore it to keep us safe. I couldn't keep it through one lousy audition.'

'But… I thought *Andy* wore it.'

'He knew I had auditions today,' Zack shrugs. 'He wound it round my frets. For luck, I s'pose.' He winces like it hurts to think about it. 'I only found it when we started setting up in the gym. Then some crazy girl with a clipboard hustles us into the changing room, and next thing I know, it's gone. I tried to call you, Kat. I looked everywhere, but it's gone.' His voice cracks. 'She's gone.'

"S OK, Zack.' I press my hands against his chest. Feel his heartbeat, wild, against the suede of his jacket. 'Me and Lees will find your mum's chain. After the auditions, we'll *crawl* over every inch of floor. We'll find your St Christopher, I promise. Just don't treat it like a bad omen, yeah?'

'But—'

'But nothing. Your mum would never want to be some sad thing that hangs round your neck. She's in here.' I press my hand against his pounding heart. 'And here...' I move my hand to his face. 'In these ridiculous cheekbones! Though *this*, she would not like.' I rub his soft-rough head. 'She'd have told Andy to PUT THE CLIIPPERS *DOWN*.'

Finally, he laughs. 'Yeah. My bro went in hard. Wanted me to look sharp.'

'You do.'

'You think?' His eyes flash like broken glass.

'Zack.' I feel my breath catch. 'You're a force to be reckoned with. *Not* that you look it.' Briskly, so as to have something to do, I straighten the front of his jacket. 'Pull yourself together.' I slot the vintage brass zip into its slider. 'You can *do* this.'

'Says who? This is mad, Kat. I'm nothing, I'm—'

'Zip it.' I take the runner up to his chin; make the suede *snap*. 'You're not playing the O2 Arena, Zack. It's a smelly school gym. You're up against Year 9 jugglers, facing a judging panel that is frankly mental.'

He juts his jaw out over his collar. 'How mental?'

'Well, there's Gina of the Blessed Nose-Ring...' I tick off on my fingers. '...Harriet West aka "Crazy Girl with Clipboard." Plus Zara Khan, who's so kind she'll give full marks to *everyone*. Then there's me.' I take a bow. 'Your Vote in the Bag. Plus Lees, who's just taken up Morris dancing.' He frowns. 'You know...' I raise my knees, and start kicking.

'…but imagine I'm on a chair.'

'*Zack!*' Nick Harcourt shouts from the shed. 'You dumping us for a girl?'

'Not cool, Nick.' Zack shouts back. 'Ignore him,' he tells me. 'He's got abandonment issues.'

'Yeah right, like his sister,' I cross my arms. 'Now she's passing you Diet Cokes during band practice?'

'Yeah.' He ducks his head. 'I was gonna tell you about that.'

'When?' I beady-eye him.

'When you wouldn't explode 'cause I've got some girl's number.'

'YOU'VE GOT HER NUMBER?'

'Cool it, can you?' He glances back to Nick Harcourt.

'Does *he* know you got his sister's number?'

'I didn't *get* anything, all right? Stella put her number in my phone.' He tucks his chin back into his collar. 'In case I needed help today.'

His shoulders droop. They don't look so broad suddenly. 'Forget it.' I sigh. 'I can kill you later. Today's about the gig — and you…' I look him dead in the eye. '…sooo needing help.'

A laugh escapes him. We're that close, his breath tickles my neck, soft as a kiss.

Maybe that's why I do it.

I hook my hands into his pockets. Rising up onto my toes, I press my mouth against his. Softly at first, then surer as he starts to kiss me back.

'*Zack,*' shouts Nick. 'We splitting?'

'No!' I yelp, rocking back on my heels. Zack catches me. 'Get back up there,' I plead. 'For me?'

He laughs, his eyes lighter than I've ever seen them. Not exactly a "yes", but…

'Grab your gears, guys,' I shout over his shoulder. 'Boy's back in!'

Credit to Nick and Sam, they don't need persuading. Gathering their kit, they lead a mad stumble up the fire stairs. Heaving amps and trailing cables, we burst into the changing room to find everyone filing out to the gym. 'Quick. Get set up,' I tell the guys, 'it's showtime!'

I run across the gym to re-join the judges. Lisa's sat with both legs splayed out on the table. 'How's the cramp?' I ask.

'I may never dance again,' she puffs. 'You find him?' I nod. A bit too quickly. She frowns, bringing her legs down.

'Here…' Harriet butts between us. '…your personalised scoresheets.' She hands out printed slips. 'Let the judging begin!'

The first act steps up. The others wait their turn on the benches by the changing room. Any second I'll see Zack again. Feeling the warmth of his kiss, I BURY MY BLUSHES in my scoresheet.

KAT PARKER'S SCORESHEET FOR TALENT AUDITIONS:

ACT 1: Dean Bovery, Year 7, Juggler

Kat's judging notes: Boy throws balls, catches them.

Score: 6/10

ACT 2: All-male a cappella group THE CHORD-U-ROYS

Kat's notes: Full marks for matching outfits (purple corduroy flares, what's not to like?!) But uh-oh... they've started singing. Singing in hiiiiiigh falsetto. Now one of them's produced a set of maracas.

Score: 4/10 I'd give them a '5' but I can't un-see those maracas.

ACT 3: Acrobat Allstars (St Edwards + Winsham Gymnastic Teams)

Kat's notes: 12 kids bounce round the gym doing back flips . . . 'shorty shorts' doesn't cover it. Seriously, DOES NOT COVER IT. Things start falling out. When a large boy goes full gallop at the horse, Harriet intervenes 'on health and safety grounds', and Lisa has to pop a Nurofen.

Score: 7/10

A lull follows while Harriet tots up our scores so far. 'Where's Zack?' mutters Lisa, scanning the remaining acts. 'I don't see him or – what's his band called again?'

'Branded.' I check the changing-room door. 'They'll be out any second.'

'They'd better be.' Lees checks the clock. 'Or they'll blow it.'

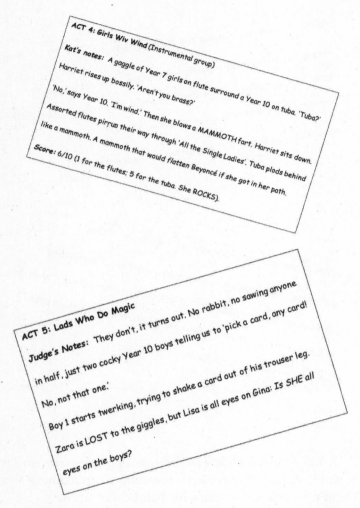

ACT 4: Girls Wiv Wind (Instrumental group)

Kat's notes: A gaggle of Year 7 girls on flute surround a Year 10 on tuba. 'Tuba?'
Harriet rises up bossily. 'Aren't you brass?'
'No,' says Year 10. 'I'm wind.' Then she blows a MAMMOTH fart. Harriet sits down.
Assorted flutes pirrun their way through 'All the Single Ladies'. Tuba plods behind
like a mammoth. A mammoth that would flatten Beyoncé if she got in her path.
Score: 6/10 (1 for the flutes; 5 for the tuba. She ROCKS).

ACT 5: Lads Who Do Magic

Judge's Notes: They don't, it turns out. No rabbit, no sawing anyone
in half, just two cocky Year 10 boys telling us to 'pick a card, any card!
No, not that one.'
Boy 1 starts twerking, trying to shake a card out of his trouser leg.
Zara is LOST to the giggles, but Lisa is all eyes on Gina: Is SHE all
eyes on the boys?

'What?' Gina clocks Lees looking at her. 'If *this* is how Winter Wonderland pans out, I say we bail NOW.'

'No!' I jab Lees. '*Ask* her.'

'Ask me what?' says Gina.

146

'Nothing.' Lisa glares at me. Gina glares at Lees. 'Wanna be my date?' blurts Lisa. 'For a laugh.' Silence. 'Stupid idea,' gabbles Lees. 'Forget it.'

'Forget it?' Gina practically shouts. 'I love it.'

'You do?'

'Screw this retro dating fascism. We girls don't need no schmucks in a tux.' Gina twiddles her nose-ring at the Winsham magicians. 'If a rabbit doesn't hop out of those trousers, I'm in.'

No rabbits hop out.

Gina's my date for the ball. Glory be! Lisa's eyebrows express to me.

'Now for our final audition,' announces Harriet. There's a stir of excitement by the changing room door. Kids are rising up from their benches. This next talent is *hot!*

But it's not Zack.

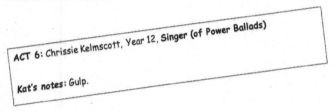

ACT 6: Chrissie Kelmscott, Year 12, Singer (of Power Ballads)

Kat's notes: Gulp.

'Someone take the mic off her,' hisses Lees, as Chrissie steps up to sing. 'The set of lungs she got on her; she's St Edward's answer to Adele.'

'*Helloooo.*' Chrissie booms. '*It's me. Can you hear me?*'

YES, WE CAN HEAR YOU. Even Gina's sitting up. Craning to read my fellow judges' scores, I clock 9 after 9 after 9, then...

'Zero? No way.' I snatch Lisa's pen. 'Zack doesn't need us to cheat for him.'

'You reckon?' She glances across at the changing room.

'Zack can't seem to open *the door* for himself.'

Chrissie nails another number. Reluctantly, Lisa takes back her pen, and amends '0' to...

'0.5. But I hate myself.'

Totting the scores, Bossy Harriet inform us judges that Chrissie Kelmscott is 'the clear winner!'

'Oh, yeah?' Gina queries. 'You might want to tell *that* lot.' From the changing room, troop three Winsham boys, lugging amps.

'Looks like the band got back together,' grins Lees.

ACT 7: Year 10 / Year 11 Winsham, rock band Branded

Kat's notes: WHAT TOOK YOU SO LONG?!

'Sam Chung, Nick Harcourt and...' Rattling her clipboard, Harriet strains to read through the line she's struck through them. 'Zack Mel—'

'—waaaay-oh-way-oh-way-oh-way,' sways Lees like she's in a football stadium.

'Sit,' I pull her, 'd*own*. He might bolt again.'

'No way.' She laughs. 'Not now you've worked your juju magic on him.'

'Some magic,' says Gina. 'That one can't find a plug point.'

She's (annoyingly) right. While Sam tunes his bass, and Nick looks slick at his drum machine, Zack's fumbling at his guitar strap like he's never played before. When he fiddles with his amp – releasing a screech of feedback – Gina leaps up.

'Screw this.' She lurches off down the gym.

'Figures,' I mutter. Then she stops; at the band. Starts bending over amps and plugging in the guys like she was a roadie in another life.

'Don't ask me.' Lisa laughs at my stunned expression. 'That girl's past is A Closed Book. All I know is...' She watches Gina hook up Zack's guitar. '...Now I *really* want to kiss her.'

'Please.' I wince. 'Let's not talk about kissing.'

'Uh-oh.' She twists round. 'Wotcha done?'

'Nothing. Everything's fine.' Isn't it? I mean, Zack's ready to rock. He raises his hand to give the guys their cue – and drops his plectrum. Guitar swinging, he scrabbles for it. When he rises back up, I catch his gaze. And I don't let go. Not until he's got a grip of his axe. The electricity surges through him, and he rips into a riff. Then another, each lick leaner and means than the one before.

As the storm builds, the gym goes quiet. It's not just me feeling it, is it?

How Zack makes the air come alive.

Sinews straining against suede, he strikes a killer chord, and blows the world away.

Sure, his bandmates follow – Sam steady on bass, Nick not bad on vocals for a vaper – but it's Zack driving them. He shreds his guitar like he's entering another dimension, and we are gone. Whoever Zack's playing for, it's not us.

He crashes into a last chord, riding the reverb like a wave. Then he looks up dazed, as if returning from somewhere far away. Finding me, his eyes go from dark to light green, like a mountain lake getting touched by the sun. 'Was I all right?' they ask.

'YOU ROCK!' Lees yells over my head. As the gym erupts, Harriet chucks down her clipboard. Screwing up our score sheets, she thrusts a load of health and safety forms at Nick Harcourt. ('You can't play at the ball without them,' she says, her face beaming. 'No, you can't smoke backstage! Are your guitar straps reinforced?').

Through the chaos I hear Chrissie Kelmscott asking Sam Chung if they need another singer. Gina's bearing down on Zack. ('Tell me you've got your gig merch sorted: baseball caps, t-shirts. What d'you mean, *you've got no logo*? You're called *Branded!*')

It takes me a second to see the shadows massing outside – Tag-Hags, fogging up the glass. They're huddled out in the yard; must've seen the whole gig. Now Keisha's elbowing out Carly, who's jostling Natalie, who's tossing her hair like she wants to catch a boy in it. The only one *not* trying to get spotted is Stella. Not a glance for her brother, she stares past Lisa

who's jumping up and down, hugging Zack,

who's laughing, and reaching over

to bring me in. As I disappear into a mad group hug,

I get the weirdest feeling:

Stella's pressed against the glass

looking at *me*.

Next day, things get weirder. Starting with double gym. Yep, I hear you: thirty girls doing teddy bear rolls, when *isn't* that weird? But today, numbers are down: the hockey girls have been drafted for a final practice before Friday's regional, so it falls to Olivia and Carly to lead the locker room in a HILARIOUS game of Toss Kat's Stinky Shoes. Hooking plugs of soggy Sellotape out from each toe, they're about to stick it to me proper when who should come to save me?

Spoiler alert: *not* Lisa.

'Grow up, can you?' Stella clatters in from hockey training, mud flying from her boots. 'Give Kat her shoes back.' Carly just stands there, dangling a streamer of wet tape. Olivia blinks, like she can't compute. '*Now.*'

Jerkily, like she's malfunctioning, Olivia jabs the sticky plug back into my shoe. Carly copies, looking so blank, I can't help it…

I get the giggles.

Turning away, I catch Stella's eye. She gives me a perfectly mascara'd wink.

A wink? From Stella Harcourt?

Still not weird enough for you? Grab your lunch trays,

people, and prepare for Things to...

Get...

Freaky.

The scene starts normally (but then doesn't it in *every* horror film?). A storm's blowing outside, so the canteen's packed. Lisa's off with Gina talking balls (hockey/Winter Wonderland/cheese corn) so I hunch over my sorry excuse for a phone. This Nokia brick ain't getting any smaller, but it *is* receiving texts, mostly from Zack. We've not spoken since his audition triumph. Group-hug over, things between us felt... weird. (I really need to get me some new words.)

I click back through his messages from this morning.

Yesterday was crazy. Like something from a film! (Felt real though.)

Does he mean his 'Guitar Hero' moment? Or when I... Blushing, I hit *DELETE.*

I'm still rushing. Call me.

And say what? 'Sorry, Zack, wasn't thinking!' (And now I can't STOP thinking...)

DELETE.

Kat, you ghosting me?!

DELETE.

Seriously, you ghosting me?

'Kat!' I look up to see Zara. 'Weren't Branded great yesterday?' she says. 'The way your friend played.' She pretends to shiver. 'It was goosebumpy!'

'Kinda.'

She smiles shyly, and hands me a carrier bag.

'What's this?' I ask, feeling warmth come through it.

'From my mum,' she says. 'I was telling her how we made your shadow dress together. You laughed at my pics of little Fazli and Hasan...'

'...Your nutty nephews,' I remember. 'Having a samosa party.' My belly rumbles. 'Sorry!'

'So tuck in.' Zara laughs, tugging open the bag to reveal a Tupperware tub topped by tiny, tinfoil parcels. 'My mum's chicken korma is LEGEND.'

'But I can't...'

'You must, or Mum will make *me* eat it. Top secret now,' she drops her voice, 'I'm a jalfrezi girl.'

'Okaaay.' I'm laughing, taking a sweet sniff of curry – in danger of getting close to a hot meal – when an alarm sounds across the universe.

'Kaaaaat!' The shriek rips through the canteen. 'We can seeeeeee you!'

Stella's stood on a bench by the Cool Table. 'You DEAF OR SOMETHING?!' she waves. 'Get over here!' Half the canteen's watching, as I set off (anything to shut her up). I don't realise I've got Zara at my back till we reach the Cool Table.

'You OK?' she murmurs.

'Er, probably not,' I mutter, as Stella jumps down from the bench.

'Don't you *want* to sit with us?' she cackles. I look at her like she's mad. Which just makes her cackle more. 'Bad enough you bolted from McDonald's the other day!'

'I didn't *bolt*.'

'And now you've been dumped by Lisa.'

'Have not!'

'So, sit with us,' she shrugs. 'Or d'you wanna be sad *all* your life?'

So I show her. I sit myself (and my curry bag) down at the cool bench (and pray nothing leaks). Zara, rigid-backed, sits down with me. When the Tag-Hags won't budge up, she shakes out her headscarf. Cue Keisha chewing cloth while Stella dispenses with Nat. ('Oi, Nat, *shift*.').

Too late, my rational brain kicks in…
    a) How did I get here?
    b) What does Stella want with me, and
    c) will it hurt?

The Tag-Hags look on tenterhooks too. ('What is happening here?') A crack of plastic makes us all jump: Stella opening her prawn salad box. The Tag-Hags relax. ("Salad time. *This* we know."). *Pop, pop, pop*, their boxes open. Carly pokes at her rice. Keisha prods a cherry tomato. Only Natalie actually forks something into her mouth. 'Hungry much?' smirks Stella. 'You're, like, bulimic but keep forgetting to puke.'

Gusts of laughter turn the air green. Frills of salad fly skyward. Rocket shoots into the air. Natalie stares down at her lunch, so hard her eyes start to water.

I know that look.

Removing a serviette that Zara's mum has tucked in with my curry, I slide it across to Nat. Slowly, so as not to draw more fire, she brings the napkin up to her face.

'Bin time!' Stella crushes her £5.99 Pret box. 'No way I can eat this lot AND stay a size 6 for the ball.' Seeing the succulent king prawns trashed, I let out a noise. 'My bad,' says Stella with a laugh. 'You want?'

'Your leftovers?'

She shrugs. "'S just, you weren't eating at McDonald's, and—

'I'm sorted, thanks.' I smile gratefully at Zara. Placing my silver foil parcels on to the table, I pull out the Tupperware tub. Peel back the lid to reveal chunks of creamy chicken dotted with plump raisins and roasted cashews. 'What *is* that?' cry the Tag-Hags, recoiling.

'Gross!'

'Ew…'

'*Mmm*…' The sweet, spicy scents of korma sauce waft down the bench. We share a warm intake of breath. Then Stella flicks her hair, and…

'That sauce is rank,' says Carly.

'Looks like vomit,' says Keisha.

'It *looks* home-made,' sneers Natalie, throwing down her paper towel (she's back in the game!) Inspired, Keisha starts tossing tinfoil parcels. As they bounce down the table, they explode, showering Carly and Natalie with bits of onion bhaji.

'You *bitch*,' shrieks Carly. 'It is ON!' Laughing, she scrapes up a handful of smashed crumbs, and hurls them at Keisha.

Now Nat's piling in. Ripping open Mrs Khan's neat package of samosas, she throws them at Carly. '*FOOD FIGHT!*'

'Please, no!' cries Zara.

'Give it back.' I snatch a samosa off Nat. She shoves me back on to the tub of curry, sending it skidding across the table —

Into Keisha's lap.

They stop laughing. Slowly, Keisha stands up. She's got chunks of chicken and apricot splattered across her chest and a thick, oily pool of sauce sliding down her kilt. When she looks at me, her face is one hundred per cent hate. And her hands are round the curry tub.

Aargh! The hard, plastic edge whacks into the bridge of my nose. Chicken korma explodes everywhere. Through burning tears, I see Keisha and Jayden high-five. Shame sears through my bladder, like I could wet myself *in front of everyone*—

'I'll go get towels,' says Zara. Head down, she battles past girls pressing in for a better look. A crack opens in the crowd, and I see Mrs Cribbs bearing down on us.

'KAT PARKER,' she roars. 'DETENTION NOW.' But legs are shaking. My chest has turned to sludge. As I mop at my jumper, fat slugs of sauce ooze out through my fingers. 'NEVER in all my years of teaching have I seen such a HORRIFIC DISPLAY! Who else participated?' Cribbs glowers down the table. The Tag-Hags stand to innocent attention, Keisha holding her blazer over her splattered skirt.

I stick my chin up.

'Fine,' says Cribbs. 'Kat Parker, you force me to put EVERY SINGLE GIRL FROM 10W INTO DETENTION.' The crowd surges behind me. I feel thirty daggers go into my back. 'Or will your fellow perpetrator step forward?'

Nothing.

A clink of cutlery.

I'm on my own,

drowning in the *drip, drip* of chicken korma

when a girl steps up.

St Edward's has its own rules. No one knows *why* lunchtime detention happens in the science block, but believe Lisa (who attends detention like the rest of us go to the toilet), 'It pays to sit by the door, because the lab windows are hermetically sealed. And the supervisors can get a bit loose with the gas taps.'

Camel Cribbs dumps me in Lab 1, then ducks into the tech room to warn the teacher on detention duty, 'There's another one coming, once she's cleaned up the canteen.'

I'm left to rinse my mess in the chemicals sink.

Daubing off chunks of chicken and clots of congealed sauce, I reduce my jumper to a sopping rag. Then I slide down behind the nearest bench. Gas taps OFF (*check*), I sneak a glance at my fellow detainees. Ranged down my row is a bunch of Year 12 vape-heads. Behind us sit a bored-looking Year 11 and two terrified Year 7s, fresh out of a marker-pen fight, I'm guessing – their hands are covered in red scribbles, and the smaller girl is rubbing at her forehead, trying to remove a huge "POO".

I give her a wobbly smile, and watch her recoil. I stink, don't I? *Ugh*, I pull off my jumper. Peel off my claggy wet shirt beneath. Who cares I'm down to my vest? Half the school's seen me splattered in chicken korma. I could stride down the halls in a Dolce & Gabbana suit tomorrow, and the girls would *still* see me wearing a curry.

'Hey, cool top.' Miss Bloxam appears from the tech room. 'One of your upcycles?' She nods at my sequinned poppy, stitched into snowflakes of frosted lace, then clocks my ruined jumper. 'Jeez, Kat, *you're* the food fight?' She approaches me with a stack of detention assignments. 'That kinda stunt isn't you.'

'No,' a voice comes from the door, 'it's more me.' Stella waits until All Eyes Are On Her, then she swishes in like this *isn't* lunchtime detention she's navigating, but the VIP area of a nightclub. Waving me down the bench, Stella settles on a stool, then holds out her hand to Miss Bloxam like she expects her to put a frappuccino in it.

Miss Bloxam slaps down a test paper instead. 'Yer not in the canteen now, Stella. Yer in a lab rammed with chemicals and one angry Australian. Pull any crap,' she glowers, 'and I put yer in the fume cupboard.'

I wait until Miss Bloxam moves off, then hiss at Stella. 'What are you *doing*?'

'Fractions, looks like,' she glances down at her test, 'or is it French?' She pulls a face. Then pulls a pack of gum from her bag. 'Spearmint?'

'No!' I splutter. 'I don't want your *gum*. I want to know what you're playing at: why take the rap from Cribbs back there?'

'*Ha*, did you see her eyes bug out when I stood up? Cribbs thinks I'm trouble?' She cracks her gum. 'I'll give her trouble. Besides . . .' She shrugs. 'I got it. That Tupperware party you were throwing?' She trails her manicured nails through her hair. 'I've been there.'

I'm lost.

158

'The packed lunch club, yeah? I was stuck there most of Year 7. My mum's fault,' she grimaces. 'She'd make these fancy dinners for Dad when we all knew he'd not be coming home. Working late,' she explains hastily. 'Mum would have to pack the lot into Tupperware tubs for me and Nick to take into school the next day. *Sad.*' Sad is how her eyes go for a second. 'Whatevvs...' She pops a fresh gum. '...things change, don't they? Like you.'

'*Me?*'

'Putting yourself up for the catwalk? Jonah asking you to the ball?' I blush.

"S all right...' She puts up her hands. '...he's all yours.' Flipping out her phone, she starts scrolling.

'What are you doing?'

'Giving him to you. There!' She hits a key. 'I've just sent him your number.'

'My—? No! How've *you* got my number?'

She cackles. 'I've got *everyone's* number.' As she slides her phone back up her sleeve, I put my head in my hands.

'I can't believe you did that.'

'Relax, he likes you.'

I pull up my head. 'So *that's* what this is? 'The whole "canteen buddies" act ...Jonah Kerrigan says I'm cool, so I *must* be?'

'Cool? Hardly!' She eyes my vest. 'You ...*sewed* this – this poppy thing?' She jabs my motif. 'What's the white stuff?'

'Old lace.' I look down. 'From my gran.'

'OMG.' Her eyes widen. 'You really *are* broke.'

'You can't say that!'

'Why not? 'S true, isn't it?' She flicks back her hair, and sharpens her shirt collars. 'If anyone's a fake round here, it's you.'

'Me?'

'Acting so superior. That little black dress you wore outside the Savacentre?' She toys with her neck chain, hooking her nails into the Pandora pendant heart. 'I saw how you knotted the back to make it tighter.'

'But I—'

'Save it, Queen Kooky. With your thrift clothes and choppy bob…' She tugs at my home-cut hair. 'Like you're a sustainable style influencer in, I dunno, Paris. Ugh…' She shudders. '…put a beret on it! Ever since Year 7, you and Lisa have been in this sad huddle, giggling at some secret the rest of us can't get. When you *do* come out with us, to Norbridge Bowls, you turn up in scuffed DM boots that should NOT GO with a skater skirt, but sort of do…' She frowns. 'Like the rest of us are stupid for buying into it.'

'Buying into *what*?'

'We know you call us the "Tag-Hags". But what's *wrong* with shopping at boohoo?' Stella raises her voice over sniggers from down the bench. 'What's wrong with wanting to look hot? So I'm popular!'

'Stella!' barks Miss Bloxam.

'Not so popular with *that* lot, am I?'

She means our teachers, I guess. But the Year 10 vape-heads are whispering, chanting. '*Tag-hag… Tag-hag…*'

Stella fingers lock in her chain.

'*Barbie doll*,' coughs one.

'*Slag*,' splutters another.

Stella sticks up her nose, flicks back her hair and— disappears behind it.

'*Daddy, can I have a tit-job?*'

'Hey, back off.' I jump up without thinking.

'Oooh, scared,' hiss the vape-heads. Loud enough to launch Miss Bloxam. Under cover of Ozzy fire, I sit down to find Stella playing with her flash, silver heart. But now I don't see bad-ass and bling.

I see Zack clinging to his St Christopher. 'You working your sparkly charm?' I say.

She frowns; looks down. 'Oh, this? Don't realise I'm doing it!' She gives a half-laugh. 'Drives my mum nuts. Probably 'cause my dad gave it me.'

'Oh.'

'Him and Mum are *schlittt*,' she scrapes her pendant across her throat. 'Now he's in Birmingham – some BIG business deal. Makes it hard for him to get back.' Her heart drops.

'Mine's stuck in the attic,' I say. 'My dad, I mean.'

'Right.' She stares at me. 'What happened? He went too soon with the Santa suit. Now he's wedged in your chimney?' She hoots suddenly. And I hear an answering hoot from me.

Now the vape-heads are scowling at both of us. 'They're just jealous,' says Stella with a sigh, pulling out a lip balm. She applies the shine from our gas taps. 'Because I don't look like I sleep in my clothes. Girls are bitches.'

I eyeball her. 'You think?'

'I *know*.' My eyeballs are lost on her. She's too busy applying lip balm in the shine from the gas taps. 'Boys, on the other hand…' She pouts. '…They're obvious. Some are all right though. Big Mike and what's his mate called?'

'Little Mickey.'

'They make me laugh.' She smiles… a bit wistfully seems to me. Maybe that's why I blurt out:

'You got a date for the ball?'

She cocks an eyebrow. 'Let's say I'm working on it. How 'bout you? Finished your gown yet?'

'I'm working on it.'

161

'I bet you are.' She picks up the maths paper. 'A girl's gotta work her angles, right? In my case, that's...' She drops the maths paper, '...hot bod plus flash gear.'

'Plus attitude?'

'Sure beats fractions.' A cackle bursts out of her. And like it's catching, I hear one burst from me.

'STELLA HARCOURT!' Miss Bloxam yells. '*Shift.*' Rolling her eyes, Stella rises up and does her best runway walk to the back of Lab 1. I'm not sorry to see the back of her. Laughter subsiding, I calculate she's cranked up my troubles by ten. I'm dashing off the World's Fastest Maths Paper when my phone beeps in my bag. With one eye on Miss Bloxam, I fish out my Nokia brick – to see a text from a new number.

You free after school tomorrow? Fancy coffee? X

My heart starts to race. It can't be... *it must be...* Jonah?

Sure.

I hit send.

A beep sounds from the back of the room. I spin round to see Stella, eyes down, thumbs flying.

It's a date, bad girl.

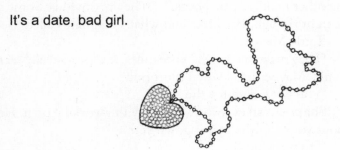

'Are you nuts?' cries Lees. 'INSANE IN THE MEMBRANE?' She opens her locker, releasing an avalanche of sweaty skorts. 'You cannot hang out with Stella. *Pew...*' She picks through her sports bras. '...Help me find one that's *not* honking, can you?'

Its sensitivity levels like this stopped me seeking out Lees after detention yesterday. When she didn't answer my texts, I ran home to my "concerned and interested" parents. Who, it turned out, couldn't peel themselves off the heater.

Yep, remember the grubby box heater my dad bought to save the day, and waft warmth up the "family trouser leg"? Turns out a toaster would produce more heat. 'Yet *still* it sends our electricity bills into orbit?' marvels Mum (in a tone that shows she is NOT finding it marvellous).

Getting home yesterday, I find her setting the timer for our "daily hour of heat". ONE HOUR we huddle together as a family. Then the timer rings, the heater goes off, and we splinter apart like icicles.

'Ouch,' yelps Lil.

'Gimme!' cries Daisy. Playing tug of war with their blankie, they trot from our draughty kitchen back into the loving glow of the TV. Mum warms her hands on the kettle as it boils.

'What's up?' She clocks me hovering.

'Nothing.' I pass her the mugs.

'And?'

''S just…' I pass her a teaspoon. 'Stella Harcourt.'

'That blonde madam?' She frowns. 'What's she done now?'

'She's, um… she's asked me out for coffee.'

'Coffee?' Mum says with a gasp. 'You're kidding.'

'*I know.*' She gets it. 'Stella's Miss Popular, and I'm like—'

'A frothy one? Sprinkled with chocolate?' Mum shuts her eyes. 'Oh, I dream of such a thing.'

'Christ, Kell.' Dad gives a hollow laugh across the table, making Mum and me jump. (He does this now – disappears until a burst of sadness reveals his location.) 'Five days to find the cash for this boiler,' he says, 'and *you're* thinking about Starbucks.'

'Right.' Mum's eyes snap open. 'It's my OUT-OF-CONTROL COFFEE HABIT screwing us, not the fact that you've failed to earn a penny since—'

I'm outta there. Escaping upstairs to my gown, I slide down behind my sewing machine. Running my hands over the sea of blue silk, I feel a wave of calm flow through me. Then reality crashes in:

Five days, my dad said. Five days or my folks will, like, shatter.

It's make or break time. In forty-eight hours I'll be striding down the Winter Wonderland catwalk, heading towards a "dazzling" £500 prize – or a nasty fall (no safety nets in my corner). It's down to me. So I snatch up my dress and worry the zip. Worry the Stella situ. All night, feels like, I'm snagging it, unpicking it… Getting nowhere fast.

*

Now here I am, back at school. Another day closer to the catwalk, yet no further on. 'Help me, Lees.' I spin her around from the lockers. *What should I do?*

'About this coffee date with Stella? Easy.' Lees rams in her gumshield. 'Runabruddymile.'

'But she's got "new ball info".' I get out my phone, and scroll through Stella's texts from last night:

> We can cruise Crown Mall.
> Meet u 4pm under the clock!

But Lees sees only the texts I've left *unread*. 'WasswivZack?' She jabs at a stack of unopened envelopes.

''S nothing,' I say. Just letter bombs ready to explode. 'Stella says: lattes are on me.'

'Great,' puffs Lees. 'So now she's spiking your coffee.' I roll my eyes.

'With what?'

'Stella's usual poison.' She shrugs. 'Nail varnish. Fake tan. Or—' She spits out her gumshield. 'What's that thing Russians put in their drinks?

'Er, vodka?'

'Novichok!'

'Stella's not a *spy*, Lees.'

'You sure? Because seems to me it's *her* wanting the information.'

'About what?'

'Your dress, doofus! This top secret gown you're sewing! Think about it.' Lisa screws her curls into a top-knot. 'You're not an ant under Stella's shoe any more, you're *the competition*. The girl who could trip her up on the catwalk.'

'So why stick up for me yesterday then? In the canteen.' Lees looks at me blankly. 'I texted you! The Tag-Hags attacked me. With curry. You're saying it *didn't* hit the locker room?'

'No. Yeah…' She frowns. 'But—'

'What?'

'I didn't believe it. I mean, you with a *curry*?' She turns red. 'Sorry, that came out—'

''S fine.' I bury my face in her kit. 'I don't "go" with nice stuff.'

'Hey—'

'You weren't there.' I fold her vests. 'Stella was. We did detention together.'

'Cool.' Lisa snatches back her vests, SHOVING them in her locker. 'You jailbirds bonded.'

I can't believe this! She's jealous? 'I go off with Stella one time. *Weeks* you've been trailing round after Gina. You don't read my texts—'

'What,' she grabs her stick. 'Like you're *not* reading Zack's?'

'That's different—' But she's heading out to the hockey pitch already. Through the open doors, Gina's beckoning to her.

'Wait!' I cry.

'What for?' She turns. 'Zack can't stay locked in his room forever, Kat. Cool as Marie Melway was…' Lees tips her stick in salute. '…she's gone. But Zack's *happening*. You saw him smash that audition. When he rips into Winter Wonderland, the reaction he'll get from the crowd?' She takes off. 'It'll blow his world open.'

'*So?!*' I shout after her.

'You might not be the only girl he lets in.'

4.20pm, and I'm outside Crown Mall getting peed on; rain mostly, though a dog's just tried to give me the full lamppost treatment.

Grrr. Twenty minutes I've been stood waiting for Stella. Stood *up*, more like. My guts start up a familiar grind, and I hope it's just hunger. Christmas shoppers bash past me, sucking on milkshakes; the windows of the M&S Foodhall gleam with giant mince pies, so I swivel round to face Sweatzone, Norbridge's glass-fronted gym. A large man in a vest starts wobbling on a trabelator, and my queasiness goes into overdrive. Sure sign my period's coming.

'Please, oh Boob-Mighty Goddess of Womanhood,' I pray to Katy Perry, 'let me not bleed tomorrow! Saturday, I will happily sit in a bucket, but Friday night is BALL NIGHT.' If I can get to Winter Wonderland, the magic *will* happen. Through the twinkle of Christmas lights, I can almost see it: our school gym transformed into a glittering ballroom, Jonah Kerrigan rocking a tux. He's getting all the glances, but has eyes only for me. Tossing back his hair, he clocks my dress and...

Brrr. Cold beads trickle down my back. I had to leave my coat at school (no way can I hang out with Stella in that ripped, old thing). Now I'm splattered with rain and turning icy with panic: my gown still has no swish, *no zip*. Now Stella's left me freezing my fanny off when I should be sweating at my sewing machine…

Unless that's her idea?

'Quick, grab the kid!' The doors to Sweatzone slide open. A squad of burly men spills out, shouting. 'Wanna play with the big boys?'

'Hey,' a muffled cry comes from their midst. 'Give it back.'

'Come and get it, yer little dick.' A huge, bullet-shaped bloke holds up a Nike sports bag. A skinny, hoodied youth is trying to snatch it back. But he's got no chance: moving up the street towards me, the men start chucking the bag between them, jostling the kid. The big bloke takes a swing, and the kid whips round, scared eyes glittering inside his hood. *'Jonah?'* I catch him.

'Oi!' A clean-cut guy in a 'STAFF' shirt emerges from Sweatzone. 'What's going on?'

'Nothing,' says Bullet-Head. 'Just messin' with the new kid. He moved in on our weights, didn't he?' He makes another lurch, laughing as Jonah shies back. 'We just wanna see what he's got.'

'You OK?' the Sweatzone guy asks Jonah.

'It's cool.' He ducks into his hood. 'We're cool.'

'You're sure?'

'You heard him,' says Bullet-Head. 'Kid just had to learn, there's a code. Whatever crowd you run with...' He retrieves Jonah's Nike bag. '...there's *always* a code.' He throws the bag hard at Jonah. The whole squad jeer as Jonah doubles up, then they swagger off, swinging their kit bags over their shoulders like heroes who've seen action.

Some heroes. 'You OK?' I bend over Jonah, as the Sweatzone guy retreats to the gym.

'I'm *cool.*' Coughing, clutching his Nike bag, he rights himself. Then he swings his bag onto his shoulder just like the men had done. 'What are you *doing* here?' he says angrily.

'Nothing. I... just meeting Stella—'

'*Stella?* Where?' His eyes dart down the mall. 'The crew aren't along, are they?'

'No, just me.'

'Cool,' he repeats like a mantra, "cool." He tugs on the strings of his Tommy Hilfiger hood, and I notice his fingers for the first time. They're slender. Sensitive...

Shaking. 'I didn't know you worked out,' I murmur.

'Why? Want to take a swing at me too?'

'No! I'm just glad.'

'*Glad?*'

'That I was here, I mean—'

'To *save* me?' He rears.

'No—' Why am I the bad guy here? 'You rescued *me*, Jonah. My sisters – outside the Savacentre, remember? You're their hero!'

He's listening.

'Then at McDonald's…' I gabble. '…asking me to the ball. Stuff like that doesn't happen to me. Seriously. It Does Not.' He nods, like we're back on track.

Phew, I breathe again.

Now what? 'So… You do the gym thing?' I peer into his hood. 'Work out, I mean.'

'A few times a week,' he shrugs.

'You're kidding!' He tenses. 'No, I mean – you're fit…' I start gabbling again. '…obviously. Muscles everywhere! It's just I don't get to see them, NOT THAT I WANT TO SEE THEM.'

Nooo, now he's pulling back his hood and—

Laughing. At me? I don't care! Not if it means I get to see that cute, crooked smile of his. Half cocky, half shy; *fully* meant for me. And yay, those dreamy blue eyes. With his soft, fluffy fringe… er, where's his fringe gone? 'Oh.' I bite down on a cry. His hair's turned to a dark, sweaty slick, the price of trying to keep up with those… 'Stupid muscleheads!' I say, diverting the conversation away from embarrassing, and trying to stop myself thinking about the lack of fringe Jonah currently has.

'Stupid's right. They think they're jacked?' He hunches his shoulders. 'They wouldn't last ten minutes in the Meat Locker.'

I peel my eyes off his hair. 'The *what*?'

'Winsham weights room – our rugby squad call it the Meat Locker; you can't get them out of it.'

'Ah.' The penny drops. '*That's* why you come here?' He shrugs.

'Beats having a load of Year 12s rip into me.'

'Rip? But—' I open my mouth. Shut it again as I recall the torn belt loop on his Burberry. The protein powders I found in his pocket. The page torn from *Men's Fitness* magazine. 'Idiots,' I say. 'They *wish* they had your style.'

'Yeah, that's why they kick the crap out of me.'

'No—'

'Once's all.' He flicks back his crinkly knot of hair. 'No one saw.'

'Right, like *that's* what matters?'

He looks at me. 'It matters.'

I blush, feeling stupid. Like I don't know the rules, and now I'm blowing it—

'Hey.' He leans into me. 'We're still on for the ball, yeah?' His fingers lace into mine, his grip cold and surprisingly strong. 'We can hang out properly... and you can wear that hot dress!' He lets go. 'Oh, and this whole scene outside Sweatzone... Nothing happened, yeah? You didn't see me.' Pulling up his hood, he turns to join the stream of Christmas shoppers.

As he disappears, I can still feel the pressure of his hand.

'Kat!' Stella pounces. 'You're shivering.'

Brrr. I reel around to find her transformed. Whatever trick she's pulled in the toilets after school, Stella's now glowing. Her blonde hair shines, her cheeks shimmer with bronzer, and her eyelids flash gold. Her St Edward's uniform is hidden beneath a silver Puffa jacket with white fur hood. She's also switched into sharp bootie

heels – and picked up two takeaway
coffees. 'Seriously, Kat.' She passes me
one. 'What's with the "wet jumper" look? You not got a *coat*
now?'

'I left it at school.' Warily, I take the coffee. 'Not *everyone*
can pack a spare.' I frown at her Puffa. 'D'you keep it stuffed
in your locker all day?'

'What, like some try-hard?' She laughs. 'I make Natalie
keep it in hers.'

'Lucky Natalie.'

Stella shrugs. 'She thinks so.'

I take a cautious sip of my coffee. Mm, I'm not *tasting*
nail varnish… or Novichok. In fact, it's good. SO good.
Hugging my cup, I think of my mum: hunched over our
kettle, dreaming of *just one* frothy coffee—

'Watch out!' shrieks Stella, as foam comes bubbling up
through the hole in my cup lid.

'Wow, you do NOT care.' She watches me slurp up the
spill. 'How you look, I mean. If *I* had your attitude, I'd be,
like—'

'Getting burned for it?' The coffee scalds, and I'm back
there: wearing curry, channelling hot shame. 'Lisa's right,' I
wipe away the froth, 'what *am* I doing here?'

'Er, drinking my coffee?'

'Thanks, but no thanks.' I thrust the cup at her. 'So we
did detention together? You've been a bitch to me since
Year 8. 'S going to take more than a latte.'

'Fine.' She rolls her eyes. 'I'll say it.'

I freeze. Stella Harcourt will she actually say, "*Sorry*"?

'Shoes,' she pouts. 'You got a pair? For the ball. 'S just…'
She tosses her hair. '…seeing Keisha and Nat chuck yours
round the locker room yesterday—'

'I have *got* other shoes, you know.'

'Right.' She cocks an eyebrow. 'Like you've got another coat? Call me a bitch, but I like a fair fight.' She hands back my coffee. 'You wanna hit the catwalk in a pair of Lisa's gross Reeboks – or borrow my killer heels?'

I take the coffee. But I don't drink it. 'What's the catch?' I ask.

'No catch.' She fluffs up her fake fur hood. 'We'll go back to mine now. Don't worry,' she adds quickly, 'my mum's never home. It'll just be my brother Nick and his band—'

'The band!' I slap my forehead. 'Tonight's their last practice before the ball – I meant to text Zack.'

'Oh yeah, that's right… Zack Melway's a mate of yours.'

There's something about the way she says it. 'Stella.' I frown. 'A girl *can* be mates with a boy.'

'You reckon?' Her voice catches on a gust of cold wind. 'Come on, Cinders.' Her eyes glitter. 'Let's go get your shoes.'

Walking through Crown Mall with Stella, I feel like a star. Actually, strike that, I feel like the dorky *friend* of a star who gets cut from shot when the pics are sold.

I can't keep up with Stella's supermodel strut, but I do catch the looks glancing off her. Little kids stare at her shiny hair like they want to stroke it. Old ladies frown at her short skirt. Passing Gamezone, we're accosted by a bunch of Year 12 lads from St Joseph's. Though they clearly know Stella, she doesn't stop for them.

Nestling into her silver Puffa coat, though, she smiles.

'You go for older boys?' I ask.

'They go for *me*. Starting from when I got these.' She gestures at her shiny, silver chest, like it's a trophy she never wanted to win. 'I was ten when they appeared, like overnight. Year 6, I'd walk home from school, and clock these, like, *old* guys slowing down in their cars.' She halts us at the bus stop. 'They'd stare at me, and I'd start checking my shirt for spilt ketchup or ice cream.'

'Gross,' I say.

'I got good with it. Pity parties aren't my style,' she says with a shrug. 'But the Winter Wonderland Ball?' She hails the bus. '*That* I can work with.' Hailing the bus, she buys both our tickets, and swings up to the top deck. Shaking down her hood, she pulls out her phone and turns the back row into the Stella Harcourt Social Office.

'Carly's having a hair crisis,' she says as she skims her first text. 'Major frizz.'

She types back…

Superdrug do a gloss serum – really works. It's on the rack by "Hair Masks".

Beep, another incoming text:

Natalie needs a push-up bra for the ball.

R U mad?
Your dress is a halter-neck. You want stick-on fillets.
Try Ann Summers on Market Street.

Beep. From Carly:

Keisha's stormed off on me for, like, NO reason.

Stella replies:

She's hangry. Off carbs till she can fit into her dress.

She frowns into space for a second, considering options, then:

Feed her a bag of Haribos. Wash it down with fat Coke.

'*Man*. Running a squad,' I say, 'it's full-on.'

'Tell me about it,' she mutters, as another text pings in. Stella taps her screen, and I see her face turn blank. She puts away her phone. Shuts up into herself. As our bus grinds up Redmond Hill, Stella stares out of the window like she wants to lose herself to the dark.

Her phone beeps again.

And again.

'Someone really wants you,' I say.

'Let them.' She rises up, and hits the bell. 'Here's me.'

The bus drops us at the bottom of a long, sweeping avenue. I've never been up to the Redmond Hill estate before. The houses still look brand new. Proper mansions they are... or temples (to the God of Cash!). Grand pillars flank every front door; tall columns prop up each garage. Front lawn statues rear up at us from the gloom. Striding ahead, Stella triggers automatic lights like torch-bearers guiding our way. 'We're going back to ancient Rome!' I laugh. 'Next we'll get jumped by a muscly gladiator in a short skirt and leather thongs.'

But Stella's not laughing. She's rummaging in her bag – '*Crap*, forgotten my keys.' – and swinging off the main drag into a small cul-de-sac. No fancy streetlamps here, just darkness and rain.

'Here's me,' she crunches up a gravel path towards a house cloned like the others except... it's skinnier. Skimped. The lights are off, and the black windows sit too close together, like a mean pair of eyes. No garage with ornamental columns here, just a couple of council wheelie bins. We pass a blank-eyed woman, naked and stony cold, sinking into the grass. 'Is that Venus?' I peer at the statue. 'Waving?'

'Drowning, more like.' She pounds at the front door.

Then rings. Then pounds harder—

'Stell, why is it *always* a drama with you?' The door's swung open by her brother Nick (thankfully *not* sporting a short skirt and thongs). 'Great,' he clocks me, '*you* again. Well, you're out of luck.' He turns and pads back down the hall. "S'only me and Sam here.'

'Ha...' Stella follows. '...like we wanna hang around your stupid band!'

It's left to me to shut the front door (already I'm sensing the Harcourt siblings prefer to *make* an entrance). When I look back up the hall, Stella's disappeared, leaving a trail of muddy prints up the plush, cream carpet. I gulp. If this was *our* hallway, my mum would be grabbing a wet rag while my dad dropped to his knees ('We have a *carpet*?!'). But I'm guessing the Harcourts don't "do" rags. I settle for pulling off my own (leak-tastic) shoes, then squelching in my socks after Stella.

Where's she got to? I hazard a quick check behind each door: there's a cupboard rammed with coats. A toilet (*woah*, thick with hairspray). A weird, small room with nothing in it but a yoga mat (rolled up) and a drinks cabinet (wide open). Sticking my head into the MASSEEEVY kitchen, I fight the urge to body-surf across its sleek chrome surfaces. Zero biscuit crumbs clutter *these* counter tops! Forget "Final Demand" bills, the only sign of life is a growling dishwasher. 'Stellaaaaaa!' I back up. '*Where are you?*'

'*Here!*' I follow her voice round a corner: Stella's fighting a closed door. 'Nick!' She yanks on the handle. 'Let me in!' The door opens an inch, then slams shut. I realise Nick's holding the handle on the other side, and get a weird urge to giggle. It's like watching a stand-off between the twins (except the twins would have TOTALLED that door by now).

'Aargh!' Stella lets go. 'He's such a *loser*. At least me and Mum use the lounge for NORMAL STUFF,' she shouts through the door, 'LIKE GETTING READY TO GO OUT. My sad brother daren't come out from behind his drum machine. Can't take the fact I'm more popular with his Year 12 mates THAN *HE* IS.'

The door swings open. 'Those guys are *not* my mates,' says Nick, 'and "popular" is *not* what they're calling you.'

'Meaning?'

'Mathew Coles,' says Nick. 'He had half the class huddled round his phone today. Bragging he could get some girl to send him "hot pics".'

She goes stiff. 'So?'

'Sam heard him say "Stella".'

'Big deal.' She shrugs. 'I'm not the only Stella in Norbridge—'

'—who's gone out with Mathew Coles *and* Dean Shipman? And is "*well* fit for a Year 10"?'

'Seriously? They said that?' I'm trying to gauge if Stella's mortified or made up when a crash sounds overhead.

'Oh, yeah.' Nick looks sheepish suddenly. 'Mum's off on one. I tried to keep her out of your room but—'

'*She's in my room?*' cries Stella. 'Nick, you promised!' Turning, she pushes past me to take the stairs two at a time. High heels wobbling, skirt hitched-up: this is so not Stella – none of this is. It's like her cool cracked the second we walked in here. As Nick pulls the lounge door shut, another slams upstairs. I hear muffled voices being raised.

Now what?

Slowly, I squelch back towards the front door. This place, it's a hall of mirrors: a big, gilt-framed thing by the stairs… an oval looking glass above the sideboard… a full-length mirror opposite the toilet. But I can't see one picture of Stella or Nick – or their parents.

And that's not the only thing missing.

My skin prickles as I scan the stark walls, the deserted rooms... where is it? *Where's Christmas?*

It's 17th December. Winter Wonderland Ball is tomorrow, yet the Harcourts haven't put up a scrap of tinsel, not so much as a star. Which is, like, nuts. Even my shonky family hauled our wonky plastic tree out of storage last week. We strung up our battered baubles, and even Dad who, if he's not "clinically depressed" (yes, Mum, I can Google) should *not* be trusted with scissors, cut out little paper snowmen. 'Look, girls,' he cried as he made them dance, 'I *can* bring the page alive!'

'*No!* Please,' Stella shrieks overhead. 'Let *go!*'

I'm up the stairs so fast I set the mirrors rattling. My feet sinking into the snow-white carpet, I cross the landing towards the source of the screams. 'Stella?' I push open the door. 'You all right?'

She's dazzling. Talk about "quick change"! Stella's lighting up the room in a glittering gold gown.

'Wow,' I murmur. Even with her back to me, I recognise the dress – it's the one she tried on at Charlton Mews. A thousand sequins shimmer like golden scales down her fishtail skirt. I can't resist the urge to touch them. 'So beautiful.'

'You think?' She swishes round with a flick of her tail, and *woah,* I whip my hand back. Her eyes are blue as ever, but her face... it's shrivelled. Her skin's cracked like leather. Stretched over her cheekbones, it pools in wrinkles round her neck. Her arms are brown and spotted.

This mermaid is *wrecked.*

'Surprise!' A sarcastic cry comes from behind me. I spin round to see Stella, the *real* Stella backed up against the wall. 'Kat,' she says, 'meet my mum.'

'Don't *call* me that,' snaps Stella's mother – crikey, I can see it now. She's the image of Stella, but all washed-out. 'All girls together, aren't we?' Her mum gives me a watery smile. 'I'm Gabrielle, and you're…?'

'Kat.'

'A friend of Stella's. *At last.*' She flutters her bony fingers. 'She's brought one home! And a pretty one at that.' She hooks a dark red nail into my hair. 'Want to play dressing up?'

'This is not a *game*, Mum.' Stella pushes between us. 'That's my gown for the ball. Take it off!'

'*No.*' Gabrielle sways back on her heels, swimming with her arms to stay upright. I catch the bitter-sweet waft of alcohol. 'I'm meeting Stefan for drinks tonight,' she says. 'He told me to wear something nice — and what have I always taught you, darling?'

Stella bites her lip.

'Quick now…' Her mum flicks her tail. 'You don't want these sequins to unravel.'

'All right!' Stella flushes. '*Never disappoint a man.*'

'He'll disappoint *you*, of course.' Gabrielle laughs. 'But you're not to show it. No frown lines.' She waggles her finger. 'No sad face, or *pouff*, he'll be gone! Just like your father.'

'Dad's not vanished, Mum. He's in Birmingham.'

'Well, Stefan's *here*. At least,' the old mermaid checks herself in the mirror. 'He's waiting in a bar off the Southbridge Road. That'll be my cab now.' She giggles as the doorbell goes. 'You'll get your dress back for the ball, darling, good as new. After all,' she eyes her daughter up and down, '*I'm* not the one who stretches things round here.'

OUCH! A last flick of that tail, and Stella sinks down onto her bed like a beautiful, burst balloon. Then I realise she's looking for something. 'The *bitch*,' she rifles through the clothes tossed on top of her bed. 'She's nicked my new black bra.'

'That's OK,' I catch the clothes as they fall. 'You can't wear a black bra under those gold spaghetti straps!'

'Unless it's in the wardrobe.' She leaps up. Extracting a key from a tiny china pot on the windowsill, she goes over to her glossy fitted wardrobe and jiggles the key furiously in the door. '*Stupid lock*. You're supposed to keep Mum out,' she mutters, 'not *me*.'

'Give it here.' I take the key. 'There's a trick to it. My gran taught me.' A deft turn, and I click the door open.

'Skill.' Stella flashes a wicked smile. 'Now it's my turn...' She puts a hand on my back. '...to show *you*.' She shoves me into the wardrobe.

'*Hey!*' I trip forward, clutching at the air – and feel fabrics ripple through my fingers. Forget "walk-in" wardrobe, I'm proper spinning, running my hands along the hangers: ruby red skirts, emerald green tops, belts studded with gemstones. 'Talk about Aladdin's Cave!'

She shrugs. 'Credit card heaven, more like.'

'Or Cinderella's closet *after* the ball.' I slide a pink maxi-dress off its hanger. 'When she's bagged her happy ending!'

'You're mad.' Stella shakes her head, but she looks pleased. And she hangs the dress up carefully when I'm done twirling. 'Is it always the fairy tale with you?' she says.

'Me?' I rummage through another rail. '*You're* the one living the dream.'

'Some dream,' she mutters. I'm shaking out a pair of skinny velvet jeans, when she pushes past me ('*yess*, my black bra'). I stumble against her shoe rack, sending Nike platforms crashing down onto summer sandals onto party heels onto—

'Here,' Stella catches the last, tumbling pair. 'These are the ones I was thinking of – for you, I mean.' She hands them to me. 'For the ball.'

They're beautiful – shimmery and silver – proper princess slippers! But with a spike.

'Beginner heels,' Stella says. 'Unlike *these*.' Bending down, she slips on shoes that appear identical twins to mine. Then she stands up, and *woah*! She's towering over me. 'My bad heels.' She laughs.

'No kidding! Those stilettos look deadly. How can you walk?'

'You learn.' She struts off down her room. 'I'll teach you.'

'You will?' I frown. 'Why?'

'Why d'you think? So you don't fall on your—'

'No, I mean why *help* me? This catwalk contest – there's £500 at stake. Or does that not mean anything to you?'

'Winning? Oh, it means something all right.' She turns on her heels. 'That's why it has to be fair.'

'Funny. I never had you down for the Girl code.'

'Girl code?' She strides back towards me. 'What's that?'

I shrug.

'You either get it…' I place her shoes back on the rack. '…or you don't'.

She stops, like she's trying on something new for size, when something growls at her from the bed. '*Man*…' She snatches up her vibrating phone. '…can he not leave me alone for ten minutes?'

"'S that Year 12 boy?' I guess. 'Mathew Cole?'

She chucks down her phone. Steps down from her heels. 'He wants me to send him pics.'

'*Hot* pics...?'

'Well, duh. It's not a close-up of my *brain* he's after.'

'That's why you want the black bra? For bedroom posing?'

'I'll wear something on top,' she shrugs. 'Off the shoulder at least. So you can stop looking at me like that.' She rams her heels back into the rack. 'It's just pics he's after.'

'Which he'll share with all his mates! Seriously, *this* is why you like older boys?'

'*You* said that.' She slams the wardrobe shut. 'Not me. I just want a boy with experience, 's all. Who gets it.'

'Gets what?'

'That life *isn't* a fairy tale.' She locks her wardrobe door. 'Count on people sticking around?' She hides the key back in its pot. 'You set yourself up to lose.'

'Riiight...' The phone growls again. 'And posing in your pants makes you a winner?'

'Like you'd know?' She snatches up her phone. 'Squelching round my house in socks that belong in a bin.'

I flinch like she's hit me. And see a flush rush her face... like it's me that slapped *her*.

'Please, Stella. Don't pick up.'

But now *the whole room* is shaking. Crazy music is blasting through her window. Guitar chords crash and crescendo, turning the air electric. 'What the—?' says Stella.

'Zack,' I say with a grin. 'He's down there.'

'In the *garden*?'

'Strollin',' I nod. 'He does that.'

'But it's sub-zero out there.' Chucking down her phone, Stella helps me wrench open the window. 'He must be—'

'Freezing his nuts off?' I giggle. 'Do you think he *means* to serenade us?'

'Who cares? No boy's *ever* serenaded me before.' Stella cranes out – just as the patio door shuts below: Zack's gone back inside, taking his sounds with him. 'What's he playing?' says Stella with a frown.

'"Foxy Lady". Come on.' I laugh, pulling her after me. 'It's our cue!'

I ride Zack's reverb the whole way down. I'd forgotten how much the STOOPID boy makes me... vibrate! What was I *thinking*, freaking out over one stupid kiss? Ducking his calls?

'Are you *trying* to freeze a guy to death?' Nick's bolting the patio door behind Zack as I crash into the lounge. 'What were you doing out there?'

'Cooling off,' says Zack, shaking rain off his jacket. 'This gig, it's getting to me—'

'Zack.' I move towards him.

'*Kat?*' He spins round. 'What are you doing here?'

'Seeing you!' I edge past a lampstand. 'But also, you know ...Hanging out.' I squeeze past a huge, white leather couch. 'With Stella. *Oof!*' I trip over a white leather foot stool.

'Stella?' He frowns. 'I thought you and her were—'

'Mates. *Ow,*' I clip the edge of a glass coffee table. 'We're mates now, I think.'

'You *think*?'

'Yes.' Aware that Nick's in full glare mode (does he have any other?) I lower my voice. 'Zack, can we talk?'

185

'Fire away.' He crosses his arms. Like I mean to do him damage when I CAN'T EVEN GET PAST THIS COFFEE TABLE.

'Aargh.' This place isn't a home, it's a lounge set for Love Island. 'Stuff's happened,' I tell him. 'Turns out Stella can be, you know…'

'What?' He glares at me.

'Cool.'

'*Cool?* What, like Jonah?'

'I didn't say that!'

'Yeah, well, you don't say much these days.' His eyes go dark. 'Not to me.'

'Yeah, about that. I'm sorry.' I try to reach him, but he is *not* meeting me halfway. Soddit, if I can't get round the furniture, I shall swing my leg *over* it.

'Down, girl!' Stella breezes in. 'What's our coffee table ever done to you?' I blush, wobbling furiously. She tosses her hair – freshly mussed – and I realise why I beat her on the stairs: she took a mirror-stop, didn't she? Now I look like a furniture-straddling loon, while she's all lip gloss and sheen. 'Hiya, Zack.' She flashes her best cheerleader smile. 'Big band practice tonight! You don't mind us girls crashing?'

Before Zack can answer, Nick leaps up from his drum kit. 'You swore, Stell.' He blocks her. 'You'd give me this last band practice. *One night* without your games.'

'Hey, bruv,' says Zack. 'She's just hanging.'

'Yeah, hanging round *you* since we started.' Nick turns to his sister. 'I told you to back off. Now suddenly you're dragging Zack's little friend in too?'

'Hey,' I say, 'less of the "little".' I adoped a dignified crouch on the coffee table. 'And you can drop the "dragging".' Everyone looks at me. For like a nano-second, then it's back to the Harcourt Sibling Show.

'We had a deal,' Nick scowls at Stella. 'You'd stay away from the band, if I kept Mum off your back.'

'Well, she's taken *the dress* off my back instead,' hisses Stella. 'So now what? I can't even keep a *friend* for myself?'

I'm her friend? Her BFF? Carefully, I dismount the coffee table, so Stella and I can girly-skip off into the sunset together.

'Fancy a Diet Coke?' she asks Zack. 'Even rock stars need to take a break! Or we've got a thousand cans of tonic,' she adds quickly. 'My mum sticks them in her gin.'

'Niiiice,' says Zack warily. 'I might skip the gin.' He catches my eye, but whatever he sees there, he's not interested. 'Thanks,' he turns to Stella, 'a Diet Coke could be good.'

No coulds about it, Stella swoops him off to the kitchen before I—

Can—

'*Ow!*' I knock my shin against an empty magazine rack.

'Careful,' says Sam. 'It's all sharp edges in this house.' Opening his guitar case, he pulls out a bulging McDonald's bag. 'Fancy a burger? I bought two.'

'Thanks,' I sidle past, 'but I've lost my appetite suddenly.' I go to the kitchen, only to halt, like there's an invisible line I can't cross. Here's me in my damp, stinking socks. There's Zack and Stella laughing like they're something out of a Diet Coke ad. They're leaning against the Harcourts' shiny chrome fridge. He's rolled up the sleeves on his white school shirt, and is swigging from his can while Stella shows him something on her phone – something hilarious, I'm guessing, because she's giggling, and Zack smiles as he leans down to look. Shy, but at the same time...

Not.

'Hey,' I say, 'what's so funny?'

'Nothing.' Stella looks up, eyes are shining.

'Zack?' I move towards him. '*Woah.*' I skid across the kitchen tiles in my wet socks. Hitting the Harcourt's huge island, I try to laugh, try to connect with Zack, but he's frowning into his Coke can. Like he'd rather look at *dregs* than at me.

'Wow,' I say. 'So late already?' "18.35" dances on the oven clock. 'The twins will be screaming for their tea!'

They don't try to stop me leaving.

In fact, it's like I was never there at all. Now Stella's doing her trademark hair-flick, and I see a spark shoot from her to Zack. An actual spark!

Quick as a flash, Zack shoots up a hand to catch it.

'You're fast,' marvels Stella, as he opens his fingers to reveal a sparkling hair slide. 'Thanks,' she reaches for it. But the hair slide, it must be a fiddly thing to get hold off. Because as I turn to go, her hand is still in his.

Running down the hall, I feel my stomach cramp. My insides are turning out. At the front door, I pull on my sodden shoes.

'You got your coat?' Stella sticks her head out of the kitchen. 'Oh, sorry – forgot you didn't have one. *SO SAD*,' she raises her voice. 'TAKE ONE OF MINE, *I'VE GOT LOADS.*'

'No, thanks.' I practically fall out of the door to the street. 'See ya!' But it's Zack's face I can't shake the whole way home: how his eyes went hard on me…

How he couldn't stop looking at *her*.

The world's gone dark. Fierce winds hound me down Redmond Hill. The R3 bus roars past, and in the pale glow of the top deck, I pretend I see Zack. Zack as he used to

188

be: riding solo up front. Then walking me home, sharing his Fruit Pastilles as I let off steam about Stella: how she'd cut me. All those times she'd been a bitch.

Well, she's not being a bitch now, is she?

She's a hot blonde princess.

It is 6.00am. My eyes snap open. Winter Wonderland
– *it's tonight.*
Tonight.

I lurch out of bed and start ransacking the
bathroom. Dad's rusty razor goes flying, the twins'
chewed toothbrushes take off, but nope – no brand
new box of Tampax appears MIRACULOUSLY on
the shelf. I'm back to wishing as I slide down onto the
loo. Wee, wipe... *phew.* No blood. Not yet...

Pulling up my tights, I hop over to the basin and
pray once more to Katy Perry, Goddess of
Womanhood, *please don't let my period strike until
MIDNIGHT!*

'Kat,' Mum yells up. 'You ready?'

'*So* ready! Destiny's calling,' I tell the
girl in the mirror. 'You ARE the most
Dazzling Look.'

'Yeah right,' the girl answers back.
'Have you SEEN that bobble hat
you're wearing?'

So I whip it off – *all of it.*

the bobble hat,
    Dad's thickest sweater,
        Mum's warmest PJs,
            my woolly school tights,
                layer after layer until there's
nothing left but—
    a skinny girl in a baggy tee.

Hitting the shower, I feel a thousand icy daggers pierce my skin.

Stella and Zack. Together...

Tonight?

For once, I'm glad when the cold turns me numb.

'Gotta run!' Mum shouts up, as I emerge wrapped in a towel. 'Dad tells you've been taking the twins to nursery.'

'But, Mum.' I lean over the banisters, '*I can't today!*' The front door slams. Mum has obviously ignored me. The twins come skidding out of the kitchen in their Maggie Simpson babygros.

'*Kat!*' Lil hurls herself at the stairs. '*We commin.*'

'TO JUMPONOOOOZE!' Daisy follows.

'Dad!' I call up to the attic. '*Just once*, can you take the twins in?' Nothing. Must have his headphones on. But he's not the only one creating around here! I slide behind my sewing machine.

Hands shivering, I start to hemstitch round the edges of my skirts. I rev out the bad voices in my head, and focus on the £500 prize. As the twins tumble into my room, I picture them dancing round our new boiler, skipping naked through our hot house. Mum is, like, *melting* into Dad's arms. Mission successful, he whips off his balaclava like James Bond! Fast as flowing silk, my imagination runs away with me... Now Lisa's in our kitchen, wearing summer shorts and passing an ice cream to Zack.

He grins, turns to me and says, 'Can Stella come round for a bikini party?'

Aargh, the needle chews up my skirts. As I pull at the threads, another cramp bites. *Please, no.* I hurt so bad last night, all over. I couldn't work, but if I don't work, I can't win...

'No!' Lil climbs up into my lap. 'No sad.' She pats my tears. 'Stop dat.'

'Esss,' says Daisy with a nod, clambering over her. 'Stop dat, Kat.' She squishes my cheeks. 'We want BEKFUSS.'

'You do?' I take my foot off the pedal. I'm shaking. 'What are you thinking?' I rest my forehead against hers. 'Cornflakes?'

'Noooo.' She nuts me. 'ZackandAndys.'

'Esss.' Lil tugs at the crumpled silk. 'Nuff of diss. Nuff!'

'*Enough*, you're right.' I can't fix my dress while my head's this shredded. I need to make things right with Zack. Whatever's gone down this week, he's still my best mate in the world. I *can* mend us.

I scoop up the twins. Taking the stairs, I swing through the kitchen and out the back door. Feet stumbling, heart racing, I run to find Zack.

'Sorry, Needle Girl. You've missed him.' Andy opens the Melways' back door in a t-shirt and boxer shorts, his afro all squashed. 'Zack left first thing,' he yawns, scooping up the twins. 'Got in late last night too.'

'How late?' I grill Andy as he sets the twins up to cook breakfast. While they smash eggs into a pan (and a fair bit of the cooker), he shrugs; Zack went straight up to his room apparently. Andy was woken this morning by the sound of the front door closing on the latch. Now it's like something slams shut inside me. I can't eat – can't stay still – as the twins wolf their eggs. 'You look fried,' Andy jokes. When I don't laugh, he puts away the pan, and insists on coming back with me to help. 'Wassup, Kat?' he asks, as we get the girls ready for nursery. 'Has Zack done something?'

'No! Yes – maybe…' I bundle Lil into the buggy. 'But it's OK, I'm happy for him. That's what I want to tell him…' I heave Daisy in beside her. '…how happy I am.'

'Right. Happy.' His kind eyes hold mine. '*That's* what this is?'

My bag beeps. 'That might be him now!' I say, rifling through my school books. '*Yes*,' I fish out my Nokia brick. 'No, I mean, it's Jonah.'

'Jonah?' frowns Andy. 'Who's he?'

'My date for tonight.' *Finally,* he texts!

Tonight's gonna be chill. C U there.

'He's a lucky guy,' says Andy, manoeuvring the double

buggy out onto the street for me. 'Kat, take care, yeah?' he shouts as I go. But the wind buffets his voice, so I can almost think it's Marie Melway calling after me, *Take care, child. Watch how you go.'*

I bite down on a sob. Desperately I zigzag up the road to the twins' nursery, my seven-year-old coat hanging off me as I try to get through to Zack. Over and over I call. Until all that's left is to text:

Please, Zack, call me!

Twins dropped off, I pick up speed.

Zack, I'm so sorry FOR EVERYTHING

Hurtling down Norbridge Hill, I try Stella.

Text me! What's the plan for tonight?

Nothing. Crashing into the Year 10 locker room I find Natalie flashing her new acrylics to Keisha. 'Where's Stella?' I ask.

'Skiving,' says Keisha with a shrug.

'She's off with Zack Melway,' smirks Nat. 'They're coming to the ball together.'

'Great,' I flush. 'We can go as a gang.'

'In your dreams.' Keisha flicks her new braids. 'The only one who wants you there tonight is Jonah Kerrigan – and *that's* gonna change when he sees the state of you.' She takes in my dishevelled coat. 'That little black dress?' She checks the holes in my tights. 'It won't cover enough.'

'You look like a skank,' says Nat with a snigger,

'who's lost a fight with a dog.'

'*Woof.*' They push past me. But it's me howling by lunchtime. My cramps are killing. It's all I can do to limp to the toilets (the grotty ones in science block that *no one* visits). Crouching in the cubicle, I check my knickers. Phew, nothing... *yet.* Just in case, I scrunch up a wad of toilet paper and shove it into my knickers. Then I scrunch up more paper and scrub at my face. Great snotty chunks come bursting out of me. *Zack... he's off with Stella. He likes her. And she* never *liked me*! I tear the toilet roll. *She was just using me to get to Zack, wasn't she? His sad, trash friend*, I scrunch up the paper, *now I'm chucked.*

It takes a while, but I get the sobs out of me. Drained, I hit the flush – who needs them? *I can do this.*

Exiting the science block, I waddle my toilet paper fanny towards class: double textiles beckons, with Keisha and Nat. Ugh, just the *thought* of them makes me stick my head in my bag. I swear there's an ancient paracetamol at the bottom somewhere. Yay! I tear open the tinfoil.

The pill crumbles in my hand. *Gah*, where's Lees with her shin splints, cracked ankles and PACKETS OF NUROFEN EXTRA? Where's Lees *full stop*? I huff—

No. *Noooooo, how could I forget? Today's regional trials!* Lesson bell clanging in my ears, I pull my phone. I'm texting, though I know it's too late: St Edward's 'A' team went into action hours ago. After months of hard training, Lees will be charging down that pitch knowing her best friend couldn't spare her a thought.

GOOD LUCK! KNOCK 'EM FLYING!

I bowl into the textiles studio.

195

'A walking disaster,' mutters Miss Bloxam, as I knock into her desk. Beautiful bottle-wing butterflies tumble from her tray stack.

'Sorry.' I try to catch them. 'I'm so sorry.'

'Yeah, that's what you said in detention.' Miss Bloxam folds up her wings. 'Then Stella Harcourt swans in, and suddenly I have *two* pains in the butt. GOT YOUR PROJECT PIECES, GALS?' she shouts over my head.

I shuffle to my desk, but my teacher's not done with me. When I don't *instantly* produce my project work, Miss Bloxam bawls me out in front of everyone. Then she leans over me, criticising my stitch work, and questioning my colours. When she starts on my fabric swatches, I blink furiously and see a stain bloom on my scrap of taffeta.

'Here.' She passes me a tissue. I look up. '*My* turn ter say sorry,' she says. 'I lack the sensitive touch.'

"S all right,' I sniff, scrubbing my face (again. I'm, like, losing a layer of skin today!) I try to laugh.

'That's bedda. My bad.' She grins ruefully. 'Growing up in the outback, yer develop a hide like leather. Good for when emus are pecking your butt, less good for teenage guidance. Come here.' She gives me a brisk, emu-crushing hug. 'I do get it, yer know. Yer wanna change! But the trick is to turn into your *best* self! Become a beautiful butterfly, don't morph into... waddya Brits call it?' She screws up her face. 'A biddovadick?'

I snort. So does she. Then we're back to business. 'How's it looking for tonight?' she asks. 'You finished your dress?'

'Hardly.' I screw up my tissue. 'No hems yet, just raggedy edges. As for the back...'

'Yeah?'

'I've *still* not put in a zip.'

'Jeez,' she hoots. 'Tonight's gonna be interesting. *So* interesting.' She drops her voice. 'I might forget to lock up the sewing studio after school. Work hard enough...' She nudges me. '...who knows what can happen? Get to Winter Wonderland, and you might just—'

'—fall apart?'

'—*take off.*' A last, rib-cracking squeeze and Miss Bloxam goes to check on her other students. 'Keisha, watch where yer waving those fabric shears. Yer supposed to be creating a collage, *not a HOLE IN NATALIE'S FACE.*'

The afternoon shoots by. Still no word from Lees. As school streams out, I pace up and down outside the gates, torn between needing to race back to my sewing machine and wanting to THROW MYSELF in front of the hockey team minibus. If it *just* gets back in time, I can make it up to Lisa. If she'll let me . . .

I peer at my phone through the settling dusk. Still nothing. I've been universally ghosted. My schoolmates stream past, and it's like I'm not even a shape to them. I spot the KS3 girls, giddy and giggling, splitting off into gangs to get ready for the ball. Across town, first-floor windows will soon shine like the Christmas lights – cosy bedroom after bedroom glittering with girls' gowns, Claire's Accessories and tidy wishes coming true.

Schluck! The R3 sails past, sluicing me in cold water. I see laughing kids lit up inside. Then *whoosh*, they're gone. Miss Lipscombe comes out to move me on: the minibus is delayed; no, she doesn't know how the team did. Don't I have a home to go to? She claps her hands excitedly: a *ball* to go to?

I split before she can break into song. No Disney princess here. No fairy godmother at hand. Two hours until

Winter Wonderland, and my dream dress is just that – a dream. My reality is a lonely trudge home, past shops teeming with people. It's only Armitages that looks half-empty. As I cross Market Square, it looms up like a shipwreck.

And it hits me – there *is* someone who can help me. My hair lifts with the wind, as I start up Norbridge Hill.

I'm not the only girl Gran taught to sew.

'**M**um, you in?' I dump my bag in the hall. 'I NEED YOU!'

Nothing. Where *is* everyone today? Hanging up my coat, I hear the twins chuntering in front of the TV, but... 'Dad?' I shout up the stairs. 'Mum?'

Silence.

A crash sounds from the kitchen. But when I spin round, the door's closed.

It's never closed.

Stomach turning, I move towards the kitchen door. It gives a creak. A woman's hand curls round the door jamb. Her nails are chipped, fingers stiff like a corpse. 'Mu-um?'

The door swings open, and a naked woman lurches out at me. She has mad, staring eyes. Her body's streaked with scratches – chunks of flesh gouged from her chin and nose. As she sprawls on me, I thrash wildly, catching her mop of blonde hair *which starts to slide from her head.*

'*Aargh!*' I scream.

'Surprise!' Mum appears behind her. 'Meet my new friend, Dolly.' Giggling, she holds up what I see (now I'm NOT CACKING MYSELF) to be a battered shop dummy.

'Whoops, Doll.' She tugs its hair. 'Keep your wig on!'

'Jeez, Mum.' She's giving off fumes. 'You've been drinking?'

'*One* cocktail I had after work,' she hiccups. 'The other girls in*sssssis*ted on paying. Plus I had to drink Dolly's here. She wouldn't touch the stuff.' Mum's voice drops to a whisper. 'Do you think she's a Mormon?'

'I THINK she's a mannequin! **Property of Armitages**,' I read out the label stuck to her back. 'Mum, what are you *doing* with her?'

'Teaching Armitages a lesson,' she stumbles. 'Fankslove.' I prop her up. 'Not only are they slashing overtime, they're cancelling our Christmas party!'

'Oh, Mum.' She leans against me. I stroke her sad, flattened curls.

'There was going to be a free bar,' she says into my shoulder, 'with finger food and a dancefloor. D'you *know* how long it is since I had a dance?' She staggers away from me, Dolly in her arms. 'Me and your dad, we used to cut some shapes. To crap indie rock bands, mostly, but still...' She twirls Dolly around the kitchen table. 'I've been *hanging on* for this party – one night of escape. A chance to dress up, you know?'

I know.

'When I heard it was cancelled...' She crashes into the pedal-bin. '...I got mad, and took off with Dolly here. She spoke to me, didn't you, girl?' Tenderly she brushes a piece of potato peel from the shop-worn face. 'You were pretty too, once.' Eyes shining, Mum turns to me. 'Catch!' She throws Dolly. 'She's all yours.'

'*Me?*' I grab Dolly.

'Thassright. Not so dumb as I look.' Mum taps her finger at her head, missing it slightly. 'I know you've been sewing away in your room. I've heard your Singer singing up there!' A giggle turns into a sigh. Turning to the sink, she rolls up her sleeves, and starts running the taps. 'I know you've plucked up courage to make your own gown. I'm so proud of you, love.' She squirts out the dregs of the washing-up liquid. 'Winter Wonderland's next week, isn't it?'

'Mum,' I croak, 'the ball's *tonight.*'

'What's that?' she shouts over the rushing water. 'You'll be fine! And I'm still quite nifty with a needle.' She clatters the dirty dishes in to soak. 'I'll help you finish it, love, even if we have to Sellotape your skirts together! *Memo to self*,' she shuffles off to the front room, 'find money for Sellotape. Oh good,' she subsides in front of the TV, 'CBeebies.'

Dolly and I look at each other. Two dummies with nothing going for them...

But a dress.

'Agh, come on.' I batter us upstairs to the attic. Dad *must* be up there. Dad knows what it is to dream. *'Dad!'* I push open the door. *'Can you give me a lift into school?'* He turns a blank face to me from his screen. 'Andy Melway was going to drive us,' I pant. 'Me and Zack, I mean, plus his band gear—'

'Woah, hold up.' Dad pulls off his earphones. 'Why exactly is Zack trying to get into St Edward's? And why's Andy helping him? The library's only for you girls.'

'Library?' I frown. 'The ball's being held in the gym, Dad.'

But he's not listening. 'I do *care*,' he talks over me. 'I read the emails from school: it's great they're keeping the library and computer room open late – to help girls like you.'

'Like *me*?'

'You know…' He plays with his headphones. '…girls who are struggling. With homework, I mean – since you lost Mum's laptop.'

'I didn't *lose* it – you sold it.' He flinches. 'Now make it up to me,' I plead. He's wavering, I can tell. Then Dolly seals the deal by doing a face-plant in his lap.

'All right!' He batters her off. 'I'll go find the car keys. But I warn you, tank's nearly empty.'

I run down to my room. Kicking my rag bag out of the way – ditto Sheila's sock-frock – I prop Dolly against the wall by my Singer. My gown lies where I abandoned it, beneath the raised needle of my machine. Drawing out the thread from the bobbin, I cut the bunched silk free. Carefully, I lower my gown over the mannequin. *Yes* – the seams are *sharp*, the waistband nips! I shake out the shimmering skirts, watch them float through the air—and sink. *Still no swish.* Spinning Dolly round, I confront my gown's gaping back. The snarled zip sticks out like a tongue, taunting me. I grab my scissors. *I'm done with being laughed at.*

Stitch by snarled stitch, I tear out the zip. There's still time – I can start again, *try harder*...

'Keys, found 'em!' Dad shouts up the stairs. 'I'll grab a cuppa, then go and start up the car.'

I can *fix* this.

Twenty minutes later, I'm ready. My heart's kicking against my ribs, but my head is straight.

I've done what was needed.

This girl's going to the ball.

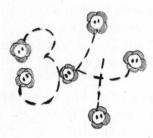

Soon as I hear Dad going out to the car, I head downstairs in my dress. Where's Mum's handbag? There, dumped by her shoes. I rummage for her spare pair of work tights.

'Kat.' The twins totter from the front room. 'Watcha doin'?'

'Nothing!' Bare legs fine, I decide. Mum's shoes are still warm from a day on the shop floor. They're also flat-heeled and scuffed, but at this *precise* moment in time (clock ticking, ball fleeting), it's them or my school pair. I slip my feet in, holding my breath... Do the shoes fit?

Nope.

I have to *jam* my toes in. 'Ouchy,' cries Lil.

'OFF!' Daisy tugs.

'No,' I lift the twins aside, and start rifling through the hooks by the front door. There, Dad's long, black raincoat. He's had it since his teenage Goth days. Knocking dust off the shoulders, I pull it over me like a cloak.

'Where you goin'?' asks Lil.

'To the ball,' I say brightly, 'to meet Prince Charming! Well, he's called Jonah, but...'

'You don't look like a pwincess.' She frowns. Daisy sticks out her lip.

'Where your pwitty dwess gone?'

'Under my coat, you noggin!' I bend down to kiss her. 'I've got to get into my carriage, haven't I?' As Dad beeps his horn outside, I hustle the twins back into the front room. 'You look after Mum.' She's nodded off on the couch, CBeebies blaring. Plonking the girls down either side of her, like safety bolsters, I fight the urge to throw myself down beside them. Quick, before the ache inside me can grow, I tiptoe to the front door. Tripping over the hems of Dad's coat, I feel like a little girl again. Heart skipping as Mum helped me climb into her high heels and let me swish round in her skirts!

We did *do* that? It's not another dream I've stitched together from wishing?

No, I fling open our front door and breathe in the crisp night air. I *was* that girl – whirling, laughing... loved. I can be her again. *Who cares if my shoes don't fit?* When Jonah sees me in this dress, he won't be looking at my feet!

I reach the car to find Dad in the driving seat. 'Thanks for taking me.' I tap at his window.

'Sorry, love,' he winds it down. 'Car won't start. Petrol's down to zilch.'

'No. *No*.'

'It's OK, love.'

'No, Dad, *it's not OK*.' I turn and start walking. 'What's the time?'

'Er... seven thirty. *Wait!*' Dad calls after me. 'You can't just take off!'

'How else am I going to get there?' I hobble furiously up the street.

'Not on your own, Kat! Two miles in the dark?' The car

door slams. 'I'll walk with you,' Dad shouts. Already he sounds far behind me.

'The twins need you,' I shout back. 'Mum's in no state to fix their tea.'

'Christ, what now?' I hear the ker-lunk of our car lock. Dad's voice veers off up our path. '*Kell, you OK?*'

I cross Keyton Road, then Skew Bridge, past the abandoned offices and the old guy who sleeps in the doorway of "Faster Print". By the time I make it through the industrial estate, my feet are shredded. Skin's scraping off my heels, blood's squishing between my toes as I limp down Norbridge Hill. But I'm getting there! I round the corner to school, and *woah* –

The street's come alive.

Horns blast; station wagons roll in. Headlights beaming, proud parents drop their daughters off for the ball. Gangs of girls giggle in their finery. Booted and suited Winsham boys lope past in twos and threes. Playing it cool, they check themselves in the car wing mirrors. Shrinking against the wall, I follow them up the drive to Winter Wonderland.

Flickering tea-lights pick out our way. Strings of glowing roses adorn the flung-open doors of the gym; a pounding bass beat draws us all in. Boys loop their arms round each other's necks, whooping as they disappear into the flashing lights of the party. Some girls stop to shake out their long skirts – magenta, cerise, electric blue. Others slink over the threshold in curve-hugging bodycons.

Me? I'm hunched in a cloak like some story book crone. Trolls will strike. I jump as my phone beeps. *Jonah?* I fumble for my Nokia brick. *He'll save me! Sweep me up—*

Hey bad girl.

It's not Jonah.

Soz, been out all day – left phone behind

Stella, she's not bailed on me!

Where U? We're all at ball already ♠♣♥♦

I'm trembling, jabbing a response when she texts again.

Got to fly. Left heels on top of your locker.
C U on the dancefloor!

I'm dancing already, hopping from one foot to the other. Pulling off Mum's tatty toe-mincers, take off round the back of the gym block. Laughing, splashing through puddles, I'm a barefoot Cinderella... ready to transform!

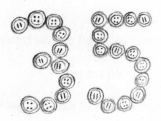

I find the Year 10 cloakroom deserted, its walls pounding to the sound system in the gym. Reaching for the *New Look* bag on top of my locker, I feel the spikes of Stella's "beginner heels" pierce the plastic.

'*Watch out.*' A girl shouts behind me. 'She's after us.' I spin round to see Zara. 'Wow.' My shy sewing partner's turned into a swirl of glittering gossamer! Her school shalwar kameez have been magicked into a shimmering pink trouser suit. She glides towards me in a lilac headscarf traced with gold thread.

'You look amazing, I say. 'I look *scared*.' She presses her forehead nervously. 'How can one girl rule our lives like this?'

'S'OK.' I clutch my bag of shoes. 'Stella's not the bitch she makes out.'

'Stella?' She frowns. 'I'm hiding from *Harriet*. She keeps bossing me with her

208

clipboard: "Put out more chairs, BRING ME MORE WOTSITS!"' I giggle. 'No joke, Kat, I need back up!'

'Sure. I just need to...'

'Lose the coat, maybe?' she suggests. I tug at Dad's belt, but the buckle – it's tricky. My fingers—

'Kat, you OK?'

'Yeah, 's just...' I look up at her concerned face, swathed in folds of lilac gossamer. 'It's easier to hide, isn't it?'

'Hide? Oh, you mean *this?*' She pats her headscarf. 'This is sooo the opposite of hiding.' She smiles. 'My hijab shouts, "*Look, world, this is me!*" So when people don't like it...'

'Must be scary.'

'Sometimes, yes.' Her eyes glitter like her scarf. 'But, Kat, scary isn't always bad. Dare to wear what you feel. What you truly feel *here*,' she pokes a button on my coat, just above my heart, 'then no one can touch you.'

'*ZARA!*' The cloakroom doors crash open. 'Must I drag you back into that gym? *Kat, at last!*' Harriet explodes into the room. 'A gang of Winsham boys have raided the refreshments table and started shaking our giant Fanta bottles. *One more lid* comes off...' She turns purple. 'THE ROOF WILL BLOW.'

'Shh now! Show me these BAD BOYS.' Zara bustles her off. 'I've survived Mixed Debate Club, I can peel a Year 10 off a fizzy orange. Kat,' she shouts over her shoulder, 'catwalk contest starts in thirty minutes. You need to get ready.'

But that's where she's wrong – I *am* ready.

Ball ready.

Goodbye Sheila's sock-frock...

Hello little black dress! Shedding my coat, I twist the mini-skirt straight. The viscose still slithers (that I *couldn't* fix while Dad rummaged for his car keys) but the tucks I put into the back are holding; ditto the modesty lining I speed-stitched into the mesh front! It's a "sock-frock" no more. Label needed? Try "the hot dress Kat wore to the ball."

A pink track starts rocking out from the gym, and I take it as A SIGN. Flashing sparks and crackling static, I scoop up my "beginner heels" and pad down the hall to the gym, so fast my stomach has to turn cartwheels to catch up with me!

The gut-churn started that moment in my room, when I saw my designer dream for what it was: a joke. Too right it belonged on a dummy! No way was my gown catwalk-ready. *No way am I.* Winning's not on the cards for someone like me. But this way, I'll pass – pass for a normal girl. In a normal dress with normal shoes. Pushing through the doors to the dancefloor, I feel my heart beat to the spiralling bass track! The teachers have allowed us to use the glasses from the canteen, rooky error! Glass is already glittering the dancefloor.

Tugging on Stella's shoes, I crash into the pulsing darkness and, in a horror split second, realise

my skirt's riding up again, and

these are the BAD heels.

alling forward, I grab at a sleeve. It throws me off, plunging me into a group of St Edward's girls. As they shove me away, I windmill desperately to right myself.

Agh, a huge lad crashes into my shoulder. His mate slaps me with his sopping wet hair. I'm in the mosh-pit: the hardcore scrum beneath the DJ decks. Music's deafening, Pink's turned nasty. Winsham boys are hurling themselves at each other, jolting my back, jarring my neck. My face gets shoved into shirt-fronts sticky with sweat. Fighting for air, I clamber towards the calmer part of the dancefloor – and spot Zack. The only boy here who's *not* in a tux.

Biker jacket zipped, collars scraping his cheekbones, Zack stands head and shoulders above the crowd. He's the cool, green eye of the storm – the boy who's always centred me. So why does my stomach flip harder than ever? Why do I move forward like I'm drawn to a stranger... a really *hot* stranger. *Aargh,* my heels twist under me.

'ZACK,' a voice peals across the crowd, 'THOUGHT I'D LOST YOU!' I wrench my head up to see Stella, cutting a swathe through the dancefloor. Her blonde hair cascades over her shoulders, her sequinned dress clings to her curves.

A golden mermaid, she glides towards Zack.

'*Zack*,' I wave desperately. '*I'm here!*' But his face is hidden by Stella's hair. She's murmuring something in his ear. She's—

Boom, the beat drops. The whole dancefloor starts jumping... Everyone but me. Swaying on my heels, I rock like a target in the wind. Through the bouncing bodies, the Tag-Hags spot me. They're dressed to kill – Keisha's in a lethal red bodycon; Nat's in a purple halter-neck; Jayden is slashed to the thigh. They shoot me daggers, but tonight they can't hurt me. *I'm with Jonah.*

Who is where exactly?

I practically cry out when I see him, leaning against the stage. He's rocking a tux, and looking straight at me. The movie that's been playing in my head, over and over since he asked me to the ball – we're in it. It's happening! I laugh as our eyes meet... at least I *think* they meet. Jonah's fringe falls over his face as he starts towards me. His crew follow – Daniel, Liam, Karl – drawing the Tag-Hags in their wake.

Now Jonah's close enough to touch, and I'm nervous suddenly. Tugging my skirt down over my bare legs, I feel a rash of goose bumps. He says nothing, just stands there, like he'd cast a shadow over me if he could. And I feel something shift deep inside me... somewhere between an ache and a knowledge. Then Jonah tosses back his mop of blond hair, and smiles at me. *Yes*, I teeter forward into his Safe Orbit of Cool. My skirt's riding up again, but hey – just needs a yank. '*Whoa*,' I topple into Daniel, 'my bad.'

'Hey,' he shoves back, 'mind the threads!'

'Sorry!' I bounce into Keisha.

'Freak,' she pushes me off. I sway, like I'm flying. *I got this!* Then a blow hits me in the back, sending me crashing.

The crowd tilts; the floor comes up and my face smacks into it. I'm stinging all over, and spitting out grit. The gym boards stink of feet and Fanta Orange. Peeling my cheek from the dirt, I see a ring of kids staring down at me. The whites of their eyes glow in the strobe lights. But it's not my *face* they're looking at.

'Gross,' someone cries.

'I'm gonna *gag*.'

'Tell me that is NOT—'

'On her knickers?'

'Blood.'

As I try to push up from the floor, something sharp pierces my palms. Hand stinging, I scrabble round to pull down my skirt.

'Are you getting this? Check her butt!' Hoots turn to howls. My fingers brush the back of my legs, and I feel a wet stickiness. A sob bursts out of me, propelling me up. I clutch at Natalie's skirt. She tries to shake me off, but I hang on. *I hang on.* I'm getting back on my feet when the Tag-Hags start screeching. A perfect, bright red bead is rolling down the inside of my thigh. I rub at it, only to spread a swathe of gore. How the…?

I flip up my palm – it's slashed to ribbons. My blood glitters with broken glass.

'Naaaasty!' The Winsham boys recoil, but they're revelling in it.

Screw you, I make ragged fists. *Screw all of you*. I take a step forward, and feel my legs buckle. My feet are skidding out from under me – my killer heels, they've snapped. Glancing down, I see one stiletto spike has torn off; the other's hanging by a string. I'm crashing down when someone yanks me up.

'Jonah!' I cling to his sleeves. 'Thank you, *thank you*.' I press my cheek against his suit jacket, smearing snot down his flash lapels. Someone sniggers: Daniel and Liam, they're shaking their heads at the shame of me. Let them. I'm safe now. Jonah *rules* this crew. Sure enough, I feel his shoulders go back. He brushes back his soft blond hair, and I prepare to melt into his dreamy blue eyes, so full of...

Fear? *'Jonah?'* I'm losing him. His eyes dart, scared, through the crowd. Suddenly we're back outside Sweatzone, just me and him in the rain. The ball, my crush – it all dissolves.

'Sorry, Kat.' He melts away. 'You're on your own.' I watch him disappear into the crowd, and it's like they're pulling a hood over his head.

Swaying on my broken heels, I scan the hostile faces of the St Ed's girls. 'I'm one of you!' I want to cry. 'Help me'. I reach out to a Year 9. Megan Kelly, she's tiny. Lees has been known to haul her up Norbridge Hill by the straps of her back pack. 'Hey, Megan—' But her friends snatch her back, making me stumble.

'Ha,' shrieks Keisha. '*Social cripple!*'

It's the signal they've been waiting for. Two hundred kids surge forward, and I feel my legs knocked out from under me. '*No,*' I thrash. 'Stop—'

'Easy.' Zack scoops me up into his arms. 'I'm trying to help here. Ready?'

'For what?' I cry, dazed.

'This!' He flings me heroically over his shoulder. I slide back down again. 'Sorry,' he staggers. 'Not done this before. It was always Dad putting *me* into a fireman's lift.' He attempts another boost.

'No!' I yelp. 'Mini-skirt, remember?'

'Oh, yeah.' He swings me back down. 'Better?' He bounces me in his arms like a baby. 'Hey, don't cry, Kat! It was just a bit of blood.'

'*Don't say it.*' I bury my head in his chest.

'Say what? Bet half the girls here are on their period.' He nudges the top of my head with his chin. 'You're making a – what would Lisa call it?'

'Feminisd sdademet,' I mumble into his suede, 'hashdag girlpower.'

'Sweet.' He swings us round to the exit – and gets whipped in the face by my shoe straps.

'Sorry! *Ugh*,' I kick off a heel. It flies up, glittering through the air, to hit Keisha in the nose. She squawks, outraged. The girls around her gasp.

'Score!' says Zack loudly. The girls start to giggle. He whispers in my ear. 'Again?'

This time, I aim high enough to clear the whole damn crew. 'Great kick!' A Winsham boy whistles. Another leaps up to catch my shoe.

'Hear that?' says Zack, as their mates cheer. 'You've got fanboys.' But it's the girls I'm aware of. They swish their gowns as we pass them, their faces glowing, eyes sparkling… at Zack.

Just like Stella's did.

'This isn't funny, Zack.' I squirm in his arms. 'Put me down.'

'No way.' He strolls us off the dancefloor. 'Kick all you like, Kat, I'm not letting go.'

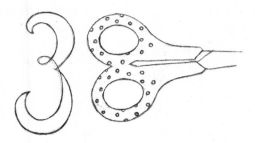

Next thing I register... Zack is setting me down by the school gates. Behind us, the ball rages on: gym's rocking, bass is booming. Kat Parker's forgotten, *I wish.*

I'll be viral by midnight.

'See the freak take a dive.'

'SAVAGE!'

'Disaster, *period.*'

'Kat?' Zack cuts through my doom thoughts. 'What happened? Where's your gown?'

'Where d'you think? In a heap on my floor,' I sniff. 'You should've seen it—'

'I've seen it,' he frowns. 'Seen you working on it enough! It was coming together.'

'It was a mess! *I'm* a mess.'

'It was beautiful! *You're*—' He touches my hair.

'I'm what, Zack?'

'Mad.' He brings down his hand to reveal a crumpled sweet wrapper. 'You're mad to give up now, Kat. You've done magic with that silk! It's easy for the haters to trash stuff, but *you*... you see how things *could* look — with the

217

right kind of love.' Gently, he brushes the dirt from the gym hall off my cheek. 'You can turn unwanted gear to gold, remember? You're Needle Girl.'

It's too much. He's making me *feel too much*. Too late. 'Oh, Zack, I wrecked myself out there. Wrecked any chance of winning for my folks.'

'They won't care!'

'They won't find out. Swear?'

'Kat—'

'Don't. Don't look at me like that.'

'Like what?'

'Like you're sorry for me.' I rub the dirt from my chest; tug down my scrap of a skirt. 'I don't want you to *see* me like this.' A riotous racket starts up from the gym: a track's reaching its crescendo, everyone's shouting the chorus. Soon they'll be shouting for him. 'Go play the rock star!'

'Kat, I'm not playing.'

'Really? Told your bandmates that, have you?' I don't care that I'm hurting him. We're not the same any more. I've been kicked out of Winter Wonderland. He's still got a shot. 'Aren't you due on stage?'

'Crap. The guys,' he pulls out his phone. The screen's lit up with missed calls from Nick. 'But,' he looks up, 'I can't leave you like this! How you gonna get home? You're shivering.' He puts his arm around me.

'No!' I twist free. 'Go impress your new girlfriend.' My bare feet scrape on the tarmac. 'Tell her, *thanks for the shoes.*'

'Kat, what are you talking about?'

'Those heels I kicked off — the heels that took me down?' I watch his face. 'They were Stella's.'

'*Stella's?*'

'Her "killer heels", she calls them.'

'And you *put them on?*'

'I thought I could handle them! Could handle you bringing Stella to the ball.'

'But...' He frowns. 'I didn't come here with Stella. I came in the back of Andy's van, buried under Nick, Sam and a ton of band kit.'

'No Stella?'

'Er, does she *look* like a roadie?'

'She *looks* like a model. But you'd know that after today,' I choke down a sob. 'Bet your gallery's full of her!'

'I — I don't—' He rubs his head like something's melting in there.

'Come on, Zack. You and Stella today? Everyone *knows* you bunked off—'

'*With the band*. I bunked off with the band.' He looks at me. 'You were right, Kat, tonight's our big shot. Last night, I couldn't sleep for working through a new set list.' He shakes his head, like the music's still in there, bursting to get out. 'First thing, I went round to Nick's. We got Sam over, and only stopped practising when Andy turned up with the van. No more hiding! We're gonna kick off with 'Seven Nation Army', then rip into 'Teen Spirit'—'

'And 'Foxy Lady'?' I rip into *him*. 'Zack, what exactly went down with you and Stella last night?'

His face shuts down. And suddenly I don't want to know. I just want to get out of here.

'Wait,' he stops me. 'You wanna do this? Fine. How about we start with that stunt you pulled outside the talent auditions: kissing me, then acting like a prize b—'

'Go on.' I dare him.

'Let's just say it rhymes with rich.'

'Ha, well that can*not* be me.'

'No? Because it felt rich, having you mess me about like I'm just some boy you... some you—'

'I *what?*'

'*I don't know.* That's just it!' His eyes flash. 'When I tried to talk, you shut me down.'

'Because I didn't want to make everything weird between us! I'd done this… *crazy thing*, and I – I couldn't handle any more drama. But I was wrong, Zack,' I move towards him, 'so wrong.'

'We kissed.'

'I know, Zack, I'm sorry—'

'No,' he jerks his head up, 'me and Stella, we kissed. Last night.' He addresses a space above my head. 'After band practice, Sam and Nick got sucked into the Xbox. Me and Stella got chatting in the kitchen, and she…'

'What? Pinned you to the wall?'

'No,' he tells the space. 'I wanted it…'

'I bet you did.'

'…for one second. Then I stopped it. Stopped being mad at you, and got mad with myself. I mean, what a dick move.' He shakes his head. 'Stella's been all right to me. She doesn't need another guy treating her like some trophy.'

'*Poor* Stella — that must feel terrible!'

'You don't know what she feels, Kat.' A muscle flickers in his jaw. 'I'm just saying, when I pulled the ripcord, Stella looked proper hurt. I didn't want to be that guy, so I told her the truth. About you.'

'Great, how did that go?' I try to laugh. '*Sorry, Stella, I can't take you to the ball. I'm stuck looking after Kat, the charity case.*'

'*No*, I told her how I feel about you, all right? How you're blocking me — driving me crazy… when all I want to do is this.' He pulls me in, and kisses me. Like this was what he was made to do. Then he pulls back, unsure.

'Hey,' I tug the sleeve of his biker jacket, 'don't stop

now.' His eyes blaze into mine, and I fall into a wild darkness lit with sparks. Zack's lips are pressing against mine; my heart's going crazy – screeching like car brakes, hooting like horns. Next thing I know, he's swinging me clear of on-coming headlights. Dazzled, I watch a Transit van skid to a halt beside us. Pumpkin-orange, it's strangely familiar.

'Bruv,' Andy bobs his head out of the driver's window. 'You got company!' The twins are strapped into their car-seats beside him.

'Yay,' shouts Daisy. 'Iss KatandZack!'

'AND DEY KISSIN',' yells Lil.

The van door slides open and I don't know what hits the tarmac first: my jaw, or my folks. Dad jumps out first, then turns to help Mum, who does *not* require help. 'I am A MOTHER,' she declares. 'My girl needs me – *whoops*...!' She falls sideways into a bush.

'What are you doing here?' I cry, as Dad fishes Mum out of the greenery.

'What does it look like?' he asks.

Er... it *looks like*

      a) My mum is now beating my dad over the head with her handbag,

      b) My dad is fighting a STRONG urge to leave her in the bush, and

      c) Zack doesn't know whether to help or hide, having nearly been RUN OVER MID-SNOG WITH THEIR DAUGHTER.

'Evening, Mrs Parker, Mr Parker,' he manages before disappearing into the collar of his biker jacket.

'Smooooth,' Andy can be heard chuckling from the van.

'Kat, we came to help,' says Dad, picking twigs off Mum. 'When we saw you'd left your gown—'

'Which is GORGEOUS by the way.' Mum wheels round to me. 'Christian Dior with a Vivienne Westwood edge! Why didn't you say the ball was tonight, love?'

'I did!'

'When?' She frowns.

'*Weeks* ago.'

'Ach, what good is that?' She bats her hand. 'I've been buried in Armitages for months. I only knew Christmas was coming because the mortgage went out. Just.' She frowns at my dress. 'What's this *rag* you're in? And why are you running round in bare feet? Your poor legs! What's that smeared on them...?' She looks up. 'Oh, love.'

'I got my period, Mum.' She folds me into a hug. 'I – couldn't – stop it.' I sob into her shoulder. 'We ran out of Tampax.'

'But...We can get more!' She rocks me. 'Your dad and I aren't *that* broke.'

'You are, though. And it's *me* who broke you. Your gazillion-pound IVF baby. You were so happy before me!' Mum tries to ssh me, but I push her away. 'Your wedding pics. They're like a dream.'

'Nightmare, more like,' mutters Dad, steadying Mum. 'Remember, Kell? All that business with your dress. Your Gran,' he explains to me, 'she wanted to get the bodice perfect, kept doing it and unpicking it. Meanwhile, the guests were starting to arrive. Forget being romantic, your mum and I had to roll up our sleeves and prepare the buffet. Neither of us had made more than a sandwich in our life!'

'Oh Chris, that shellfish dip,' shudders Mum. 'I *said* we shouldn't microwave the prawns.' Dad pulls a face at me.

'Gave half the guests food poisoning,' he confesses.

'So...' I look between them. 'Why'd you chuck it all away?'

'The shellfish dip?' frowns Dad. 'It honked, Kat—'

'*No*, your perfect-looking love! Why blow all your cash on getting some stupid kid?'

'Hey, what's with the "stupid"?' Mum pushes back my hair. 'And who cares about perfect *looking*? When those pics were taken, I was still working on the till at Woolworths. Your dad only had one pair of jeans. Twenty years on, look at us!' She slaps the back of her hand at Dad. 'He's a writer who can't write.'

'Harsh.' He pushes down her arm. 'But fair.'

'I'm a fashion buyer who can't get out of ladies' knickers. But we're still *trying*...' she wobbles. '...Together. Only now, I grant you...' The van behind her starts to rock. '"Together" has got a whole lot bigger.' Through the open passenger window, we watch Daisy and Lil wrestling Andy into a headlock.

'What your mum's trying to say is...' Dad sighs. '...Kat, *you're* our happy ending. The rest is definitely a work in progress.' He looks at Mum. She looks at him. A pale glow spreads across their tired faces, like magic returning. And I realise the door to the gym's swung open. Light beams dance out, silhouetting the figure of Nick Harcourt in the doorway.

'Zack? Get in here.' He gestures furiously. 'We're on stage NOW.'

'Just a minute,' shouts Zack. 'I've got to—'

'Go!' I push him. 'Blow them away! I'll get my folks home.'

'You will *not*,' Mum protests. 'It stops now.'

'Wha—?'

'This whole "carer" role we've dumped on you. Kat, it should be us helping *you*.'

'Mum's right,' Dad says firmly. 'I'm sorry, Kat, I've been so busy losing faith in myself, I gave up on the best job I could ever have: believing in *you* guys.'

'*Aaargh,*' a toddler-sized roar comes from the van. 'ME GONNA SIT ON YOUR HEAD!'

'You girls have got this.' He grins. 'Kat, you're an incredible designer. You should NOT be turning up to your school ball in… in what looks like a bin-bag,' he frowns at my hitched-up skirt, 'for a *really* small bin.'

'Great pep talk, Chris.' Mum rocks on her feet. 'No wonder your wife's a raging alcoholic.'

'Kell.' He rolls his eyes. 'You've had *one* cocktail.'

She growls. 'It was *massive.*'

'OK!' He puts up his hands. 'I concede, you are a very glamorous, *dangerous* alcoholic. Mrs Parker, please consider this an intervention.' Solemnly, he lowers his hands to her shoulder. 'Stop your cocktail habit, and I promise, *promise* to get paid work. Stacking shelves, sweeping streets, *I shall raise the cash* to bring you the most precious gift of all.'

'No,' she staggers back, 'not…?'

'FULL childcare for the twins.'

'It's a Christmas miracle!' She hugs him. He rests his chin on top of her head. For a second, my folks look… well, how I *want* them to look. Then his chin starts to jerk violently. Mum's head is shaking. My parents, they're cracking up IN FRONT OF ME.

Sort of. 'They're *laughing*?' I turn to Zack. 'Seriously? This is *funny* to them?' He shrugs, but now he's chuckling too. 'Gah, I give up! I mean it!' And I feel a weight lift from my shoulders. I can't save my folks, can I? It's down to them – and whatever weird thing they've got going on: call it "love" or just a lifetime of making each other laugh when THEY SHOULD BE ACTING SERIOUS.

Because, seems to me, we're still stuck outside the gym. My mum can barely stand up, and our getaway driver is being savaged by two rabid toddlers. So quite *how* this rescue is going to go—

The open door of the van rattles, and out bobs a mass of strawberry blonde corkscrew curls.

'You just gonna stand there in your period pants?' says Lisa. 'Because that catwalk contest ain't gonna win itself.'

'Lees,' I run towards her, 'you came!'

'Of course.' She jumps down onto the drive. 'Not much point sticking round at regionals once we, well…' She sighs.

'Oh, Lees,' my voice cracks. 'All that training…'

'It paid off. WE WON!' She jumps me up and down. 'Cruised to the final, then destroyed Wenborough High, 9–4.'

'You're kidding? You're the best,' I cry, 'and I'm THE WORST for not texting you before the game started.'

'Or wishing me luck.' She drops me. 'Lucky for *you* I'm so insensitive.' She turns back to the van. 'Or I'd be sobbing now, not saving your ass. Come on, Dolly.' She hauls out the Armitages dummy: chipped feet first, then billows of blue silk and finally, Gina.

'*Gentle*, Lees!' She holds up Dolly's head. 'Don't mess the dress.'

'I'm straightening her skirts,' puffs Lisa.

'You're pulling them off!' Gina jumps down beside her. 'Kat's spent hours on this gown. She doesn't need you mauling it. Am I right?' She turns to me, so does Lisa, so there's no missing it. They're wearing matching tuxedos.

'Woah!' I laugh. 'You're power-suited—'

'And booted.' Lisa hoiks her trouser leg to flash the scuffed toe of her Doc Marten. Gina straightens her lapels.

'Now *that*,' says Zack with a grin, 'is a feminist statement.'

'And ON the subject of outraged womanhood…' Lisa sticks her hand into her tux pocket, and pulls out a pair of

226

my clean knickers. 'Hoiked them from your room. Couldn't find any Tampax, so I had a rummage in my kit bag.' Proudly, she flourishes a furry tampon. It's exploding from its torn wrapper, and looks snapped in several places. 'Granted, it's lost its string…'

'Ugh, give,' says Gina. 'Here,' she tucks my knickers into Mum's coat pocket, along with a sanitary towel she's pulled out of her sleeve. 'Eco-friendly. Biodegradable,' she winks, as Andy strolls round the front of the van with the twins.

'Slick.' He holds up the twins to high-five Gina and Lees.

'Didn't I say you'd rock a tux?'

'You're in on this?' I ask him. He beams.

'Who do you think found the suits?'

I laugh, turning back to the girls. 'It's *you two* should be storming the catwalk!' I can see the neck of a T-shirt under each jacket. 'No shirt and tie?'

'No way,' says Gina. 'Symbols of male oppression.'

'Like *that* sad number. That dress is so not you,' Lisa tells me. 'Your period came to your rescue, I reckon. Yep,' she sees my face burn up through the dark. 'Group chat is on fire. Whole world has seen your upskirt. Up*side*…' She punches my arm. '…we knew where to find you!'

'*The second* the whistle blew on our match,' groans Gina. 'Lisa was, like, WE'VE GOT TO GET BACK FOR KAT AND THIS STUPID BALL. She forced our minibus driver to drop us off at yours.'

'Only to find you'd split already,' Lisa evil-eyes me.

'There was Dolly wearing your dress, with your mum passed out on the couch,' continues Gina. 'Next thing our phones start going crazy with your dancefloor take-down. Lees goes ballistic. So *I* fill in your folks, who are like, "What's with the tuxedos? And, why is Lees—"'

'"Going ballistic?"' Mum takes up the story. 'When Gina

explains, Dad grabs Dolly, while I run to the Melways. Luckily I catch Andy pulling up in his van.'

'Actually,' confides Dad, 'he ran her over slightly.'

'Oh, Mum,' I say, '*that's* why you can't stand up straight? Not the cocktail!'

'Kat, you've got to understand.' She clutches me. 'It was MASSIVE.'

'Jeez,' mutters Gina. 'Can we focus?'

'Kat.' Lisa shakes me. 'You've got a catwalk to storm.' She starts tugging my dress off Dolly.

'I can't wear that!' I try to stop her.

'Why not?' Lees bats me off. "'S got skirts, hasn't it? And a boob thing—'

'Bodice.'

'So, what's the problem?'

'*Er...*' I snatch up the the ragged skirt edges. Yank at the gaping mess round the back.

'Stop,' cries Lees. 'You're making it worse!'

'How can she make it *worse?*' snorts Mum. Then she turns her back on me, muttering. 'Good grief, aren't we done *standing round?*' Watching her lurch back up into Andy's van, Dad puts his arm around me.

'It's OK,' I manage a smile. 'Time I learnt when to give up.'

'Never,' he says, at the same second Mum falls out of the van, clutching a wickerwork box.

'Buttons!' she cries. 'That's what your dress needs . . . or Velcro, maybe?' Ribbons and rhinestones spill out over her hands. Pins fly everywhere.

'My sewing box?' I gasp.

'Thought you'd need it.' Handing over my toolkit, Mum turns sober suddenly. 'Dreaming's the easy bit, love. It's hard work that makes thing happen.'

I wish…

I wish…

I squeeze my eyes shut. Open them to see my few followers huddled round a battered, pumpkin-orange van. Nothing's changed…

Except me.

'Come on.' I set off towards the school building. 'Clock's ticking!'

'For real?' Zack catches up. 'You're gonna try and win?'

'What's to lose? I've just flashed my pants to THE STRATOSPHERE. I think I'm done worrying how I look.'

'Yay, we're gonna storm the ball!' whoops Lisa, scooping up Dolly. 'Can I set off a fire extinguisher?'

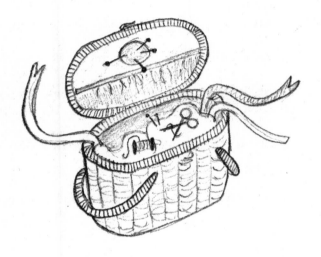

Zack, I dispatch first. Proper shove him into Winter Wonderland.

'About time,' says Nick Harcourt, pulling him through the gym doors.

'Wait.' Zack turns to me. 'I thought we were storming the ball?'

'You first,' I say, tugging up his biker collars. 'Play your heart out. Then *keep playing.*' Our eyes lock. 'Buy me time, yeah?'

'I'm gone,' says Zack. As the gym door closes on him, I catch it.

'Andy?'

'Here.' He towers behind my folks, still jiggling the twins.

'Get after him,' I say.

'You what?'

'This is Zack's first gig.' I push open the door, releasing the screech of feedback. Sam's on stage, setting up already. 'You can't miss this.'

'Nah,' Andy shakes his head. 'He doesn't want his big bruv cramping his style. Besides, the twins—'

'Give 'em here.' Dad takes Daisy, passing Lil to Mum. 'You've fed that boy, Andy. You've clothed him, bought his sodding amp. You've earned the right to dad-dance at his first gig.'

'Get up there.' Mum bounces a bawling Lil. 'Or we'll give you these two back... FOREVER.'

Andy's off into that gym before Mum can say, '*Ew*, she's done one.'

'Hey,' Lisa resists, as I push her in too.

'Sorry,' I say, 'but I need you and Gina to be my catwalk spies. The *second* the contest looks like it's starting.' I take Dolly from her. 'Come get me.'

'But...' Lisa shouts as the door swings shut. 'Where are you going?'

'Guess!'

I sprint across the schoolyard to the tech block, swinging a mad-eyed store dummy. But I know I'm on track when I find the fire door "magically" wedged open for me (with a book: *Koalas, And How To Avoid Them Biting You*).

First stop, the toilets. Mum hands over my sanitary SOS kit. I go in a mess; come out ready to take on the world.

Next stop, the textiles studio. Bouncing Dolly off the walls, I run upstairs. '*Yes...*' The door opens for me. 'We're in.'

'Woah,' mutters Mum over my shoulder. 'You sure about this, Kat?'

The tech studio has disappeared. In the darkness, fairy-tale creatures reign. Fantastical insects shimmer against the walls; magical creatures stretch their plastic-bottle wings.

'It's OK, Mum,' I say with a laugh, 'this is *my* Winter Wonderland.'

I enter our sewing room, drawn like a moth towards a bright light on the first row of desks: the sewing machine I always use, it's been left turned on for me. A sheet of A4 paper is taped to the handwheel. Carefully, so as not to break the spell, I unfold the paper and read the loopy scrawl of my Aussie textiles teacher.

Be your own label, Kat. Fashion has no rules.

Only she's scratched out "no rules" to add, <u>one</u> *rule:* DON'T SHOW YOUR PANTS.

'Yer drongo, that was some ball entrance!' The overhead strip lights buzz on, and Miss Bloxam emerges from the stockroom. 'Yer supposed to be showing off yer tailoring, not yer toosh! Mr and Mrs Parker...' She nods at my folks. 'We missed yer at the last parents' evening.'

'There's been a parents' evening?' says Mum.

'Christ,' Dad shakes his head, 'we need to get on this.'

'Agreed,' says Miss Bloxam, 'but not on Kat's time. Because tonight *is* your time, Kat.' She looks from me to the wall clock. 'Crikey, it's ticking! Wait there.' She ducks away, leaving me to shake my gown off Dolly. I'm a heap of sliding silk when a crash comes from the stockroom—

'*Da-naaaaa!*' Miss Bloxam appears in a puff of white tulle. 'Shove this lot under your skirts,' she bundles the giant springy ball of netting at me. 'Granted, it's not the posh

232

stuff, but teacher's wages and all that.'

'You bought this – *for me*?'

'Call it an investment in your talent,' she shrugs. 'Just don't tell the other judges.' I splutter through the netting.

'You're judging the catwalk contest?'

'Along with Cribbs and some serious-looking stiffs.' She looks worried suddenly. 'Twenty minutes to fix your gown, Kat, then you're outta time.'

Whisking out of the room, she claps her hands, whipping up the butterflies inside me. They're knocking against my ribs, nudging me towards the sewing machine. But my heart's racing so hard, I can't think…

'Kat?' Mum looks at me anxiously.

'Ssh!' Dad holds his finger up. 'Listen'. A drumming sounds beneath our feet. An uncertain cheer goes up from the gym. Branded, they're starting their set! As Zack pounds out the relentless loop of 'Seven Nation Army' – sure, steady – my heart pounds with it. Sure, steady, I work out what I need to do.

~~Stitch List~~ *Swish List*

1. Find stretch of elastic; tie it round waist.
2. Loop Miss Bloxam's netting over elastic to create a CLOUD of underskirts!
3. Hem edges of gown. But that's a serious amount of silk, and I've only got one pair of hands…

'Muuum!' She's on it already, sliding down behind the sewing machine as I finish my instructions. Foot on the pedal, she feeds the ragged edges of my dress under the darting needle. 'These I can fix.' She whizzes down the hems. 'But how are you going to pull together the back of your gown? I know what your gran would say, "*Nothing holds*

233

like hooks and eyes, but…"

'There's no time! I can't be stitching in a row of tiny fastenings.'

'Seventeen minutes,' says Dad helpfully.

'What's the trick?'' I mutter, laying out my dress on the desk. As Mum feeds the skirts through the Singer, the bodice twists and twirls. Now the desk is dancing too. The gym below us is bouncing, kids going wild, as Zack slashes through 'Teen Spirit'. As the studio windows start to rattle, fabrics unfurl themselves from the shelves. Cotton goes reeling.

'*Ow!*' Mum yelps as a bulldog clip hits her.

'What the——?' cries Dad, as a giant dragonfly lands on him. Display boards rattle with bottle-top bugs, toppling from their perches. Tin-can moths cascade down the walls.

'Butterflies!' I jump  up. '*That's* how I do this. Catch them,' I urge my parents, as I dive for a Red Admiral with Fanta orange wings. Baffled but willing, they join in.

Mum's scooping up curly-winged Sprites as they bounce off the desks. Dad grabs a window pole to flick purple Ribena moths from the light fittings.

The twins toddle between us, chasing butterflies as they skitter across the floor, their fairy wings rippling to Zack's spiralling riffs.

'Quick,' Gina bursts into the studio with Lees. 'Camel Cribbs keeps trying to start the catwalk contest, but Zack won't stop playing.'

'He's got the Tag-Hags killing each other to get front of stage – their gowns are wrecked,' says Lisa with a grin. Then she sees my folks collecting plastic bottles. 'Er, what's with the litter-pick? Shouldn't we be focusing on your—'

'Gown, I know,' I tumble my catch of butterflies onto the desk. 'I'm on it. First to get this dress *off.*'

'With pleasure,' says Mum grimly, helping me to peel off my slithery black frock. Raiding our classroom supplies for a decent-sized piece of elastic, she ties it round my waist, and gathers the white netting over it. Like a wobbly primadonna in a giant ballet tutu, I rise up on my toes! Only now does she drape my shimmering blue gown around me, holding it together at the back while Gina and Lisa shake out the silk folds. As they drop them down over my stiff underskirts, I twist at the waist, and produce a swoosh of skirts, a *whoosh* of air…

'Do you hear that, Mum?'

'The swish? You've got it! Can still see your pants though…' Desperately she yanks the back parts of my dress together.

'That's right! Keep pulling,' I tell her. 'Dad too – pinch the back of my dress together, tight as you can. Lees, Gina – take the butterflies, and start clipping.'

Lees frowns. '*Cwip,*' explains Lil, holding up a bulldog clip. Daisy hurls another at Lisa's head.

'*CWIP!*'

Luckily, I can feel Gina working her way down my back already. Deftly she clips butterflies along the silk ridge produced by Mum and Dad's power-pinch. I'm holding my breath… can the butterflies hold *me*? At a stately pace, I exit the studio.

My dress holds.
I twirl down the hall.
Still holding!

I'm at the top of the stairs, teetering on my toes… dare I?

'GET A MOVE ON!' Bossy Harriet appears in the stairwell. 'Winsham boys have spilled all the Fanta,' she bellows, her eyes wild, her hair *frizzed*. 'Liam's sat on my Wotsits, and if one more Tag-Hag laughs at my balloons, she will TASTE MY CLIPBOARD.' She rattles it at me like a sabre. 'Time to take back the ball!' Irt seems like our nickname for the Tag-Hags has started to make its way around the year group after my detention stint.

'But Kat,' cries Mum, 'you've still got no shoes.'

'Great, isn't it? Means I can't lose a slipper!' Hitching my skirts, I take off down the stairs.

We run down the hall in convoy. Gina with Lisa, Dad joggling the twins, Mum holding up my hems so they don't trail on the dirty floor. 'Your poor bare feet!' she's still wailing as we enter the gym.

"S fine, Mum,' I pant, 'I've just got to get down that catwalk.'

'Which is *where* exactly?' shouts Dad, as we hit a wall of sound – and a wall of backs. Everyone's mobbing the stage, going wild to the opening lick of 'The Immigrant Song'. The kids ahead of us are punching the air, crashing down on Harriet, who beats them back with her clipboard. She's laying into some boy's kidneys when Zara glides out of the darkness, her scarf glittering in a flash of strobe.

'Catwalk's this way. Follow me.' She threads us through the crowd towards the far end of stage. 'Contest can't start until your friend here lets it.' Centre-stage, Zack is shredding it. He's ripped off his biker jacket, and is tearing up the wires while Sam pounds on bass. Nick's drums drive them on to a thrashing crescendo. Zack swings up his axe, and I catch a flash of silver sequins.

My baggy tee, it's turned into a skinny rock vest; my angry slogan now a hard blaze stretched across Zack's broad chest. I'm whooping, Mum's laughing (and crying!). Daisy hurls herself against Dad's arms as the last chord dies.

'*Zackie,*' she bounces, 'we *here*—'

'*FOR HEADBANGIN',*' Lil roars into the reverb. Zack's head shoots up. His fans follow his glance.

'*Look,*' someone spots me, '*it's Face-Plant Girl.*'

'*She does* NOT *know when to give up!*'

'*Now she's brought her parents?*'

My mum and dad close in, shielding me from view. I've got so far, but I can't do this. Not again. I'm shaking, the crowd's turning – when a screech of feedback hooks them back: Zack. Having got their attention, he reaches into the back pocket of his jeans. Pulls out a fresh pick, and scorches through his favourite lick. Soaring through 'Thunder Struck', he takes two hundred kids with him.

'Come *on.*' Lees pulls me. 'He can't hold them forever.' I catch a last glimpse of Zack, his sinews straining to lift the crowd; a dark V of sweat blooming across his chest like a torn heart. Then all I see is the inside of Lisa's armpit.

'Move!' She puts me in a headlock, and bumps me through the crowd until we reach the furthest corner of the stage. From here, a line of blocks extends like a gangplank into the surging sea of kids. This is to be my Katwalk. Above it, Darwin's banner dangles like a flag – Darwin's Dental presents *MOST DAZZLING LOOK!*

Ranged down the far side of the catwalk sit the judges. Camel Cribbs and Miss Bloxam are flanked by three dentist stiffs, none of whom are smiling (and all look like they could be handsy with a drill). I jump at a crash-out drum roll from Nick. 'A big cheer for Branded!' Harriet shouts into her mic, as she mounts the stage. 'Give it up, people!'

As the crowd erupts one last time, the guys raise an exhausted fist to their new fans. Then Sam and Nick fold back into the shadows, leaving Zack rolling his shoulders under the fading spotlight. Weary, wired, he waits for me to step up.

'All contestants to the catwalk, please,' commands Harriet, starting a frock stampede. As girls push past us, hoiking at their strapless gowns, Dad steadies me ('You're good, love! Clips are holding'). Mum shakes out my skirts ('Your gran will be so proud!') Harriet puts her hand over the mic. 'Go on, Kat,' she nods me towards the foot of the runway stairs.

I take a breath – then a first wobbly step.

Nothing.

My skirt's gone taut. Like a wall of silk, it blocks me. I try another step; feel something rip.

'Stop,' cries Mum, 'you're treading on your hem!'

But how——? No heels! *No wonder* my skirts are tripping me up. Pedalling my filthy, bloodied feet, I free one stretch of hem, only to trample another.

'Cool dance moves,' a familiar cackle cuts in. 'Very street'.

Stella appears, still working the "gold mermaid" look: hair glossy, fishtail shimmering, she'll glide down that catwalk. I can't even reach the steps. 'It was *you,* wasn't it?' I say.

'Me?' Her blue eyes shine.

'On the dancefloor.' I kick at my skirts. 'You shoved me in the back. When it looked like your killer heels might fail. You *wanted* me to fall on my face.'

'Hurts, doesn't it?' She shrugs, and looks past me. Like I'm so dull she'd rather watch a empty stage. Except, I check back, Zack's still up there, unhooking his guitar strap. I turn round to Stella, and see it's not hate making her eyes sparkle...

It's tears.

'*Stellaaaaa!*' A screech goes up from the foot of the catwalk: the Tag-Hags have spotted their leader. '*We can't go up without you,*' shrieks Jayden.

'Ew,' the others spot me. 'Gross alert!'

'Quick, Stella, get away from the period skank.'

'Bet she's *rank* under that dress.'

'*Miss...*' Keisha screeches across to Camel Cribbs, 'you can't make us share a catwalk with her. It's not hygienic, *Miss*—'

'Shut up, can you?' Stella stuns them all with a glare. 'All right,' she turns back to me, 'so I wanted you to fall, but not like that. Not on your period, for all the Winsham boys to see.'

'Girl code, right?' I bunch up my skirts.

'Something like that.'

'Right. Well...' I push past. 'I've got a contest to win.'

'No way. You're not winning anything tonight.' She grips my arm. 'Not in bare feet. Here.' Wobbling slightly, she bends down to remove her shoes: silver, sparkly, not too high. 'Take them,' she says.

'Your beginner heels?'

'No tricks this time.'

'But...? I don't get it—'

'YOU DON'T HAVE TO GET IT, KAT.' Lisa butts in. 'YOU JUST HAVE TO PUT ON THE SODDING SHOES.' She grabs them off Stella. 'Soon as I've tested for booby traps...'

'Quick,' mutters Gina, as Lisa tugs at each sparkly heel. She's shoving her hand into a toe when the sound system kranks back up. Keisha hustles down the catwalk to squeals from her fellow Tag-Hags. Meanwhile, my crack team is nose-deep in a shoe.

'She could have stuck a dead mouse in here...' Lees squints. '...or a frog.'

'Ha, I'm done kissing *them* for a bit,' says Stella. 'Not a prince among them.' She looks at me. Dead on. 'Last night with Zack,' she says, so quiet only I can hear. 'The way he talked about you? No boy's ever... *Nobody's* ever—'

'Stella—' She tosses her hair.

'Just take the shoes, will you?'

Lees gives me the nod. I stoop down to put on the fierce, fairy-tale heels, and when I rise back up, Stella looks like just another girl, curling her toes. 'What about *your* catwalk run?' I ask.

'Hey, I'm already winning *all* the prizes. Let that lot scrap it out.' She shrugs off the Tag-Hags tussling on the steps. 'I'm taking the night off. Ain't that right, boys?'

'All right, Stell.' Big Mike shoulders his way out from the crowd, scattering Year 9s like skittles.

'So,' cackles Stella, as Little Mickey skips up behind, 'where are you two taking me?'

'Erm...' Big Mike considers her bare feet. 'Norbridge Bowls?' he consults Mickey.

'Everyone hands in their shoes,' nods Mickey. 'They're asking for a pair to get nicked.'

241

'Borrowed,' Big Mike corrects him. As the three of them head off, I can hear Stella putting her order in ('No tatty trainers. Only sandals with a wedge'). A last flick of her golden fishtail, weirdly, I feel a spark go out of me.

'Uh-oh.' Lees jabs Gina. 'She's bottling it. Didn't I warn you? Time for Plan B!' Each hooks me under the arm, like they've practised it. Badly: toppling Tag-Hags out of our way, they set me down at the start of the runway. Then leave me PLONKED LIKE A CHRISTMAS PUDDING while they fumble with their jacket buttons.

'What Are You *Doing*?' I mouth.

'Being Motivational. *Forget the haters! Love your planet! And...*' Lisa checks with Gina.

'... *Be your own label,*' says Gina with a grin. In a slick, synchronised move, they turn to face down the runway. Flicking up their collars, they part their jackets to reveal the upcycled tees beneath:

'GAY,' bursts in gold letters across Lisa's tie-dye top. And Gina? She's rocking a rainbow.

'Yes,' I yelp at Lisa. 'You told her?'

'I guessed,' says Gina. 'She kept sitting on my lap in Sprinkles—'

'Did not,' Lees blushes.

'—and tried to hold my hand, like, a hundred times!'

'So this,' I nod at Gina's rainbow, 'is *you* saying...?'

'I'm holding her hand right back.' Before I can ask what this means (sisterly solidarity? Or snogging?!) they lock fingers, and take off down the runway. To a chorus of catcalls and cheers, they turn together, and stomp back triumphant.

A bit too triumphant for Camel Cribbs's liking. She's up off her seat, shouting for the volume to COME DOWN.

'Go *on*.' Lees shoves me, but the tide's turning. The sea of kids stirs mutinously as the music's killed. I brace for the wave to break on me and feel a thrum of electricity instead. It's coming from Zack, he's picked up his guitar again.

I know that tune.

'Foxy Lady', I strut. Past the upturned scowls of the Tag-Hags; beyond 'Face-Plant' boy and gross Daniel. Head and glittering heels above every kid who's ever made me feel small! Taking off down the runway, I see Mum below, cheering; Dad getting his head mashed by the twins.

Propelled by my team of crazy, beautiful butterflies, I reach the catwalk's edge. Stretching out my arms, I start to spin. Faster, faster my skirts *swish*, sweeping away my haters in a swathe of silk!

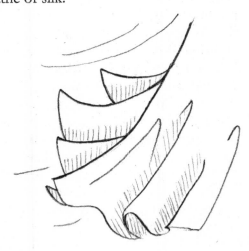

Well, we Parkers get our Christmas wish. Come 25th December, we're gathered round our MASSIVE new boiler, celebrating! In our coats...

That's right, people, the boiler is NOT yet pumping out heat to our happy home. It's parked in the hall with a load of dodgy-looking wires sticking out of its butt. (Just how second-hand *is* this thing?)

Von *was* supposed to come and fit it yesterday, but she rang from the hospital to say she'd broken her toe on a spanner. ('She wasn't even plumbing!' wailed Mum, hanging up. 'She was doing Zumba in her lounge to *Strictly Come Dancing*'s Festive Mega-Mix.')

Christmas morning, we're all still wrapped up in scarves and bobble hats, apart from Gran, who's tucked up in her wheelchair. Having got her out of the car, Dad's spent the past twenty minutes levering her past the "new arrival", as he calls it adoringly. 'Should we sing a carol?'

'It's a boiler,' says Mum, 'not baby Jesus.'

'Baby cheeses?' Lil's ears prick up.

'WE WANN BABY CHEESES.' Daisy dispatches me to the kitchen for another Mini Babybel. Yep, *get us*, eating label cheese! We had to allow ourselves a couple of treats when I won.

I won!

Handing over my prize, Judge Bloxam said my dress had shown style, verve and guts, '*and* Kat sewed it herself, which is more than can be said for the rest of yer unsustainable, sweatshop-fuelling, FAST FASHION FOLLOWERS.' (Cribbs turned Miss Bloxam's mic off at that point. And could be heard loudly telling Harriet to remove ALL cans of Red Bull from the judging area.)

Me? I'm still spinning. Bringing home a £500 cheque, me and my folks had a proper, grown-up chat (i.e. argued loudly) about how to spend it. Parkers being Parkers, every side reckons they've won.

I persuaded Mum to put £200 towards "Having A Proper Christmas".

Finally we got to enjoy a mother–daughter shopping trip! True, it was for the twins, but I got to wow Mum with my scavenger skills – no secondhand shop was safe! We bagged anything purple or bouncy, or that honked when you hit it. ('Toddlers don't care if a toy's new,' says Mum, 'just that it's throwable.') And I got a new coat!

Next, Mum filled the car with *actual petrol* (not just prayers) and we bombed down the Savacentre for a trolley-load of festive grub, plus (world faints) *toiletries*. We're talking fancy-pants shampoo, posh deodorant and A BILLION BOXES OF TAMPAX. ('So no teenage pregnancies,' says Mum, slinging them in to the trolley, 'because I'm not shifting this lot on Ebay'). She was joking... I think. She does that now (joking, I mean) because DAD'S GOT A JOB.

It all comes from Winter Wonderland. Dad was that excited when I won, he bopped up to thank the judges, and discovered Mr Darwin (of Darwin's Dental Health) is, like, his biggest fan! Well, not of Dad's second book so much, but that rock 'n' roll tale with a sauna in it? Legendary! (Poor Mr Darwin, turns out he wanted to be a drummer when he was younger, but his father made him go into teeth.)

Mr Darwin BEGGED Dad to write a piece about the catwalk contest for the Darwin's website. Which Dad *actually did*, so now Mr Darwin's paying Dad to "overhaul all their company literature". Dad's put aside his Great Unfinished Work to become an expert on molars. Mum's less stressed about money, and Dad's happy because (to quote Darwin's new company literature) "it's good to have gums".

Best of all, Dad's out of the attic. He's still glued to his laptop, but now he takes it into:

a) The bedroom, when Mum needs him to rub her feet after another long shift;
b) The kitchen, when I'm home from school, and
c) The front room, when the twins are in nappies and can't wee on his keyboard.

'Hellooo.' Our back door slams and the house rings with the loud baritone of a Melway brother. 'Where is she? Where's my best girl?'

Emerging from our kitchen, Andy Melway staggers at the vision of my seventy-eight-year-old nan in a canary-yellow cardie. Gran giggles like a teenager. Andy grabs her "love handles" (the ones on her wheelchair) and wheels her back around the way he came. 'Got to get to ours, Hot Stuff....' He pushes her out through the kitchen. '...before the turkey dries out.'

'*Turkey?*' says Gran. 'You promised me jerk chicken.'

'Well, you're getting jerk turkey.' Andy bounces her chair

down our back step, *just* missing Zack who's turned up (last as usual) to carry the twins. As Daisy nestles into his arms and Lil climbs on to his back, my parents take off after Gran. Between us we're carting plates, bowls, Christmas crackers, mince pies and a family bag of Wotsits. Plus Dad's lugging a giant Christmas pud. No climbing through the gap in the fence today. Instead we form a procession down the Katwalk – first time I've been back since I stormed a real catwalk. Since I felt the buzz of people *liking* what I'd made—

'You're hooked,' says Zack with a grin, as a thorny branch catches my new coat collar – Marie Melway's last winter rose. Gently, so as not to hurt the velvet petals, he frees me. But he doesn't let go. We've barely seen each other since Winter Wonderland. Life's been too full-on... surviving the last week of school, for starters. Post-gig, Zack acquired a load of St Edward's fangirls. When they started riding the R3, he panicked and jumped on the R4, where he got back in with his old football crew. Zack's just played his first game for them. ('It was that or have Big Mike share my number. And I mean share.')

My end of term wasn't quite so hot. Apparently Stella's dad materialised from, like, nowhere (*now* I see where she gets it from!) and flew her off to the sun, leaving the Tag-Hags to cast me *serious* shade. Some cracks of light got through – girls coming up to say they rated my dress. Megan *mobbing* me with a bunch of her Year 9 mates. On the last day of term, a Year 11 came up to ask if I'd be in business for the summer prom. 'Er,' I flush, 'what business?'

'THE SWISH: BE YOUR OWN LABEL. That's you, isn't it?' She showed me on her phone. 'Doing an Irish jig?'

Gaaaah. There's doubtless worse ways to discover you've gone into business than seeing a YouTube clip of yourself high-kicking like a mule BUT I'M YET TO FIND ONE.

'Oi! Love birds,' Zack and I spring apart as Lees bowls up our alley from the street. 'Got time for an executive meeting? You're warned, though.' She pats her stomach, 'I've just eaten a shed-load of sprouts. Gas *might* be involved.'

Yes, my new business partner is a maverick. But she also owns a smartphone, so there's no stopping her. Luckily, I only realised Lees had posted vids from our "Katwalk Collection" *after* the "likes" started coming in. Some "hates", too, but so far my butterfly wings are holding up. As for taking off... 'Another kid's asking where they can get a pair like your embroidered jeans.' Lisa pulls out her phone. 'Time to get to work?'

'First I need to buy stock.' My folks insisted that £300 went into my bank account. "Seed money", they called it, to grow my label. Starting with a trawl of car boot sales in January, I'm thinking – all those clothes getting cleared out after Christmas?

'You're gonna go customising crazy,' Zack reads my thoughts.

'Totally! But, I mean, not all the time.'

'S'cool,' he says with a laugh. 'We can hang out while you sew.'

'Yeah, 'course!' I say, blushing (NOT helped by Lisa snorting in my ear, 'he *wuvs* you').

Now Zack's blushing too, shaking his head as he lopes up the Melways' path, leaving me to pummel Lees. 'Soooo, how's Gina?'

'Good,' she says with a grin. 'Breaking in her new nose-ring. We're going to hook up as soon as the swelling's gone down.'

'*Ew...*'

'Don't "*ew*" me! You're the one chewing Zack's face.'

'Am not.' I rattle open the Melways' gate. 'I've not got near that boy's face since the ball. I still worry he might, you know, fancy Stella. She's so hot and—'

'Stop that.' Lisa punches me.

'*Hey*, not my sewing arm!' I rub it. 'I'm a designer now.'

'Some designer.' She hooks her arm into mine. 'You never did fix the zip on that coat.'

Snuggling into my new one, I giggle and steer us towards A Proper Christmas, Katwalk-style.

Already we can hear the twins battering Andy for 'JERKY TURKEY'. Gran's complaining she can't find the TV remote. Zack's started picking out a tune on Dad's old acoustic guitar. Lees and I frown at each other: do we know that tune?

Yes! We set Marie Melway's rose bobbing: '*All I want for Christmas is yoooooooou.*'

My heart's fit to burst. And my head? It's already whirring away on a new design. For a slogan tee, a step on from "GAY"…

The End

Be your own label

Thanks for following's Kat's fashion journey so far. Book 2 is on its way!

Can't wait to create your sustainable style? Check out **theswish.co.uk**, packed with upcycling ideas and sewing hacks to get you designing and creating your own clothes.

Follow us **@theswishlist.official** *(TikTok and insta)*. Swap thrifting tips, and share your makes with other DIY fashionistas!

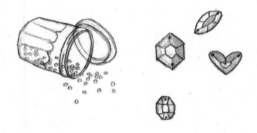

ACKNOWLEDGEMENTS

Huge thanks to all the MAJORLY talented young readers, writers, stitchers, supermodels, thrifters and grifters who've got behind *The Swish*, and rocketed it over the finish line! Together you've formed a creative fashion community, and helped turn a floppy manuscript into something with a spine.

To the bright, big-hearted readers who reviewed my drafts:
Florence Richardson, Megan Kelly, Asiya Ali, Lola Compton, Molly and George Montgomery, Laya Al-Tajer, Eliah Mathieu-Marius, Eleanor Godley, Sophia Lozano, Jacob Hatten-Pearse, Soraya Al-Assam, Crystal Haley, Lara Hayday, Ash Burlinson, Ruby Hamilton, Chloe Kearney, Tilly Pieterse, Libby Greenhill, Maria Kontou-Watson, Iris Egan-Russell, Romilly Fenwick, Cohen Baulch, Sarah Matsen, Emily Rood, Lily Porteous and Crystal Haley.

To everyone who's helped grow The Swish beyond a book, from shaping our online content to turning up to support our crazy market stalls:
Emma and Myles Curteis, Ania Westbury, Amelia Barclay, Martha Scrace, Stella Bennett, Hope Finn, Lyla Oldroyd, Ruby Caskey, Megan West, Daisy Young, Ruth 'Gazebo' Parkes and Sonya 'Wonder Woman' Griffiths.

To the next generation of the South London Massive:
Lily Thornton, Iris Hamilton, Tianna Hearn, Liv Brown, Bea Read, Megan and Charlotte Kelly, and Kirsty Adey.

For being all-round cool:
Eleanor and Matilda Wray, Huxley Woodward, Emily Widdowson, Jessica Johnson, Sienna Heath, Clarice Dunford-Frost, Mallory and Casper Denton, Emilia Jassenovics-Petre, Ivy Ellis and Bluebell Elliott.

To all the amazing charity shops which light up our high streets, and have helped *The Swish* with clothes donations and Instagram inspo, particularly Barnardos Retail, Sue Ryder shops, The Trussell Trust, Julia's House, Naomi House and Jacksplace.

To Dionne McCulloch, a fab writer and literary editor, and Katy England at Fashioning our World, Salisbury Museum, my catwalk co-conspirator!

To Bobba 'Inky Fingers' Bell, Jo Gray, the Bemerton Babes, and my Write Club posse. Plus my strapping cheerleaders Mat and Stan.

To illustrator Poppy Freer and writer Rose Freer, the sparks behind *The Swish.*

And finally, Shaun and Keren at Candy Jar. Thanks a billion xx

THE SWiSH
The ALBUM

Listen to your favourite tracks, inspired by *The Swish* on Spotify.